Chaotic Good

also by whitney gardner

You're Welcome, Universe

Fake Blood

Chaotic Good

whitney gardner

EMBER

Text and interior illustrations copyright © 2018 by Whitney Gardner
Cover art and chapter number illustrations copyright © 2018 by Kyle Hilton

All rights reserved. Published in the United States by Ember, an imprint of Random
House Children's Books, a division of Penguin Random House LLC, New York. Originally
published in hardcover in the United States by Alfred A. Knopf, an imprint of Random
House Children's Books, a division of Penguin Random House LLC, in 2018.

Ember and the E colophon are registered trademarks
of Penguin Random House LLC.

Visit us on the Web! GetUnderlined.com

Educators and librarians, for a variety of teaching tools,
visit us at RHTeachersLibrarians.com

Library of Congress Cataloging-in-Publication Data is available upon request.
ISBN 978-1-5247-2083-4 (pbk.)

Printed in the United States of America
10 9 8 7 6 5 4 3 2 1
First Ember Edition 2019

For all the geek girls,
feminist killjoys,
and nasty women

The girl section.

"Your boyfriend won't like that one." He smiles at me through his patchy, barely grown-in beard, leaning against the wall of shelved comic books. I hang my head. This is exactly what I was afraid of. I knew I shouldn't have come here. I knew I wouldn't be welcome. With a jerk of his neck, he flicks his greasy brown bangs out of his eyes. He looks me over, his arms folded tightly in front of his puffed-out chest. He hovers close by, waiting for my response, dying for me to acknowledge him, not taking silence for an answer. His name spelled out inside a bat-signal pin: BRODY.

"I'm sorry, what?" I ask, not daring to look directly at his face. I knew better; I knew better and I came into the shop anyway. I read the reviews online: five stars from the guys, two stars from the girls. I don't need his advice; I don't need a debate. Right now I need inspiration. And this guy's killin' my vibe.

"It's super girly. He probably won't like it. When's his birthday?"

"I—I don't have a boyfriend. It's, you know, for me." *Dingbat.* My fingers squeak against the cover of the latest *The Unbeatable Squirrel Girl,* holding on tight. I'm kicking myself for painting my nails sparkly pink and curling the rat's nest out of my hair this morning. I brace myself for what's coming next. All I wanted was a few new cosplay ideas without having to pass the geek-girl quiz.

"Oh! No wonder!" Brody laughs, and his expression softens. "You should check out the girl section."

"The . . . *girl* section?" I scowl, feeling my dark brown eyes turn black.

"No worries, tiger. You'll love it." He ushers me, hand on my back, toward one narrow shelf in the corner. I step away from his touch as soon as I can, but I can still feel his phantom palm resting there. The shelf is in disarray, with a few pastel-covered graphic novels and some very kawaii manga.

"Here you go," he lilts, eyes lighting up his pallid face. "All your comics lined up *just* for you. That way you don't need to get lost in the big-boy stuff." Another patron snorts from the board game section. This is humiliating. I'm trying not to flush, not to show a reaction. I can't let him know he's getting to me, but I don't think it's working. What year am I in? What kind of backwater wasteland is this? I swallow hard.

"Welp, I am a big boy, so, if you don't mind." I sidestep him on my way out of the "girl section." I try to stomp my feet as I go, but I'm wearing ballet flats, so I hardly make a sound. Brody's black leather boots echo through the shop as he follows me. Why is he following me? Leave me alone.

"Big boy in a pink dress, huh?" Why, oh why, did I wear the doughnut dress today?

"Yep." I try to sound preoccupied as I flip through an old issue of X-Men, looking for Jubilee. I've been dying to replicate that yellow coat of hers.

"So you like X-Men?" Brody stands over me, reeking of arrogance and body spray.

"Sure."

"*Gen X, First Class, '92?* What're we talkin' here?" He combs through the comics, pretending to help. I don't want to answer him, but the way he reaches over my head is a little intimidating. Maybe if I answer, he'll leave me alone.

"Whichever one Jubilee is in."

"Jubilee? Jesus." He pinches the bridge of his nose and winces.

"Jubilee is awesome."

"Jubes is the worst X-Men of all time. *The worst.* Worse than Dazzler."

"Who?" *Crap.* And with that one little word, I know I've screwed up. One little word out of my big mouth and I've sealed my fate. Again. Why should it matter if I know who Dazzler is? How am I supposed to learn without buying the comics first? I pivot over to the next shelf and cough, hoping he didn't hear me.

"I knew it! I knew you didn't know anything about X-Men. What are you really looking for? Attention? A boyfriend?"

"I'm looking for comics!" I snap at him. My black hair flies in front of my face. I brush it away. I try to channel Liv, who would know exactly what to say. She would put him in his place. "Is my *girl cash* not worth as much as your *boy bucks*?" I feel myself shrinking; he laughs at me while I try to remove the gold ballet flat from my stupid mouth. "Who said I have to be an expert to like something, or to shop here?" I wave the comics in his grinning face, trying to distract from the awkwardness. I'm a thousand percent done. I wish I were She-Hulk. I'd have smashed him and the entire "girl section" to bits by now.

"You don't have to get all snippy. Just hoping you can explain," he starts, "why you're buying comics if you don't even read them." Brody doesn't get angry. He doesn't even look annoyed. He talks to me like I'm six years old. Like he knows better. He doesn't.

"Excuse you—I read comics. I love comics," I say under my breath. I'm scared to raise my voice despite how angry I am. From now on I'll be doing all my shopping online, that's for sure.

"But you don't even know who—"

"I know enough. Okay?" I snap. "I know all their costumes by heart, and one day I'll be making—"

"Costumes?! That's what you're into, their outfits? Oh God . . . you're not one of those cosplay chicks, are you?" Brody reels back, face scrunched up as if he caught a whiff of something more rotten than his body spray. He looks me over again from my shoes to my shoulders, not bothering to look me in the eyes, disgusted. Every second I stand here is excruciating. I wish I had never come in. I should have waited to go back to Portland. I should have saved up to buy an iPad so I'd never have to leave the house to buy a comic again. I can't bring myself to say anything else. There's nothing I can actually say. Nothing that would make a difference. I'm ready to run—screw inspiration—when the staff door bangs open. Another employee stands in the doorway, balancing six boxes in his dark brown arms. Great, now he's got backup.

"Ayo, Brody! New Dark Horse shipment came in," he says, nodding toward the back room. Brody takes his cue and leaves us with one last laugh.

"Come on, I'll ring you up." I follow without questioning, keeping my eyes focused on his red Vans and rolled-up cuffs.

"Oh! Nice choice. Let's kick some butts and eat some nuts!" he chants while typing into the staff computer. I nearly choke on the spearmint gum I'm chewing.

"What?!"

"You'll see." He smiles. He's younger than Brody, with a short golden-bleached Afro. His name tag only says WHY. "It's one of my faves."

"Yeah? You shop in the *girl section*?" I growl back at him under my breath. Just ring me up so I can get out of here. The attention is getting to me. I start peeling the polish off my nails; the glittery flakes fall to the ground.

"Ugh. He brought that up? I've been trying to talk him out of that girl section since I started here—it's hella annoying." Embarrassed, Why pushes his red frames up onto the bridge of his nose. The lenses are covered in so many fingerprints and smudges I'm surprised he can see me at all.

"Sure."

"No, really. I know it's stupid, right? But his uncle owns the shop. Brody pretty much acts like he runs the place."

"Good for him." I hand Why my debit card, no receipt, and rush to the door.

"Hey, wait! Do you want to enter a raffle? It's for—"

"No thanks!" I cut him off, and get the hell out of there.

. . .

5

Atomix Comix is the only decent place left to buy comics in Eugene after Vanishing Planet vanished. Apparently, they went under without the extra income from selling board games, toys, and knickknacks. I never even got a chance to shop there. Now I'm stuck buying comics from grody Brody and the He-Man Woman-Haters Club.

I squint into the summer sun. The main drag is all washed out and white as my eyes adjust to the light. I try not to think about Liv getting to work at Books with Pictures this summer. How she'd never have her comics-cred questioned because she works behind the counter. Liv gets to be on the inside. I wonder if she kept the Lightning cosplay I made her. After all, it was *her* idea to dress as Final Fantasy characters. And yeah, I don't know who any of them are, but I liked the designs. I had no idea I was going to get called out. Not like that, anyway.

I need thread. I need buttons. Hot glue. Sequins. Armature wire. A new thimble for my ever-growing collection. I list out all the things I'll buy at the craft store to soothe my sore ego. I wish it were a longer walk; I don't want to taint the one place I like in this town with the bad vibes from down the street. The bells on the door at Kozy Corner jingle quietly as I step into the shop. The air is heady with the smell of dust and fake flowers.

I'm home. I pace the aisles, tracing my fingers along stacks of folded fabric. My mind races through the possibilities. This vinyl could be Black Canary's corset, and that intricate weblike brocade could be the lining for Spider-Gwen's hood.

And then I spot it. A summer-night-blue fabric, a blue the deepest depths of the oceans, an almost-black blue that practically glows under the shine of the fluorescent lights overhead.

This bolt of midnight-blue satin calls to me, crammed in the wrong spot between some yellow and green felt.

"Who put you here?" I ask the satin as I pull it out. I feel like fainting from just the sight of its cerulean perfection. I want to spray it with bleach and create a pattern of nebulas and galaxies. Hand-paint in stars, wire it up using fiber-optic strands so it twinkles, and, damn, what a gown it would be.

I would wear it to the premiere of my first summer blockbuster. And everyone would know that's Cameron Birch; she's the girl who designed the costumes. I fabricated them too, but I forgive their ignorance this time because I'm too busy posing with Chris Pratt for the press. I'll buy five yards of it.

"Don't you just look lovely today?" Dotty with the lilac-gray hair sighs as she rings me up.

"Thanks." I hope when I'm her age, great-grandma age, I look as cool as Dotty. She dresses sharp, severe. Slick black capes and pounds of pearls and baubles. I've never seen her wear the same pair of earrings twice.

"All pink and poofy and perfect." She kisses her thumb, her own personal gesture of approval.

"Sure."

"What's wrong? You've got a face like a wet weekend." She folds the satin carefully before slipping it into the plastic bag.

"Maybe too pink," I tell her as she swipes my debit card. I look over my pink doughnut-printed dress, the one I spent last weekend sewing after a serious bout of homesickness. I never liked the doughnuts at Voodoo Doughnut, but I loved seeing tourists with their pink boxes. I even sewed on little beads that look like sprinkles. Now I wish I had made something more normal. Maybe I should just start buying clothes at the mall again.

"No such thing as too pink." Dotty hands me my fabric while the printer screeches out my receipt.

"Thanks, Dot. See you round, I'm sure."

...

Dotty has style, but she's wrong. Pink is out. Pink is the new puke green. Get it out of here; get it away from me. At home, my closet is stuffed with fabric and costumes and all my super-girly clothes that I made and *used* to love. Now I need a major wardrobe overhaul. It doesn't matter how much I love Liberty of London prints—they're too floral, too feminine. I push aside my Zelda-from-Wind-Waker cosplay, the one that took fifty hours of work, and hang up the bag of faultless blue fabric next to it.

Zelda, of course, is way too pink. It doesn't matter how hard I worked to embroider the skirt. No more crowns, opera gloves, or princesses. I should have made Tetra's costume instead. Even if it would have been tragically simplistic, *she's* a pirate captain, a boss. I try to forget about how she turns into a princess half-way through the game, robbed of her ship and freedom. I fling the comics, still in their plastic bag, onto my bed. I belly-flop on top of them, haunted by that Brody guy and his ugly, beardy face.

I check my phone. Usually I'd have fifty notifications from Jen and Liv. When I lived in Portland, we could barely go a half hour without being in contact. Not so much lately. Not from them. Maybe it's the move. Though it's hard to blame the miles when their names, their faces, are right underneath my thumbs, only a text away. I love this picture of us, winning best group cosplay at Seattle Comic Con. It feels like we hopped on the train, suitcases bursting with costumes, years ago. But it was just this fall. I post the picture on my feed and tag them. *Miss you guise!!!* with a bunch of smiles and stars and hearts. I toss my phone aside. I don't want to know how long it'll take them to reply.

"Cameron's having a bad day, huh?" Cooper's voice enters my room before he does. He can tell when I'm in a funk without even seeing me.

"Where've you been?" I ask, even though I already know.

"Trying out that Wandering Goat coffee place with James and Krista."

"How do you have friends already? We just got here."

"Work friends, and, you know, asking people to hang out. You have to ask, Snip. You can't just wait around inside all day hoping."

"Oh, hello, fellow teen-person. Would you like to perhaps do this thing called 'hanging out'? Like that?"

"No. Not like that."

"And I did leave the house, thank you very much. That's what I'm so pissed about."

"What happened?" Cooper asks. I consider not telling him. It feels like a superficial problem, something that comes along with the territory of being a girl. Cooper leans against the door frame, his posture soft and understanding. I can't help but spill it.

"Why did I have to be the girl twin?" My words are muffled by my quilt.

"Like I know? As if it even matters, you wouldn't have been spared all that much heartache if you were me—that's for sure. So, let's hear it. What exactly is it you're mad about?" Cooper sits on the end of my bed and fishes out the comics from under me; I flip over to watch him. He looks just like me, black hair and brown eyes, pink cheeks under tawny skin.

"You're gonna have to drive us up to Portland next week. I can't go back to Atomix. The place is a nightmare bro fest."

"Um, no. I'm not. Not unless you have a way to pay for gas."

"Come on, you can't tell me you don't miss Portland."

"I don't miss our cramped-as-all-get-out apartment. I don't miss sharing a room with your messy ass. And I don't miss waiting four hours for Thai food," Coop says while flipping through one of the issues. "Squirrel Girl, huh? How're you gonna make that tail?"

"Doesn't matter."

"How much time do you want? Thirty or the full minute?" He pries his phone out of his skinny jeans.

"It's gonna take way more than—"

"Thirty seconds, then. Go." He taps the screen and holds it up. The timer starts ticking down. I get thirty seconds to mope about what happened, then I have to move on. Or at least let it go for the time being. We both have the tendency to be overly dramatic, so we put this system in place last year after the "free coffee punch card" debate dragged out for three full weeks. With seventeen seconds left, I start in.

"It's infuriating! We move down to the boonies, and it's like I'm living in a flipping time warp. News flash: Girls read comics! Girls like geeky stuff! Big whoop! Portland had me fooled, Snap. I can't believe I still, *still*, have to justify my existence to these creeps. What'd I ever do to them?! I'm never going—"

The timer cuts me off.

"Now, did you want to figure out the teeth"—Cooper rips out a page from the comic and holds it up—"or the tail first?"

Sigh. "Tail."

Girl at work.

It's stuffy in the loft above the garage, but it's all ours. It was the biggest consolation prize for moving down here when Mom got her new job at U of O. We were priced out of Portland; the rent got too damn high. In Eugene we could afford a whole house. I was incensed when I found out we couldn't stay for our last year of high school, for senior year with Jen and Liv; then I saw our workspace-to-be. Two giant skylights pouring in beams of sun like rays straight from heaven, and I swear I heard a harp plucking the "Hallelujah Chorus."

The roof is fitted with dark, wooden slats, and the floor is painted a dusty white. Built-in cubbies and foldaway tables line two of the walls. I stood in the loft, and for the first time I felt truly spoiled. Do we deserve this? Our own place separated from the house, but still close enough to pick up the Wi-Fi. It really is heavenly.

I used to build costumes in the living room of our old apartment, constantly having to repair stuff that got stepped on in the dark, losing pieces to well-meaning parents who were always shuffling gauntlets and cowls out of the way. Cooper has it easier; all he's ever needed is his laptop and a place to put it. He creates worlds in Word documents and screenwriting software. My creations need the room, and with this space I can finally build the costumes of my dreams. Big, complicated masterpieces.

Costumes that would impress Gillian Grayson, that *will* impress Gillian Grayson when she reviews my portfolio at the National Portfolio Review in six weeks. And then I'll get into CalArts, so every comic-shop-working douchecanoe in Oregon can paddle up a creek, because I'll be one step closer to Hollywood. So long, human armpits. Have fun trying to get girlfriends while I'm on a date with Thor.

"How many squirrels are we going to have to trap and skin?" Cooper asks from his workstation.

"Ew, zero. I'm not going real fur for some con costume."

"You're the one always harping about authenticity."

"Making it *look* authentic. Faking it till we're making it." I fan out a few more pages of *Squirrel Girl* on my desk. I had a decent grasp on the front of her costume before, but today's haul from Atomix completes the whole picture.

"This is the last cosplay," I tell him. "I need you to write me an original character."

"Nope," Cooper shouts, "you're gonna have to do at least *one* more!" He taps away on the keys of my laptop. Clicking and grinning like a madman. "Do you know some character named Quentin Quire?"

"No, but Google does." I thumb the name into the search bar on my phone. Marvel: pink Mohawk, punk, telepath.

"Someone saw your blog, and wants to pay three *hundred* dollars for the cosplay."

"How do you know?"

"He wrote to you; it's in your inbox." He turns the laptop around to face me, and I panic for a moment before remembering I went on a deleting spree last night. Nothing else for him to see in there but spam. But I know that won't last.

"I told you to stay out of my inbox. Stop guessing my passwords, Snap."

"Hey, good things happen when I check it."

"It has to be a scam," I say, but my heart races. I read the email again. Three hundred dollars is more money than my puny Etsy store makes in a year.

"Oh, hell no. He wants it in a week?" I let Cooper read over my shoulder. We huddle together over the screen. I bring up the client's blog. It looks legit, full of pictures of him attending different conventions. In each photo he's sporting a different cosplay, although none of them are very good. Lots of construction paper and felt; there's heart there, but not much skill.

"Aw, he's cute. And not afraid to wear tights, I see." Cooper wiggles his eyebrows and enlarges a picture of the guy in an excruciatingly form-fitting Aquaman outfit. "I'd hit it," he declares. I ask Cooper to pull up some pictures of Quentin Quire on his phone while I draft a response to the buyer.

"Is it doable? Seven days isn't all that much," Coop asks without looking up from his screen.

"Totally. It's not a build or anything. I could do most of it from

13

thrift store finds." I start pulling out my scrap bins and picking out anything black, anything remotely usable. There isn't much here, but I know I can pull it off. I have to. I sweep the *Squirrel Girl* pages onto the floor; I can make her outfit anytime. This is more important. If he's paying, I can finally call myself a legit professional.

"So what do I say to him?" I ask Cooper, feeling a little clueless.

"Ask for a deposit," Cooper directs me as I try to type a polite response.

"God, Cam, you type so slow. Gimme." Cooper takes over and drafts a perfectly worded email in under thirty seconds. Show-off.

"Okay, what else do you need to start?" he asks.

"If he sends the deposit, get his measurements. And ask if he has a specific version of the character he wants."

"Aye, aye." He hammers away at the keyboard and fires off the email.

"Thanks, now stay out of my inbox," I tell him, and I mean it.

"Whatever, Snip."

"I'll cut you in, if you'll be my stitch-bitch."

"Good, because . . ." Cooper clicks his mouse a few times. "It looks like we're a hundred dollars richer."

• • •

I love how quiet our new house gets at night. Before we moved, I had to suffer through marathons of French films and the tinny sounds of Beyoncé blaring through Cooper's headphones, singing him to sleep. Trying to block out the noise of his tossing and turning for hours. I could hear Mom pacing in the kitchen, tapping away at her laptop, planning her week. Dad's snoring was no match for our paper-thin walls. Here, it's dead quiet. Everyone is off in their own little corner of the house. It's peaceful. Until my phone jingles to life.

"Jen!" I smile into the screen. "How's everything? Did Liv start working at Books with Pictures yet? How's Portland?! Man, Eugene is so much worse than I expected. I thought it was going to be—"

"Cam, hey," she says softly. "Can you . . . You shouldn't . . ."

"What's wrong?" Usually Jen is bursting with news and gossip. I was so happy to see her name show up on my phone that I didn't realize how upset she looks.

"It's nice that you posted that picture, but could you not? Please don't tag me in stuff online anymore, okay? Don't post my screen name or anything."

"Oh. Did they start something?" I ask as Jen hangs her head. Her shoulders droop forward. She doesn't look at the screen or at me. Her bedroom is dark, and the light from her phone turns her skin an eerie shade of blue.

"Yeah," she sighs.

"I'm sorry. I never meant for—"

"I know. But I can't handle all the . . . all of it. You get it, right?" Jen asks, and I swallow the lump in my throat.

"Yeah," I croak.

"I think I . . . just need a little space. Time for it to blow over, you know?"

"Liv too?" I ask, hoping I'm not going to lose both of my lifelines in one fell swoop.

"I dunno. She's on vacation with her mom. No Internet in their cabin."

"Mm-hmm." I can barely speak. It feels like I'm losing more than a friend—it's more like losing a limb. An extension of myself.

"I gotta run. We'll talk soon, all right?"

"Okay."

She hangs up. And just like that, Portland seems that much farther away. As upset as I am, I can't say I blame her. If she were responsible for all the messages flooding my email, I might ask her for space too. I can barely handle it myself.

I open up my inbox. Cooper always guesses my passwords. I have to stop using the names of characters from games and movies. He knows all my favorite numbers, favorite colors. I never used to care; we shared everything. I'd read his emails, and he'd read mine. Our lock screens always unlock with the same four-digit code. Then I started posting my cosplay online, and I needed to keep him away. After Seattle Comic Con, I need all of it on serious lockdown. He has no idea why, and I'm trying to keep it that way.

Enter new password:

The box prompts me. It has to be good. Different. Something he won't expect. The cursor blinks, ticking the moments away. It can't be anything from pop culture, or our shared personal life. I look around my room, trying to find something worthy of protecting my one, big secret. Protecting me and Cooper all at once. And there it is, right in front of my face: my huge thimble collection. Standing like little soldiers. Ready for action.

I had tried sorting all the thimbles by style and type, but after a while the collection grew so large it would've taken a full day to get it all organized. I have porcelain ones with miniature Victorian ladies and lads painted on them. There are a few carved wooden ones, a glass one that looks like a strawberry. The silver thimbles are my favorites. Bordered with delicate filigree and sometimes inlaid with little stones or gems, they are precious to me. Each and every one.

Enter new password: thimblegirl

There are thirty-two unread messages screaming for attention. Thirty-two comments in a day. It's getting worse. I can barely even stomach the subject lines. I click each box, highlighting the messages, readying them for deletion. Every click pricks at my skin.

> You are whats ruining comics.
> attentionwhore
> fucking fake geek girl u make me sick.
> Genderswap *this* bitch
> pls write back. ilu so much id marry you
> dykebitch
> It's called research.

I know I can batch delete, and I know I can ignore my inbox altogether, but there's that dark place, deep down, that I can't help but visit sometimes. I let all the anons confirm my worst fears. That I'm a faker. Talentless. A waste of space. And when I'm there, in the dark place, there's no stopping my dye-black curiosity.

There is a part of me that misses the days when no one visited my blog, when the lack of likes was the only thing I had to worry about. Blowing up is a blessing and a curse. None of these jerks realize the time and effort I put into making the costumes themselves. They think I'm some poser with deep pockets and flat tits. I wonder if guy cosplayers have this problem.

I finish deleting the emails, not bothering to actually read them this time. I leave just one message, the one from my first client, right at the top, and star it. This is why all of this is worth it.

Even without reading the emails, I can still hear Brody's gravelly voice in my head, mocking me about my comic blind spots. I look up pictures of Dazzler. What's so bad about this one character anyway? What about her offends him so much? She's very blond and very shiny. The more I scroll, the more I fall in love with her. She's a diva; she's on roller skates; she's everything.

While I'm on an X-Men bender, I switch to researching Quentin. Gradually, the sound of Brody's voice and all the slimy subject lines fall away, replaced by ideas and plans for sweater vests and T-shirt designs.

...

It's dark, and my head aches from the Internet rabbit hole I just crawled out of. I spent way too many hours combing through way too many pictures of Quentin Quire. Even though I couldn't find any drawings of him from behind, it was worth it. Whatever happened earlier today is sufficiently buried in the feed of my life. Being hired for the first time is too exciting to let some comic shop creeps and online randos ruin it for me. I'm getting paid, flippin' cash money, to do what I love more than anything in the world. I'm winning, losers—watch out.

The cold air from the fridge soothes me as I rummage through condiments and strap on my cold mask. Headache relieved, I fumble back to my bedroom in the dark. Everyone in the house has been asleep for hours; they're all morning people. I am the night.

"Cameron Rose Birch! I'd like to drink my coffee in peace!" my mother howls from downstairs. She always gets mad when I let my alarm ring for more than ten minutes. Her voice shocks me awake in a way no puny phone alarm ever could. And *she* doesn't have a snooze button. I live for the snooze. I finally silence the beeping; the alarm has been going off for two hours this morning, but it's summer vacation. I should get to snooze as long as I want.

My hair is something to behold in the morning; it twists and swirls into black tornadoes and nests and tumbleweeds as I sleep. I like to keep it wild as long as I can stand it. Cooper has the same problem, but he tames his tresses the minute his eyes open. He's horrified when I walk into the kitchen.

"Is something living in it? That has to be the only excuse for all"—he waves his hand in a halo encompassing my face—"this."

"Yes, actually. A small family of raccoons moved in last night. I'm giving them until after breakfast to move out."

"Breakfast? It's noon." Mom pushes past me to the fridge and grabs her travel mug.

"Oh, then I guess it's brunch. Where's the lox?" I smile.

"See you both for dinner. Give your father a hand in the garden if he needs it." She has to reach up to hug us: we both dwarf her; last year we grew three inches, and she lost one. Mom takes a last look in the mirror, smooths out a kink in her own twisty gray hair, and is out the door.

"So today I thought we could hit up the Goodwill on—" I start.

"I can't help you today; I have work."

"Are you really going to get screenplay ideas working at Banana Republic?" I ask Cooper as he dashes around the kitchen looking for his keys, his wallet. Just like Mom does. Always in a rush to be fifteen minutes early.

"No, but I'll get *money.*"

"I'm earning now too!"

"So get to work, girl."

...

If I had the time, I'd knit Quentin Quire's cardigan from scratch. Buy some pink and black roving-weight yarn, cast on to my size 15 needles, and let it fly. That's the kind of effort I like to put in. I'd go down to Kozy Corner and buy muslin and chalk and create the pattern for his pants on sheets of tracing paper myself. But with only a week to create the cosplay, I don't have that kind of time. So I'm walking two miles to Goodwill, where I can comb through the bins. I know I won't find the exact sweater there—it's way too specific. But I know I can scrounge up a good base and alter it.

The bins have a smell about them, an aura. Dusty and funky, desperate and hungry. I savor it. It's hard to reach the bottoms of the bins standing at the edge. It's easier just to climb in. With yellow-rubber-gloved hands, I dive deep into the bins, even though it can get a little dicey down at the bottom.

I tell the girl shopping two bins over what I need, and I keep my eyes peeled for a raincoat without holes for her. Anything that looks remotely nice or usable I move to the top of the heap for the next scavenger. I try to spare them the dive.

I'm just about the same size as Quentin's buyer, which is a lucky break. I've already found a decent pair of black jeans that I can tailor. Now I try on whatever sweaters I can find as I dig deeper into the bin. A cream-colored knit sleeve peeks out from the pile, and even though it's missing a button on the front, I yank it out, hoping for a decent match. It's cabled, with gold buttons: it doesn't really work for the design at all, but I try it on anyway. My arm barely fits into the sleeve. It's way, way too small. I put the sweater aside on top of a purple plastic coat. No holes.

"I found you a raincoat!" I call over to the girl.

"Wanna trade?!" Her arm shoots into the air, waving a large white sweater. We both crawl to the edges and lean across the gap with our treasures.

"Whoa, this is actually pretty cool-looking." She inspects the coat. The zipper in the collar reveals a matching hood. "Nice find."

"You too!" I look over the sweater. It's really plain, and way too big, but too big is fixable. I could cut it into the shape and style I'm looking for. It's got all the right problems. "This'll be perfect." I look up from the sweater, and the girl smiles, happy to have helped a fellow hunter. She can't be much older than me; maybe she could be a new friend. Someone to thrift-shop and then grab some pad thai with? All I have to do is ask. That's what Cooper would do.

"So, what are you doing? You wanna hang . . . or chill? Or kick it?" Oh God, what's wrong with me? It sounds like I was raised in a bunker, and this is my first interaction with *an outsider.* Why am I so bad at this? I wonder why Jen and Liv ever hung out with me in the first place. If we hadn't met in third grade, would I have any friends at all?

"Um, maybe next time," she says, too politely, before plunging her arms back into the debris.

"Right. Happy hunting."

...

21

My workroom is alive with music from the speakers and, occasionally, the sewing machine. I've painstakingly deconstructed the sweater, and I'm placing straight pins in the new seams. Every now and then I carefully, carefully slip it on to test the size. One wrong move and the whole thing'll unravel. Once it's ready, I'll show Cooper how to sew it up, and I can move on to the pants, the T-shirt, the buttons, everything.

I pull up pictures of Quentin, searching and searching for the one side of his outfit I just can't seem to find: the back. The buyer wants Quentin from *Wolverine and the X-Men*, volume 1, and there are only a handful of pictures online.

In comics there are so many versions of the same characters spread across different issues and universes. You can't just put on a black catsuit and call yourself Catwoman. Not if you want to do it right. Do you add the exaggerated stitching like Catwoman from *Batman Returns*, or do you go with the Darwyn Cooke comic version? The one where she wears sports goggles and a big belt?

I like to get as detailed as possible. Unfortunately, the same few images of Quentin show up no matter what search terms I apply. And all of them are from the front. This is my problem.

My problem that was never actually a problem until we moved down here. I can't order that specific issue of X-Men online; it would never arrive in time. I need to actually go and buy it ASAP, which means going back to Atomix and facing the bro brigade. Suddenly the workroom is hot, too hot. Stifling.

• • •

Dad is hip-deep in a pile of weeds, socks pulled up to his calves, his floppy straw sun hat bobbing up and down with every yank.

His happy place. We got our workspace; he got to retire and tend to his dream garden. It's early summer and most of his plants are still young. No real produce yet, but more salad than I can stomach.

"Need a hand?" I call out to him, but I know he won't hear until I get closer. It's weird to watch your parents get older, and ours were already getting up there when we were born. Now they're pushing sixty. Sometimes I wish that they had us when they were younger. Then again, Cooper and I might not have each other if they hadn't waited. I pop a neon-yellow nasturtium blossom into my mouth—peppery and fresh—and wave to get Dad's attention.

"There she is! Can you believe all these weeds? The nerve," he jokes.

"So rude."

The garden is a mess: tools everywhere, two huge piles of dandelions and morning glories, their roots already starting to tangle together into one huge, villainous, monster plant. The dirt underfoot is beige, dry, and hard as rock. Dad has his work cut out for him.

"Is that the mail?" I reach into his wheelbarrow and grab a pile of catalogues and envelopes.

"Is it? Heh, I must've forgot to bring it in." He smooths his mustache with his thumb and pointer finger in one swift motion, leaving a smudge of dirt on his cheek.

"Oh my God, it's for the National Portfolio Review. Dad, you can't mulch my mail!" I turn the envelope over and over in my hands.

"Is that the thing?"

"The thing?"

"You know, the thing with that Jacqueline woman? The designer?"

"Dad!" I shout, frustrated. I've explained this to him dozens of times; I don't know how he doesn't understand it yet. "Her name is Gillian Grayson, and she's a teacher at CalArts. She's going to review all my work and—"

"Right, right, I remember now. She's a designer too, though; I thought you said—"

"Yes. She's both." I rip into the envelope and let it fall to the ground.

"Isn't it a bit early for that?"

"It should just be the requirements. So I can prepare and stuff." I scan the letter with shaky hands. I've been waiting for this for weeks, checking the program's website over and over so I could be the first one to get an update. This is the first, and it's a doozy.

> *Dear Ms. Birch,*
>
> *We are looking forward to your attendance at the National Portfolio Review on August 27th. Reviews begin at 11:30 a.m. and continue throughout the day with a short break for lunch. Representatives from 15 colleges will be in attendance, so budget your time accordingly. Your portfolio should include your best and most recent work, but feel free to show works in progress and sketchbooks as well.*
>
> *You have chosen the FASHION/COSTUME DESIGN track. Your portfolio should contain the following:*
>
> *Five original designs for characters that inhabit the same world, fully fabricated and photographed.*

A reimagined version of an existing character.
Any relevant sketches or prior work.
Keep your presentation simple: the work itself is
what's most important. Don't hesitate to contact us
with any questions.

"How am I gonna do all this?" I finally look up from the letter.

"All what?" Dad drops his trowel and reads over my shoulder. He smells like fresh dirt and cinnamon gum. Dad always smells like cinnamon gum.

"Five original characters. *Five?* There's no way I'll finish in time." Maybe if they had sent this letter during spring break, not six measly weeks before the deadline. How was I supposed to know?

"I'm sure you can use something you've made already. You have so many."

"They're all cosplay, Dad. All of them."

"What's wrong with that?"

"Cosplay copies existing stuff. Nothing I've made is, you know, unique."

I knew I would have to make some original creations, but five? It's impossible. Oh, and let's throw another reimagined design on top of it all. This is a disaster. I'm going to fail, never make it to design school, never make it to Hollywood. I'll be stuck here in Eugene the rest of my life, until I'm as old as Dotty and running Kozy Corner.

"I've seen you make a lot of things, Cameron. I know you can—"

"Everything depends on this. My whole flipping future!"

"I'm sure that's not true."

"Dad. Okay look. This . . ." I wave the letter in the air for emphasis. He has to understand just how big a deal this is. "This is how I'm going to get into college. They'll look at my work and evaluate, and this is, like, make or break."

"You've got decent grades. Don't those count for—"

"Hardly anything. Not for art school. Not really. This is how they're going to judge me; I need this to be the best stuff I've ever made. A bad review means I'll never get out of Eugene, and I have to get out of Eugene."

"So, you'll make your best work." He ruffles my hair, his hand still inside a dirty garden glove. Like it's that easy.

"I can't come up with five new characters. I'm not Cooper; I'm not a writer."

"Creating characters? Is that the problem?" He starts to chuckle but thinks better of it under the glare of my side-eye.

"It's *one* of the problems."

"I can help you with that. Come on." Dad adjusts his sun hat as he marches with purpose back to the house. Dad's not a creator. He would be if he ever finished anything, but when it comes to putting his big plans into action, they never seem to materialize. He's a dreamer, total Portland-hippie type. I go to Mom for work advice, Dad for life advice. I'll be impressed if he gets more than one garden bed finished before fall rolls around. He's dependable, but distractible. He's horrible at holding grudges; our fights are usually over by the time I can queue up a show to watch or a game to play. Mom, though? Mind like a steel trap.

"I know it's in here somewhere," he says, balancing on a rolling chair. I stand behind him, holding the chair in place. We have a stepladder, but that's not his style. His knees wobble as the chair rolls a bit. He laughs every time he almost loses his balance. He lives on the edge, knowing that we're holding everything steady underneath him—and I love him for it. He pulls down a box of Mom's scarves and winter hats from their bedroom closet.

"I can't copy from a book, Dad. I have to make it up myself. Or bribe Cooper into helping me."

"You won't need to with— Aha! Got it." The next box he pulls down is decrepit. The cardboard is water-damaged, with packing tape that's barely hanging on. I take it from him while he carefully dismounts. Loose bits rattle around inside. He doesn't need a knife to open it; his thumb slides through the tape like tissue.

"It's been a long time." Dad takes out a book, its pages warped by moisture, and hands it to me like it's his third-born kid.

The comic-book-loving, superhero-crushing, total geek inside me gasps. *Advanced D&D: Players Handbook.* I run my fingers across the cover. Two thieves pluck a ruby out of a gargoyle's eye. Flames leap up from a bowl in the statue's enormous hands while a group of knights discuss maps and plans in front of a giant slain serpent. It's totally badass. In that ultimate, uber-nerd way. That we-have-a-secret-club way. A code, a language, a game-that's-all-ours way. And I want in.

"You don't need to play the game, but there's a whole system for creating characters. It might be a good place to start."

"*You* played Dungeons and Dragons?" I ask. I've never played the game myself. Everyone I know plays games like this online. They leave the books and the papers out of it. Dungeons & Dragons has always seemed like the geek game I don't actually have enough cred to play. I tried to look up the rules online once, and it went way over my head. I don't think there is any one true way to play, and that's intimidating.

"You thought I *didn't*? Wasn't it you who once called me the dorkiest dad ever?"

"Probably." I thumb through the black-and-white pages. I don't know how this is going to help me, but I want it to.

"You never know. Maybe it'll inspire you."

"Worth a shot."

"I've seen you create some amazing things, Cameron. Seriously amazing. That giant sword? Come on, you're a shoo-in."

"I wouldn't go that far."

"And why not? Forget the swords and armor and wigs. Look at you! When was the last time you bought a dress from the store? You're going to sew your way right into their hearts. I promise." Dad wraps his arms around me, and I want to believe him.

"Gimme a piece of gum," I ask him.

"Here." He fishes a piece out of his pocket. "Now, come! Help me battle the level-six tentacle-weed demon in the garden."

We head back outside, both smelling like cinnamon.

• • •

I read about magic-users and bards. About rangers, clerics, and fighters. And the more I read, the more desperately I want to play. To have a group of friends gathered around a table telling a story. Creating and cracking inside jokes.

My chest hurts. I remember the last sleepover I had before the move. Sitting around on Liv's floor, Jen playing her ukulele while I attempted to paint a purple ombré pattern on her toenails. Liv would sing off-key, and we'd all join in for the chorus. Would they have played D&D with me if I asked? Liv might have. Jen would have had performance anxiety, but she'd crack the best jokes.

28

I pore over the pages, trying to forget about Jen and our last painful conversation. Dungeons & Dragons seems more open than a video game, a way to play a game with real choices instead of the fork-in-the-road approach you usually get. Press A if you want to be the good guy, B for the bad guy. On screen, that's all you ever really get.

I read about lawful evil characters who follow rules but twist them to be in their favor, not caring about the well-being of anyone else. Chaotic good ones place a high value on free will: they always intend to do the right thing, even if their methods are haphazard and generally out of sync with the rest of society. Choices, so many choices.

Page after page, I find myself more confused and more excited with every new rule and exception to it. This will help. I'll roll some dice, fill in some blanks, and *bam,* five new and original characters ready to be costumed.

But I have to finish Quentin first, so I slide the decaying cardboard box onto a shelf in the workspace and pull out some contact paper. Quentin wears a lot of T-shirts. He's different from most superheroes in that his "uniform" actually changes quite often. The client requested a specific one for his cosplay. It's red and reads MAGNETO WAS RIGHT underneath a picture of Magneto's face.

But I'm going to do him one better. Since Quentin wears different shirts, and the convention spans three days, I'm giving him three shirts. I'm that kind of thorough. I'm that kind of nice. Sadly, I don't have a silkscreen—not yet, anyway—so I have to make do with contact paper and X-Acto knives. I print out the reverse image, trace it onto the paper, and cut away the positive spaces. Stencil done, the paint goes on.

When the first shirt is dry, I try it on underneath the cardigan. I wouldn't dare do this otherwise, but my boobs are a negative-A cup and there's no danger of stretching anything out. The shirt fits perfectly. I bust out our button maker and create a few custom one-inchers. I pin them on in front of the mirror. Maybe tomorrow I'll dye the sweater.

"Whoa, I thought you were a dude for a hot sec," Cooper says, coming up the stairs.

"This better?" I pull off my headband and let my hair nest fall over my face.

"A bit. It's looking awesome."

"I need you to stitch some buttons on this cardigan while I work on the pants," I tell him, and gingerly hand over the sweater.

"A cardigan. You're telling me a superhero wears a cardigan?"

"I know, right?" I check out my reflection again. The T-shirt is perfect. It doesn't look handmade at all. I might as well have bought it from whatever store Quentin Quire shops at.

"What goes on the back?" Coop asks.

"Uh, I don't think there's anything on the back." I pace a little.

"You don't *think*?"

"Right."

"Shouldn't you know? What if there's, like, a name on the back, or some patch or something?" Of course Cooper is right; I need to know what's on the back. I can't just guess. Not with money on the line.

"Can you go to Atomix for me and—"

"Hell no, I won't. Where are your ovaries? It's just one neckbeard—be brave."

"Come on, Coop, they won't give you a hard time; you're a guy."

"A *gay* guy. If they *gave* you crap, they're gonna *kick it* out of me."

"No they won't. They wouldn't."

"Are you sure about that?" he asks, eyebrows arched, looking up from his needle and thread. Cooper is careful, and I don't blame him. He was bullied—no, tortured—when we were younger. It did get slightly better as we got older, but the scars are still there, even if the wounds have healed. At least Mom and Dad never cared. Hell, they got a rainbow flag for the front porch and a Human Rights Campaign bumper sticker for the car. Mom begged Cooper to let her march with the Proud Moms of Portland at Pride last year. He acted embarrassed, but I think he really loved it. And, of course, I don't care either; Cooper is my mirror, my alter ego, my best friend, my soul mate. Nothing could ever change that.

"No. I guess I'm not sure," I admit, and he goes back to work. I pull my hair away from my face and glimpse at the mirror again. "I should wear this," I joke. "If they hate girls so much, I'll just go in as a guy."

"Ha, show up as this Quentin character and blow their troglodyte minds with your mad skillz." Cooper leans back in his seat, imagining.

"No, not full Quentin, but just, like, a random boy. I'll wear this shirt, they'll be impressed with the reference, and I'll be all, *BOOM! I'm a girl!*"

"Let me do your makeup," he demands, his smile practically cracking his face in half.

"Do we still have that wig?"

■ ■ ■

My latest costume lies at the foot of my bed, ready for a good night's rest before its debut at Atomix. The wig doesn't look right. It's suspiciously shiny and the color isn't perfect. It would work for a comic-con, where everyone *expects* you to be wearing a wig, where people would suspend their disbelief. And while I doubt Brody or any other guy in the store will be picking apart my mismatched hair and brows, I want to look believable. Real.

My hair is short enough in the back that I could tuck most of the girly wisps under a hat. I ditch the wig for a beanie I knit over winter break.

I peek out of my bedroom door into the darkened hallway. The house is quiet. I don't know if Cooper's asleep, but I know he won't come poking his head into my room tonight. He got sucked into some just-released indie documentary, and he's plunked down in front of his screen taking notes. It's now or never. Fingers shaking, I open my laptop and log in to my inbox. Nestled between the hate, there's one message that doesn't seem too bad. I open it, hoping for the best.

SouthBySomnambulism left a comment on your photo:
I think you need to try and understand. When you dress up for a con people are going to get excited. Especially if you do a good job. Which you did! I won't begrudge you that. And then when you go on to win, over other people, other real fans, who actually love the games and shows they are cosplaying as, people are going to be pissed when they find out you aren't even a fan. You just did it for the likes, and attention that goes along with winning. So you honestly

shouldn't be surprised people are calling you an attention whore. It's what you are.

Why else would you dress up as Cloud if you've never played FFVII? Attention and fanboy-lust aside, I just don't get it. Why wouldn't you choose something you actually like? That way this won't happen. And if what you like doesn't get you the attention you're after, consider why you need all that outside validation in the first place. Because real fans can see right through your desperation. Pathetic. You're just pathetic.

Great. Thanks for all the advice that I didn't ask for, guy. Yes, I dressed up as a character I didn't know anything about. My friends love Final Fantasy, and I love a cosplay with spiky anime hair and a big-ass sword. So when we won and the emcee asked me what my favorite part of the story was, I didn't have an answer. I told the truth.

"Oh, I don't really play Final Fantasy. I just like the costumes." Why can't that be enough? How does knowing every line of dialogue or leveling up your whole party to ninety-nine make for a better cosplay? I geek out over the character design, but that somehow doesn't qualify me as a real fan? You would think I straight-up drank Stan Lee's blood with the way they're acting. This is supposed to be fun. His condescension only cements my resolve. Tomorrow I'll go back to Atomix, and I'll show them. I'll show every last one.

Return of the girl.

I'm wearing one of Quentin's shirts, the one that says WAKE ME WHEN THE HUMANS ARE DEAD inside a mushroom cloud. I'm wearing a pair of Cooper's jeans and a few swipes of his deodorant. A denim jacket, my cable-knit beanie. I'm wearing black Chuck Taylors, sunglasses, and a leather bracelet. I'm wearing dude.

Brody shelves comics while Why sorts through piles on the counter. I thumb through issues of X-Men, trying not to pass out. My heart is beating so fast and so hard I wonder if they can hear it. I'm looking for the paperback that will have Quentin's costume, but I can barely concentrate on the spines. My head is spinning. Can they tell I'm wearing a costume? Can they see that I'm a girl? It seems doubtful, because no one asks me any questions. In fact, no one says a single word. They don't even bother looking up. The shop hums with the quiet buzz of fluorescent lights.

"Where should I put these?" Why asks Brody, holding up a few issues of some comic with ponies on the cover.

"Girl section," Brody answers, barely looking up.

"I'm telling you, you gotta get rid of it."

"It's helpful!"

"It's not helpful—it's condescending." Even so, Why puts the pony comics where he's told.

"Yes, it is helpful! That girl came in and bought comics, didn't she?"

"Yeah, but I doubt—"

"Yeah, but what? I know girls get uncomfortable in comic shops. I'm trying to make it easier on them!"

"What does your uncle think about it?" Why asks.

"He doesn't care either way. He likes that I take initiative. I'm helping!"

I swallow hard, my stomach knotted up like scraps of thread at the bottom of my button bin. He's mentioned me. I'm standing right here, and he mentioned me. I guess my cosplay is accurate enough. . . . If I'm anything, it's thorough.

I'm floored. Brody is actually aware girls feel uncomfortable in his shop. I want to tell him that *he's* the one making it uncomfortable. He thinks he's being supportive.

"And you know, that way we don't have to constantly hold their hand and help them find stuff. It's annoying," Brody adds. I roll my eyes; that makes a lot more sense. He's looking out for himself first.

I keep waiting for the right moment, my cue to rip off the beanie and laugh that I'm a chick and they're all so wrong about girls, but it hasn't come. After ten minutes, it's as quiet as deep space. Brody coughs. I look at him expectantly, but he just spits into the trash behind the counter and goes back to shelving. Boys are gross. I know where the book I need is, but the lack of interrogation is making me want to browse. So . . . this is what it's like.

Finally. It's just like shopping anywhere else. It feels incredibly weird that shopping in peace should be a novelty, but I relish it. I wander around the store, taking my time. Some of the single issues are stuffed into their boxes carelessly. Covers and pages torn and bent. I don't know all that much about comics, but I know that no one wants theirs all dinged up. Everything is so poorly organized, with comics sorted by publishing house rather than alphabetically. And, of course, the ever-pastel girl section. Why is right: Brody needs to get a clue. He needs a librarian.

"Need any help, man?" Brody asks me. My shoulders tighten at the question. I look over at Why, but he's caught up reading a comic. Ms. Marvel is the only girl in the shop with his attention. I take a deep breath, trying not to blush or panic. But a chill still runs down both my arms. I shake it off and answer.

"Nah, dude. I'm—I'm okay." I feign confidence and turn my back to him. God, what if he recognizes me? What if my voice is a dead giveaway? It's not exactly manly. I close my eyes, waiting for his response, but it never comes. He just goes back to work and leaves me be. I exhale, light-headed.

My fingers shake as I run them along the spines of X-Men issues. Once I find what I'm after, I calm down a bit. I won't need to ask Brody where to find anything. I tuck *Wolverine and the X-Men,* volumes 1 and 2, under my arm. I pace slowly in front of the rest of the X-Men comics, not looking for anything in particular, enjoying the silence. I let out a small laugh when I see that Brody has stocked *Essential Dazzler,* volume 1, in the big-boy's section. I add it to my pile.

There's a display rack full of dice near the front of the store. I wander over and zero in on all the little plastic packets. Dungeons & Dragons has infiltrated my thoughts since I got the player's guide. It's fun to dream up new characters, but I don't have anyone who would ever play with me. Unless I dragged Dad back into it. Then I would qualify as dorkiest daughter on the planet. But maybe I'd feel less alone.

I give the rack a push and watch the dice spin by in a colorful blur. There were some in my dad's collection, but I'm missing that all-powerful d20. The twenty-sided die that decides your fate and so much else in D&D.

"What do you play?" Why asks, looking up from his issue of *Ms. Marvel*. It doesn't feel like he's quizzing me; he genuinely wants to know.

"Oh, um, Dungeons and Dragons," I cough out, talking as deep as I can go without sounding like a cartoon. I check for Brody's reaction, but he must have gone into the back.

"Really? Where at?" Why puts his comic down, excited.

"Ah, nowhere yet. I'm kind of a beginner." I can barely meet his eyes. Sweat prickles under my arms.

"Cool, cool," Why says, going back to his comic. He lets me continue browsing. I look over the dice, trying to find a good one. There are sets in tubes or boxes, but I only really need the one. I can't believe I'm about to ask a question, to ask for help at Atomix Comix. I walk up to the counter, dig my fingernails into my palms, and ask, "Have any d-twenties?"

"Only a whole bucketful!" Why reaches into the glass case under the counter and pulls up a tub of dice. "Fifty cents." I look through the clear plastic, trying to spy a good one.

"Here, this'll be easier." He tips some out, spreading the dice around so I can sort through them. They clatter against the glass counter like Portland rain on a skylight.

"Thanks." I nod. There's one for every color of the rainbow; some are swirled with iridescent, marbled plastic and white numbers; others are crystal clear. I'm immediately drawn to a pink one but think better of it in the moment. *No more pink.* I pick up a deep purple die, each side stamped with a number in gold. It's translucent with blue glitter suspended in the plastic. I love it. I place it on top of my stack of comics, signaling I'm ready to pay.

"Nice choice, but you're gonna want one more." Why motions to the pile.

"For what?"

"In case you get a bad streak. Always better for your luck to switch it up a bit." He tosses one of the dice over his shoulder and catches it with his other hand.

"Do you play a lot?" I ask, trying to keep my voice steady. Can he tell that I'm faking it? That underneath Cooper's clothes I'm just this poofy-skirt-wearing girl? There's no way he can't tell. It should be obvious, shouldn't it?

"We used to play once a week, but some of our players up and quit on us for, like, obligations and real life and stuff. People, right?" He rolls his eyes.

"Right," I chuckle. I consider his advice and sift through the dice for an alternate. Not that I'll ever really get to play. I'll take all the luck I can get.

"Love your shirt, by the way," he says. There it is, my opening. My time to whip out my hair and stand in the sun and scream *I am girl; hear me geek!* But I don't.

"Made it myself." I hear the reply come out without thinking.

"What?! No flippin' way." His eyes light up as he offers his hand, his wrist loaded up with paper wristbands and bracelets. "I'm Wyatt, but everyone calls me Why." I try to remember everything I was ever taught about firm handshakes and meet his palm with a slap.

"Cameron." For a moment I panic. Why didn't I think up a name? I had Cooper put a slight five-o'clock shadow on my face, but I didn't bother to think up a boy's name?

"You should get this one." Why holds up a lime-green die, and I sigh with relief, remembering that my name is unisex. "It glows in the dark."

"Heh, awesome." I take it from him, and he rings me up. Sliding the shopping bag off the counter, I start to go. If he hasn't noticed who I really am yet, I had better leave before he does.

"Hey!" he calls out. This is it—he knows. My heart starts pounding like a needle set on zigzag. "You should enter our raffle." I'm so flooded with relief I turn around and walk back toward him.

"A raffle?" I ask.

"Yeah, if you win, you get a discount for the month and a whole bag of comics."

"How much does it cost to enter?" I pat my pockets, knowing I don't have cash. I never carry cash.

"Oh, um, you get to enter when you make a purchase." He rips off a paper ticket from a roll and hands it to me with a pen. He fumbles and almost drops it when I take it from him. Klutz. "Put your name and phone number on the back."

I fill it out and drop it into a red fez. There are about ten other tickets. I like my odds.

"Thanks." I wave as I head out the door.

"Until next time." He smiles. Looking over the receipt on the walk home, seems like he forgot to charge me for the glow-in-the-dark die.

...

I head straight up to our workroom and pin up pages of *Wolverine and the X-Men*, enough to get a full picture of Quentin's costume. Turns out there's nothing on the back after all. I can't believe how easy it was, just showing up at Atomix and shopping. I felt so normal. My stomach turns as I realize that's how it should be, for anyone. I shouldn't have to suit up just to get some shopping done. But it works. For now, it works.

I take off Quentin's T-shirt and lay it out next to his cardigan, hoping I didn't sweat in it too much. It looks clean enough, but I'll iron it before shipping it off. There are only a few days left. I get out an old pair of black jeans to alter for his pants.

I rip the seams and pin them into a leaner fit, making fast work of the alterations. I've turned many pairs of thrift store pants into skinny jeans for Cooper. I snip off the black fly button and replace it with a slick red-orange number from my button tin. It's not technically canon, but I like adding little details that make my cosplays even more eye-catching. I'm planning on creating a belt to go with it that reads OMEGA-LEVEL TELEPATHS DO IT BETTER. It's an in-joke: one I wouldn't have gotten if I hadn't gone into Atomix today.

Steam puffs out of my iron as I make sure every seam is crisp on Quentin's pants. Finally ready, the pants get folded and packed, and I allow myself a moment of satisfaction as an empty cardboard box becomes the beginning of my first shipment to a paying client. My heart lightens, and I laugh. I'm really doing it.

Cooper did a nice job of sewing the buttons on the cardigan. I have more patches to add, so I leave it hanging on the wall. But the three T-shirts are ready to go, so after a quick pass with the iron, I add those to the box. Almost done. Tomorrow I'll hunt for accessories.

•••

"That dirt better wash out." Cooper scowls while trailing behind me in the garden. I'm snipping kale, lettuce, and more nasturtium blossoms, and tossing them into a basket in his arms. I kneel in the dirt, still wearing his jeans, harvesting our dinner.

"It's just dirt." I whip a dandelion at him.

"Tell me about it again," Cooper begs, recoiling.

"No one gave me a second glance. . . . It was like I was invisible."

"I would have spotted it from a mile away," Cooper chides.

"Well, either the guy working there needs new glasses, or he's too polite to say anything." I add another handful of arugula to the basket.

"Or we're really, really good," Cooper says out of the side of a smug, lopsided grin.

"Or that."

"Do the voice, do the voice again!"

"I didn't 'do a voice.'" I mime air quotes. "I just—" I clear my throat and think about scrubbing any soprano notes from my voice. A voice that's still mine, but more monotone, a more sultry alto. "'Sup?" I ask Coop, deep and steady. He cracks up, lettuce leaves flying from his basket.

I fooled every single guy in Atomix today, and Cooper still laughs at me. It stings a little. I snatch up the fallen leaves and huff toward the house.

"Real nice, Snap," I call to him over my shoulder.

"Hey! It's good! Come on!" he yells back from the garden. I know he means well, but I'm not a joke.

Mom and Dad bustle around the kitchen, cooking in tandem while I set out plates and napkins. Cooper brings in the basket and starts rinsing the lettuce in the sink. In the summer we usually eat together. During the school year, all bets are off.

"Ew ew ew ew ew!" Cooper shrieks, running from the sink. "Slug! Cameron!" He stands behind me and pushes me to the sink. Watching him squirm over invertebrates cracks me up, and I realize it was stupid to get snippy at him before.

"Don't worry, I got you." I use my boy voice to make him laugh before washing the offending slimeball down the drain. No mercy for freeloading slugs. "All better."

"What are you wearing?" Mom double-takes at my voice, and I realize I haven't washed the makeup shadow off my jawline yet. I'm standing in the kitchen in a ribbed tank and my brother's jeans. Cooper and I both crack up.

"Cosplay thing," I tell her, and she clicks her tongue and rolls her eyes. This isn't the first time I've shown up to dinner in some strange getup. Once I dined in full space-age body armor. She loves me, but I'm not sure she gets it.

"How's the portfolio going?" Dad asks, carving up a small roasted chicken.

"Haven't quite started yet. But I bought a d-twenty today."

"That's my girl."

"D'aww, our widdle girl is growing up," Cooper mocks. "Wait, what's a d-twenty?"

"How many schools are reviewing your portfolio?" Mom asks, pulling out a chair as we all take our places. Always straight to business.

"I only really care about one," I tell her, through my first huge mouthful of salad. Cooper is avoiding his, pushing it to the far edge of his plate, knowing what once lay within.

"Okay, but you're going to see more than just one school, right?" Mom's brow wrinkles. She doesn't look at me when she asks. She thinks the question is rhetorical.

"I don't know."

"All that hard work . . ."

"I know."

"There's nothing wrong with a backup plan."

"I don't want a backup plan."

"Well. Too bad, so sad, missy. There's going to be fifteen schools there. You'll go to as many as possible. And you—" She points a fork at Cooper. "I know you didn't make that writer's program. But that's no reason to laze about all summer and—"

"I thought we agreed we would never bring that up," Cooper snarls.

"Mom, he was heartbroken. Let it go."

"All I'm saying is—"

"We know!" Cooper and I cut her off. She means well, but she has the tendency to take things too far.

My phone beeps in my pocket: a text, saving me and Cooper from the double interrogation.

"Not now, you two," Dad scolds us. We've been known to text

each other during meals, classes, work, all day, every day. Cooper holds up his hands in a show of innocence: the text isn't from him. If it's not Coop, it's got to be something bad. Liv is finally back from her trip, and she's texting to say she doesn't want to be my friend anymore either. Or it's the Quentin client, backing out after scrolling through my old posts. He saw my very first, very crappy cosplay of Princess Leia—from Endor, not the bikini one—and now he knows I'm not good enough. I bet he asks for a refund. It was too good to be true. My phone burns a hole in my pocket as my mind spins around all the possibilities.

"Did you want to see that French movie, the arty one, you know, with the colors and stuff?" Mom asks Cooper. The two of them go on art-house-movie adventures together. I don't have the patience for slow, quiet movies. Not unless the costumes are outrageous enough to make up for it, and they rarely ever are. My phone beeps again.

"Yes! I'm dying to see it," Coop answers. "I'm trying to write something good like that, Mom. You know, something French, something like *Breathless,*" he sighs. I shovel what's left of my dinner into my mouth and practically frisbee the dish into the sink.

"Dinner was great. Gotta get to work." I try not to spit out any food and make a mad dash for my room.

■ ■ ■

I'm holding my phone, standing in front of my bedroom window, checking out my reflection in the black glass. I look a mess, caught somewhere between boy and girl. Long lashes, fake stubble, dirty jeans. I didn't think I would have to decide—not so soon, anyway. I'm supposed to be spending all my time creat-

44

ing original costumes, so I wouldn't need to go back to the comic shop for a while. Dressing up was a lark, a prank. I was supposed to be proving a point. But now it's become a whole new problem.

541-555-7654

Hey man, it's Why from Atomix.

Sorry to like, just text you but I thought you might be down for joining a D&D campaign.

We're gonna start something new.

You wouldn't be behind or anything.

And we need players.

Do I want to go and play? Hell yes, I do. I want to see how it's done, how all of the rules play out on a real table. But would Why have asked me if he knew I was a girl? Doubtful. I'll just text him back, tell him I was dressing up for a project, an article, something stupid ripped from a bad teen movie. We'll both laugh, and I'll show up and play like it's no big thing.

Right now it's just me, our DM, and this guy from the shop, Brody.

Brody.

...

The dollar store can be hit or miss, but it's a cosplay gold mine if you have imagination and you know what you're looking for. Quentin's costume is so close to done. I run through the final touches in my head: some yellow-lensed glasses, a pair of really long shoelaces, and the perfect shade of pink hair chalk for his Mohawk. Finding the right pair of shoes will be the hardest part. Cooper promised he would check around the mall after he gets off work.

No yellow shades, but there are plenty of clear faux-hipster glasses. I pick up two pairs along with the laces. A calculator watch calls to me—I feel like it would suit Quentin well—and I add it too. I grab some oversized safety pins and a pack of beginner-artist chalk pastels. They work great for coloring hair in a not-so-permanent way.

I make another stop over at Kozy Corner for glass paint and a few more buttons. Five minutes and a coat of paint is all it takes to transform dollar-store glasses into designer shades.

The purchases are eating into my profits, but I'm having such a good time I don't really care. The bell at Kozy's jingles, and Dotty looks up from her crochet hook.

"Cameron! How's tricks?"

"Got my first commission." I beam.

"Congratulations! You're on your way!" She claps her hands with excitement and her acrylic bracelets clack together in agreement.

Dotty goes back to hooking yarn while I browse paints and dyes. My phone buzzes, a brick in my pocket, weighing me down. I didn't know how to respond to Why's invite last night, and now I'm afraid to check it. I keep thinking about myself as dude Cameron, Cameron Boom, a Chaotic Good Rogue. Would that Cameron just go and play, for justice? For fairness? For the good of girlkind? I'd like to think so. If he would stand up for us, so should I. I take out my phone. I bypass Cooper's text about picking up pleather boots at Payless and head straight for Why's thread.

I take a moment and try to get into Cameron Boom's head. How does a guy sound when he texts? If there's a major difference, I can't tell.

Cameron

hey, would love to play.
lemme know.

On my way home from Kozy Corner, I try to piece together who I am when I'm him. Should I be the same—exactly the same—with one minor difference? Or do I start over, reinvent everything, be a person I never thought I would need to be?

It's certainly an interesting way to create a character. But the makeup, the clothes, the voice, it's all too much to keep track of in the first place. I'll just be me; Cameron Birch is every bit the geek Cameron Boom is. And hey, if they accept him, maybe, eventually, they'll accept me. If not . . . I don't know.

The girl's got talent.

The wind tosses my hair while Cooper drives and I windsurf, waving my arm through the air currents out the passenger-side window. He sings along with Adele at the top of his lungs. It's a perfect start-of-summer moment. And to top it all off, I'm about to get paid.

We're headed to the post office. Quentin Quire is finished, folded, and all boxed up. The only thing that's left to do is ship it off. My first sale ever, complete.

"When are you gonna learn to drive?" Cooper asks me over the music.

"I know how to drive."

"Your four failed attempts at the road test say otherwise."

"Whatever." I don't need to learn how to drive, or at least I didn't when we lived in Portland. We were three blocks away from the MAX, and I had my bike and the bus. Now I'm lucky I can walk to Kozy Corner and Atomix, but that's pretty much it. Cooper is tired of schlepping me everywhere, but he has to, because he loves me.

"What about that portfolio thing—how's that going?" He turns down the volume a bit, and I wish he hadn't. I don't want to talk about it, not now.

"Who are you? Mom?"

"Just asking, Snip." He rolls his eyes.

"Sorry, I just . . . I'm nervous. It's so much work. I don't even know where to start."

"Start with one, then move on to the next," he says.

"Right. I know. Right." I crank the volume back up; the next song is too good, and I'm done being stressed out. We keep singing together. Cooper sounds perfect and I sound like a goose, but we make it work all the way to the post office. I dash in with the box, and Cooper keeps the car running.

"That'll be thirty-four ninety-nine," the stocky man behind the counter says. He rocks on his heels and smiles. It's a lot for shipping, but I got all the bells and whistles. Had to. It needs to arrive in two days, and in one piece, so I'm willing to pay extra. Do I want insurance? Yes. Do I want a signature? Yes. Certified receipt? You know it.

"Be careful with it, okay?" I tell the postal worker as he takes the box from the scale.

"Of course, miss."

"It's really important."

"They always are."

"But this one *really* is." I poke the box, punctuating the

sentence, trying to seal the deal, trying to ensure no one chucks the box into a truck and the hair chalk explodes all over the costume. Not that I didn't anticipate that—the chalks are wrapped up tight in a ziplock and, like, half a roll of saran wrap.

He laughs and pats the top of the box and places it very, very gently onto the shelf behind him. Before addressing the next customer, he crosses his heart, making an X on his chest with his pointer finger. He gets it. I leave.

Cooper guns it out of the parking lot. My phone's been ringing for three full seconds. Why's name is displayed over his dorky, thumbs-up selfie. Who actually makes phone calls anymore? Four seconds. Ignore or answer?

"You gonna get that or not?" Coop reads my mind, trying to steal a glance at the screen. A few more fake old-timey rings and it'll go to voice mail. Luckily, I never set up an outgoing greeting. Why's not actually going to leave me a *voice mail*. . . . He wouldn't do me like that, would he? I clear my throat and answer deeply, "Yo, 'sup?" Cooper can barely contain his laughter. I motion for him to keep his eyes on the road.

"'Sup?!" His voice is so bright and cheery I could be blinded by it. "So, like, we were gonna start the game tomorrow night," Why starts, and stops.

"Uh, okay."

"Right, and, you know, I really want to play and stuff, but our DM says we need another player." He goes from buoyant to sinking.

"Why?"

"Yeah?"

"No, I mean, *why* do we need someone else?" I ask.

50

"Not as fun with only three players. He wants at least four," Why sighs. Cooper's face is pink from holding back his snickering.

"That sucks, bro," I say, and Coop lets out a snort, his eyes watering from my apparent hilarity. "Oh, you know what?" I ask, glaring hard at my brother. "My brother would totally play with us." Cooper almost stops the car short. That certainly shut him up.

"NO EFFING WAY," he mouths.

"Really? That would be so awesome; I was really looking forward to—" Why pauses. "Like, you know, hanging out or whatever."

"Yeah, sure. He'll love it."

"NO NO NO NO NO NO NO NO." Cooper pulls into our driveway and slams on the brakes.

"Make your characters and bring them tomorrow. See you at Atomix at eight?" Why asks.

"We'll be there." I smile devilishly at Cooper. He snatches the phone from me and hangs up.

"There is no way in high holy heck I'm going to—" Cooper looks at my phone, Why's selfie still up on the screen. "Wait. This guy is going to be there?"

"Yep."

"What should I wear?"

...

I've flipped through the player's guide Dad passed down to me a dozen times, but I'm no closer to figuring out what kind of character to make. I have no idea what kind of game we're in for.

Cooper's character comes to him so effortlessly, his writing chops fully on display. Now that we're actually going to play, I have to pay attention to the rules, and I can barely understand them all.

The font in the guide is so small and dense, I wish I owned a magnifying glass. Each page loaded with charts. What's your ability score? What's your weight allowance? What's your hit probability? My eyes glaze over.

"I thought this was supposed to be fun," I whine at Coop.

"Isn't it?" He scribbles something down in his notebook.

"I don't understand any of it."

"You got me involved in this mess, and now you're backing out?"

"Just help me, okay?" I lean into his shoulder.

"Fine. Start here and pick a race for your character. Dad highlighted it, look." Cooper talks slowly, without patronizing me. So completely different from Brody trying to mansplain comics to me.

"Which did you pick?" I ask, glancing over the list.

"Wood elf, and sexy as hell." He goes back to his paper and lets me look over my choices. Elves look fun; half-orcs do not. I could be a human, but I suppose it's not all that creative of a choice. I settle for a good mix of everything and choose halfling.

"I shouldn't play a girl character, should I?"

"Jesus, Cam. How much more complicated could you make this situation?" Cooper looks at me, shocked.

"Okay, okay. I'll be a dude. A dude halfling thief."

Cooper names his character Jade Everwood. He doesn't let me look at his stats, claiming that it's only his first draft. Writers. He takes his notebook and my glittering d20 up to his bedroom, leaving me with the handbook and a half-baked character.

I didn't think Dungeons & Dragons would be so much work. Without a board or cards or pieces, I figured you'd just make it up as you went along. I pore over the classes and the abilities again. If Brody is playing, I have to know every rule inside and out, like threading my sewing machine with my eyes closed. I have something to prove: That girls belong in Atomix. That girls belong, period. I'll be the best halfling thief he's ever seen, and then I'll show him who I really am. Cue the fireworks; cue the "I told you so."

It's not part of his character sheet, but I can't help wondering what costume Cooper's character would wear. As I lie in my dark bedroom, ideas come instantly. I wouldn't go full Lord of the Rings—it's been done; it's had its moment. No ornate scrolling filigree and silver. I'd make it more natural, from the forest, from the earth. And of course, since this is Cooper we're talking about here, I'd have to make it a little scandalous.

Maybe a dusty jade tunic with a low neckline, or it could have wooden buttons and a collar. That way he can decide how provocative he wants to get with it. I'd give him a crushed-velvet-lined vest that evokes birch bark, a pocket watch with a vine instead of a chain.

I flick on the bedside lamp and grab my sketchbook from my desk, accidentally sending Why's little green glowing d20 across the floor. It lands on eighteen. I get to work.

■ ■ ■

"Does it look all right to you?" I hand my dad the notebook with my character's stats. He runs down the list with his finger, smiling proudly, a huge mound of wood chips at his back. The entire garden smells of cedar and sunshine. His tomato plants are only shin-high, but they look healthy and strong.

"Sure, why not?" he chuckles.

"I want it to be good, Dad. It has to be perfect."

"There's no perfect in D and D, I promise you," he says, and passes the notebook back. "Especially if you have a good DM."

"That's, like, the guy running the show, right?"

"Exactly. Any decent Dungeon Master will make sure everyone shines at one point or another." As he explains, Mom weaves through the path to join us. She's getting sunburned, her cheeks flushed red. I can see the sun reflecting off her forehead, sweat pooling in her wrinkled brow. Mom hates yard work.

"Cameron! You're finally awake, good," she pants.

"It's two p.m., of course I'm—"

"Come on, I want you to show me your portfolio." Mom takes my wrist and leads me toward the garage.

"You'll be fine!" Dad calls out. I don't know if he's talking about Dungeons & Dragons, or my mother.

"There isn't much time left, right? Show me what you have so far."

"I don't need a babysitter, Mom," I protest, but neither of us are convinced. The only thing I've managed to make up until now is Cooper's D&D drawing.

"I'm curious. Humor me." She climbs up the stairs to the loft and collapses into our enormous beanbag chair. I pull three old costumes out from the Ikea armoire.

"I was thinking about showing these," I lie, draping them across my sewing table. I hold up the long blue-and-white Corpse Bride gown.

"I saw those already. Especially that zombie-wedding one. Don't bring that one; it's too scary. Where's the new stuff?"

"Jeez, Ma. It's coming."

"Look, you're not working this summer. We've moved out here and given you this lovely space. You can't waste it." She sinks farther into the beanbag chair, and my fists clench. I haven't wasted one inch of the space here. "Do you need money for fabric?"

"No, actually. I just got paid for a costume yesterday." It feels good, not having to ask her for cash. I can build the portfolio all on my own, and I won't have to answer to Mom if one of the costumes is too "scary."

"Well, that's excellent! Why didn't you tell me?"

"I don't know. Just in case something, you know, went wrong." I drape the gown over the other two outfits.

"Oh, Cameron. Listen." Mom reaches out and pulls me down next to her. We sink into the chair and look up at the ceiling. She pets my arm. "I know, I know—I get after you to do well. It's only because—"

"You want the best for us," I sigh.

"Yes, well, that's part of it."

"And hard work builds—" I do my best Mom impression before she cuts me off.

"You're talented. You and your brother both, just like your father. Not everyone is blessed with talent. I know I wasn't." She talks quietly, deliberately. Mom has always encouraged Cooper and me, but this is the first time she's praised us so openly. My throat dries up, like it's stuffed with fiberfill. I don't know how to respond.

"But talent isn't everything, Cam. Talent is nothing if you

don't do the work. And I couldn't bear to see it go to waste, you understand?" she finishes. I nod, guilt pooling in my stomach, knowing I'm going to be goofing off at Atomix tonight when I should be sweating away over my sewing machine. "Good, now how do you get out of this thing?" Mom and I roll out of the bean-bag onto the floor. She stands and clomps back down the stairs.

She's right. I get my scrap bin and start sewing. Doesn't matter what yet, I just need to work. I take a few scraps and sew them together, edge by edge, into a patchwork. I stitch fast and loose. The pieces are strangely shaped, but I find sides that fit together and make a mosaic out of the material. First the dark green scraps, then lighter and lighter, a yard of pixelated ombré fabric spits out from the machine in front of me.

My shoulders ache, but I don't want to stop. My fingers keep working, adding white fabric to the lightest edge of my miniature quilt. I hold it up. It's beautiful, but . . . what is it? Whose is it? Bits and pieces sewn up and Frankensteined into something new. Something more beautiful than the sum of its parts. In this moment, I understand why people make quilts.

"How the heck can you see anything up here?" Cooper stumbles as he gets to the top of the stairs. I've been at it so long I didn't even notice the sun had set. I'd been working by the little light of my sewing machine for who knows how long.

"Sorry, got distracted." I stuff the quilt into the scrap bin and slide it under my desk. I don't feel ready to share it with Cooper yet. He turns on the light.

"You're not ready? We have to go in like ten minutes!" He points to my skirt.

"Oh crap!"

"That's right, oh crap," he echoes. "Come on, Snip. You have permission to raid my closet."

...

Cooper's closet is immaculate, his shirts organized by color, print, and style. No wonder they love him at the Republic of Bananas. My closet erupts as soon as you open the door. Nothing I own is wrinkle-free; I can't even find one pair of matching socks. I slide the hangers across the bar, shirt after shirt, slacks and jeans. Nothing jumps out at me. I mean, I don't know who boy Cameron really is. I know what *I* like, but what if that's a giveaway? I'm on my second tour through Cooper's closet when he stops me.

"No one is going to care. Pick anything."

"How do you know?"

"You really think the gathering of the geeks is going to give one half of a shit what you wear?"

"Fine." I grab a plain pair of jeans and a color-blocked button-down. A sports bra under a ribbed tank top is enough to smooth out what little curves I have. Cooper starts fretting and flipping through his closet while I tuck my hair into my beanie.

"I thought you said no one is going to care what we wear."

"No, what I said was no one is going to care what *you* wear. I still have to look good."

"For the geeks?"

"For that cute one on your phone, obviously."

Cooper chooses a caramel-colored corduroy jacket over a white shirt and matching boots, and, damn it, Cooper is always so put together. I can create a suit of armor out of sheets of tin

57

and pop-tops, but I can never style myself. I love too many things, too many styles. He looks great and I look like a dude, but I guess that's all that matters right now.

"Let's go, *bro*." He punches my arm as we check each other out in his floor-length mirror.

"Heh. Here *bros* nothing."

A girl and a game.

"If it's not Mountain Dew, it's not tradition, man." Brody is debating over a spread of two-liter bottles set up inside of Atomix. He taps a red plastic cup against the glass counter with every syllable. "Moun. Tain. Dew. Is. Our. Brew."

"I'm just sick of it. What's wrong with black cherry?" The two boys, one I've never met, are so preoccupied with their dispute they don't notice Cooper and me standing in the doorway. I'm having my own debate: stick this out and see it through, or run. Fast. Cooper must notice my trepidation, so, naturally, he shoves me into the room.

"Ahem!" he coughs out as I stumble forward.

"Hey, man, you're Why's guy, right?" Brody smiles and opens the Dew.

"Uh, yeah. Yep. Right." My eyes dart around the shop. I can barely look at him. My head is sweating underneath the beanie.

The mess of hair tucked inside only intensifies the heat. I can feel Cooper staring at me. They're all staring at me.

"I'm Cooper. Cameron's brother."

"Ah, nice. Lincoln. I'm the DM." Brody's friend shakes Cooper's hand, and then sticks it out for me to take. It's a great hand, a handsome hand. Broad, and twice the size of mine. I can't stop thinking of his hand reaching out and palming my entire face. In a good way? A really good way.

"Hello?" Lincoln waves his perfect hand in front of my eyes, and I finally snap back to reality.

"Yeah, hi. Hey. 'Sup?" I shake his callused hand and hope that mine feels sufficiently manly. "Cameron."

"Don't worry, there are never any dragons on the first day," Lincoln says, picking up on my nervous vibes. His smile spreads across his face; his cheeks are two round, soft peaches. He's trying to break the ice, but I just end up melting. It takes all of my resolve to not tilt my head to the side and flutter my eyelashes. I straighten up and crack my knuckles just to distract myself. "We're just waiting on Why. He's always late. You guys can set up if you need to." He points to the folding table, then starts pulling little figurines out of his bag.

Lincoln is not what I expected to find in Atomix tonight. Sure, he fits the role perfectly: a SCHRÖDINGER'S CAT IS ALIVE T-shirt, pleated khakis, and boat shoes. Everything about him screams omega-level nerd, but I can't take my eyes off him. I thought I might make some new friends today, but I never imagined I'd meet one with that kind of *potential.* Forget Brody; forget Internet trolls; forget everything, because: Lincoln. Sandy-blond, peach-faced Lincoln.

Cooper and I pick out two seats at the long table set up for us and try to go through the motions of getting ready. Neither of us have any clue what we actually need to set up. We shuffle our character sheets around and line up our dice. Cooper asks if he can use mine: sure, whatever. My eyes are fixed on Lincoln's face, Lincoln's body. He's much taller than me, and he is bigger, softer. He has this great unmissable presence in the room. A hug from him could smother me, and aren't those the best kinds of hugs?

"You're drooling, Cam," Cooper mumbles under his breath.

"Shut up."

"You're being obvious—that's all I'm saying." Cooper rolls the sparkly purple die, and it lands on a ten.

"Hail, hail, the gang's all here!" Brody's voice booms across the store as Why finally joins the rest of us.

"I wouldn't leave you mageless—never fear," Why jokes.

"Hey, Why!" I call to him. Now that he's actually here, I feel more comfortable—excited even—and grateful he invited me. I don't care if it's only because he thinks I'm a dude. "This is Cooper, my brother." They exchange handshakes, and I swear I see Cooper blush. Great, now we're both swooning.

"I'm so glad you came; it's gonna be a blast. Promise." Why's overstuffed spiral notebook spills out on the table in front of him. The cover is creased and worn; I wonder how many characters are crammed into those pages.

"Dew? Dew?" Brody offers each of us a cup of the carbonated yellow drink. "Dew?"

"Make mine a double," Cooper jokes.

"Heh, good call." Brody actually laughs at Cooper, and I see him relax a bit.

"Is that . . . ? No, it can't be." Lincoln points to my pile of stats and papers.

"What?" I look at all the other books laid out on the lopsided folding table. Oh shit, we messed up. "Did we bring the wrong book?" I hold up Dad's handbook.

"It is! It's a first edition!"

"Holy shit, let me see it!" Brody grabs the book right out of my hands, cracks it open, and starts flying through the pages.

"Careful, man. That's vintage," Lincoln scolds him, and takes the handbook from him.

"Where on this planet earth did you score that?" Why asks.

"It was my dad's."

"Oh, for real?! You two are gonna slay us all, aren't you?" Why smiles.

"Slaying is what I'm best at," Cooper boasts. Why coughs, trying to hold in a mouthful of soda.

"Do we have to start over? What book are you guys using?" I ask the table.

"Three point five." Brody holds up his book. It's brown, printed to look like some ancient, gilded, leather-bound volume.

"No, we're using five," Lincoln corrects him, holding up his own copy. His features an enormous demon swathed in flames on the glossy hardcover. My version seems rinky-dink in comparison.

"I told you, I don't want to play unless it's three. Three point five was my compromise." Brody folds his arms and practically pouts. I can't believe I was intimidated by him. He's such a baby.

"So we're screwed?" Cooper asks.

"Psh, Lincoln'll make it work." Why takes our character sheets and passes them along to our Dungeon Master. Brody reluctantly forks his over too. Lincoln is flipping through the papers while I watch his overgrown blond hair fall around his soft face. He rubs his chin and reads carefully. Why keeps rolling one of his dice anxiously.

I glance around the table. Could these be my people? My new Eugene crew? The way Why bounces in his seat reminds me of Liv with her endless energy. I think she'd like him. She would call me crazy for my insta-crush on Lincoln. But that's why I have Cooper. To validate all my swoony feelings, because he gets them twice as much as I do. And there's Brody, I guess. I don't know what to do about him. Where are all the girls?

"It's great that you're here." Why leans in. "I've really missed playing."

"Can I be honest?" I huddle in, whispering in my tenor voice. Why nods. "I've never done this before."

"Try to remember that it's just a game. You'll be fine." He snickers. "Oh man, I'm almost jealous—you never forget your first time."

"Ha!" Lincoln's voice rumbles the table. I worry that he heard me and Why and is laughing at my inexperience. He keeps laughing to himself as he gathers his hair into a short ponytail. He looks a little nuts, laughing and rubbing his hands together maniacally. He's got plans for us.

"What's that thing?" Cooper asks while Lincoln sets up a folded paper screen in front of all his books and dice and pens.

"This is where the magic happens." Lincoln waggles his eyebrows. "I get to be a little sneaky, don't want to spoil all your fun."

"What are you, some sort of noob?" Brody scoffs.

"Shut up, Brody," Why interjects. Cooper smiles and relaxes a bit, relieved to have someone stick up for him.

"Let's begin, shall we?" Lincoln straightens up in his seat. The rest of us lean forward on the edges of ours.

...

"We'll start at the Brass Talon, a dimly lit stone bunker of a tavern with a long brass bar and cheap drinks. Clover, Wizzy, you are at the bar waiting on two pints of mead, each of which will surely be bigger than your heads combined. You're in for a long night of getting wrecked after escaping from the dungeons at Elkmire Castle." Lincoln is looking at me and Why. I'm playing Clover, so Wizzy must be Why's character.

I love the story and the way Lincoln tells it. I let out a laugh, but in an instant all the joy drains out of me. The sound of my own girlish giggling is a dead giveaway. Cooper, covering with lightning speed, fakes a loud sneeze, calling attention away from me.

"Sorry," he sniffles. "Damn allergies."

"Here, dude." Why offers Cooper an honest-to-goodness handkerchief from his pocket. Coop's face flashes red, and not from hay fever. Distraction achieved. How do boys sound when they laugh? Not like me, that's for sure.

"What about the rest of us?" Brody asks.

"I'll get there," Lincoln continues. "Clover, you were locked up for thievin', and Wizzy, you should've known—under drow rule, halflings aren't allowed to practice wizardry. No matter, though—you both managed to escape."

So, what brings you wee ones into the Brass Talon this evening?

THE BRASS TALON

Watch who you're calling wee, ya brute.

wizzy
AKA Wyatt, Halfling Mage

clover AKA Cameron, Halfling Thief

lincoln Our intrepid DM

mead

Yeah! We're celebrating!

What's the occasion?

mead

None of your bizzy!

Now bring us the fizzy!

"Oh God." Cooper groans at the rhyme. Why and I bust up, me laughing with my mouth closed.

"I love it," Why says.

"You would, you dork," Brody scolds. "Let's get on with it."

"Fine, fine. Clover, roll a perception check for me," Lincoln tells me. I pick up my d20, unsure about what he wants me to do.

"Just roll it and add your wisdom modifier." Brody points out what he's talking about on my sheet. He's actually being . . . helpful. Lincoln and I both roll dice, his behind the screen. I can't see what his lands on, but mine lands on a seventeen.

"Okay, then! You're having a grand time with your friend, but you can't help feeling distracted by the barkeep's golden pocketwatch chain."

"I want it."

"Yes, yes you do." Lincoln turns to Cooper and Brody. "Now, the two of you are seated in a far corner of the Brass Talon. Brody, your character is here to get some answers about the crown of Valzyr. As you know, it was lost in battle against the orc army that has been plaguing your homeland, and you want it back. The drow are terribly close to being removed from power, and you do not want to see that happen. To you or your people."

"What?" Cooper asks, confused by the backstory.

"Just go with it," Brody laughs.

Don't play dumb with me. I know you know where they've hidden it.

The orcs came through your forest.

What makes you think that?

Because you were displaced.

I, um. They, ah...

STOP STALLING, ELF!

I'm not stalling!

jane Cooper, AKA Wood Elf Ranger

I don't even know who the heck you are!

You've got to be kidding me.

I'm Her Royal Highness, Baroness of Valzyr. Lady of the Most Ancient and Most Noble Order of the Thistle.

SHRUG

THE PRINCESS.

I'm, like, Tiffani

"Roll a perception check for me, Tiffani."

"You play a girl?" I ask without thinking. It goes against everything I know about Brody. That he hates our *kind.* It doesn't make any sort of sense that he would want to play one.

"Yeah, a dumb one." He smirks, and rolls his d20. Okay, maybe I wasn't wrong. I tug my hat back down around my ears and study the ceiling tiles. No matter how much it feels like I'm fitting in, I know I don't. He rolls a measly five, but Lincoln must've rolled even worse.

"Suddenly there is some kind of commotion at the bar. You look up and notice that a halfling has spilled an entire tankard of mead. The barkeep is pissed."

"Do I see this too?" Cooper asks.

"Oh yeah, everyone sees this. But, Tiffani? You notice one of the halflings scurrying around. It appears he's trying to clean up the mess, but you look up just in time to see him steal the barkeep's pocket watch."

"Hmm." Brody ponders the situation.

"Roll a dexterity check, Clover," Lincoln instructs.

"Fifteen."

"Is that with your bonus?"

"Whoops, it's actually seventeen."

"Much better. Okay, Clover, your distraction worked, and you manage to get the watch off of the barkeep. You are out a whole pint of mead, though. Tiffani, you're impressed with Clover's skills. He might be of use to you."

• • •

The rest of the adventure plays out over the next two hours, with Brody's character inviting me and Why to join their discussion of the whereabouts of the crown of Valzyr. We all decide to team up and help Tiffani, even though I'm not sure my character would really do that. But I'm not about to rock the boat in my first game. Cooper eventually finds his footing near the end of the session when he gets us all thrown out of the tavern instead of arrested. Brody cleans up the cups and table while we wind down.

"You were killer. On point." Why smiles. "Both of you."

"Weren't they?" Lincoln puts his arm around Why, and I'm instantly jealous, even though the gesture seems purely friendly. Why must notice my discomfort, and nudges Lincoln off him.

"You'll come again, right?"

"That stupid bitch!" Brody screams at his phone. He slams it down on the counter and paces back and forth, his face practically purple. "What's wrong with her? I mean, what the fuck?" he rages.

"Brina?" Why asks him, squinting.

"Of course Brina. Who else would straight-up torture me like this? Look what she posted. Look!" Brody holds his phone up for us all to see. It's a picture of a girl wearing a Batman shirt, sitting on a couch with a boy. They both have video game controllers in their hands. The girl is looking at the boy, rather than the game they are playing.

"What am I missing?" Lincoln asks what we're all thinking.

"She's just a fucking poser. She needs to stop flaunting all this—"

"Chill out, she's allowed to post whatever she—" Lincoln steps in, but Brody cuts him off as soon as he starts.

"I'm *so* sick of fucking *fake* girls. What's their malfunction? Every single one, always pretending to be into my stuff. And for what? To *use* me."

"It's not like you two ever actually dated," Why offers.

"Exactly my point! I didn't want to be her fucking *friend*." He spits out the word with disgust. "She knew what I wanted, and she was a fake and she played me. Girls are useless." Brody pinches the bridge of his nose, and I'm transported to my first day at Atomix. When he made that same face at me, in my doughnut dress, when I didn't know who Dazzler was. My hands shake, and I shove them back in my pockets. I take one deep breath after another, trying to hold it together. Waiting for someone, anyone, to tell him he's wrong, to tell him to shut up. No one does. Not even Cooper.

In a fit, Brody swipes at a pile of comics on the counter and storms off into the staff room. Spider-Gwen looks up at me from the floor, useless, and I have to get out of here.

"Let's go, Coop," I whisper, and he leads the way without question.

"See you next time?" Why asks me as the cool night air hits my face. I shrug my shoulders and keep on walking.

That girl glows in the dark.

"He didn't notice, I promise." Cooper tries to reassure me on the way back home. He drives fast, and I let the wind screw up my matted hair. I need the air; I need to breathe.

"I know he didn't."

"Want to talk about it?"

"No." Of course I don't want to talk about it. What would I even say? I knew what I was getting into. I know Brody is an asshole. No, I'm not this Brina girl, but I could have been. Easily. I've had guy friends pissed at me when I didn't want them to be boyfriends. I don't understand it. What's wrong with being just friends? They had no problem including boy-Cameron, but girl-Cam is a useless, fake bitch. I need to get out of these clothes. They don't help anything. I'm not changing any lives or minds with my clandestine protest. What's the point? I can use the handbook and come up with costume ideas on my own. I don't need to be distracted by stupid games anyway.

"What about for just thirty seconds?" he begs me as we pull into the driveway. He sets the timer on his phone and, eyebrow arched, holds it up.

"No, Snap. Go to bed." I slam the car door, walk straight up to the loft, and watch Cooper make his way to the house from the window. I don't start crying until he's inside.

I sob and undress, Brody's voice ringing in my head. I ball up Cooper's clothes and hurl them into a corner. I stare them down. It's dark. So damn dark. I open my inbox and read fifteen of those emails just to reinforce that he's right. They're all right.

> **ScottW10K left a comment on your photo:**
> This is what fucking bugs the shit out of me with all these dumbass cosplay idiots. This isn't even creative. Creative would be creating something new. This bitch gets an award for what? Gender swapping fucking Final Fantasy. WOW. Good job. Congrats on being able to fucking trace the lines of someone else's hard work. At least her tits aren't fucking on parade like 100% of the other cosplay whores.
>
> It's all just bull fucking shit. I grew up being shunned and left out and being made a fool of by females. Getting ripped apart for not liking football or fucking pop music. I know these bitches, I can sniff one out from miles away. And now I'm pissed the fuck off by these twats capitalizing off of the attention of

nerds because being a geek is suddenly cool. This
bitch here is no different.

The floor is cold, and chills radiate from my back to my arms
and legs. I'm dotted with goose bumps, my face wet with tears.
The ceiling is covered in glowing patterns that shift when the
wind rustles the trees. Dancing shapes, dark shadows, begging me
to translate them into fabric. Inspired, I let myself get mad—no,
angry. Livid.

"How dare you," I yell at all the anons in my head. *Leave us
alone. Leave me alone. You have no idea what you're talking about!*
I don't bother finding something else to wear. I sit down at my
sewing table and get to work in my underwear.

I rip apart strip after strip of black scrap fabric. I leave the
frayed edges, and I don't measure anything. I want it to look like
it made itself out of some ancient magic. I switch out the green
thread in my machine for black. The stitching will be invisible,
erase any trace of my handiwork.

Strip after strip, the stringy fabric shoots across my lap and
under the needle. I zone out; the feel of the fabric, the hum of the
machine, perfectly match the rage pounding in my head.

KRRRRRRRTTGGGGGGG G G G

Everything comes to a grinding halt, and I snap out of my
trance. The needle is blocked up, completely tangled in a ball
of threads. The frayed edges got caught in the bobbin chamber
and made a mess of everything. I turn the knob on the side of
the sewing machine and raise the needle, which pulls up even
more thread with it. I yank the fabric away, ripping the fibers and
breaking the needle. Is *everything* conspiring against me today?

I unplug the machine and the light goes out. Black fabric

rains down over the workspace as I throw the bits and pieces away from me. I should know better than to work angry. I get careless and sloppy. The scraps and Cooper's clothes work as a decent makeshift pillow. Drained, I settle down and fall asleep watching the shadowy patterns dance across my bare skin.

...

What a mess. Daylight only makes the destruction look worse. My tantrum left nothing meaningful in its wake, just a floor full of flotsam. Time to clean up the wreckage. It's one thing to have my bedroom be a mess, but I hate when the studio gets this way. We've only been living here a month, and I don't want it to go to crap so soon.

I have a hard time working when everything is in disarray, and today I want to work. I separate out the ripped-up scraps from the rest. I may still use them; they have potential. Outside, I hear a car roll over the gravel driveway: Cooper leaving for work. I guess he took the hint, because he didn't bother coming to find me this morning.

It's not his fault. He's not to blame for Brody's bro-ness. He has no idea about what goes on in my inbox. I can't tell him. Not after all the nights he cried to me. The first time someone called him the f-word, when someone left a note in his locker threatening to kick his ass, after his best friend told him he didn't want to be friends anymore. Each moment sobbed into his pillow until it was soaked.

All of that was just as bad as, if not worse than, what I'm going through, because those were his classmates, his friends, people he knew. At least I don't have to know who's on the other end of the screen. I like to imagine they all live on the other side of the moon and I'll never, ever see them in real life, so who cares? Except I do care. Sometimes. Like last night.

I manage to get the mess under control and take up my seat at the sewing table. I blow away the threads and notice the snapped needle. Right. There's a compartment in my machine for extra thread, bobbins, and needles. I have plenty of the first two items. But the only needle left is one for sewing heavy-duty fabric like leather or denim, and it's not going to cut it.

Dad is already puttering around in the garden. I can hear him humming some old Motown song. I don't want to see him, or I don't want him to see me. He'll ask me questions I don't feel like answering. And my dad knows when I'm lying, always. If I cross the garden to the house so I can get dressed, he'll notice me. I can head straight out of the driveway and he won't. But that means I have to go to Kozy Corner in my underwear, or in Cooper's clothes from last night.

His shirt is already wrinkled, thousands of little creases bent into the fabric from spending the night balled up under my head. It looks more like mine now, softer. Cooper would be pissed. But Cooper isn't here. I leave the first few buttons undone and let my collarbone breathe. His jeans don't look too wrinkled. I like them; they're relaxed and broken in. The full-length mirror reflects a weird average of boy-Cameron and me. It's certainly not an outfit I'd normally wear, but I feel comfortable. I feel okay.

• • •

I manage to avoid Dad and Atomix on the way to Kozy Corner. I walk along back roads and side streets. Eugene is different from

Portland. Not as many condos, bigger gardens, bigger houses. It's more lived-in, more run-down. Dad says Portland used to be like Eugene, but all the techies moved up from California and started "ruining the vibes, man."

The bell jingles at the fabric store, and I'm off like a shot at the first sign of broad shoulders and blond hair. Did he see me? I duck behind a display of silk flowers and Styrofoam blocks and inch my way into one of the aisles. I thank God I wasn't staring at the ground when I walked in. I don't know what I would have done if Lincoln had seen me first. What's he doing here?

"I want it to be big, Nan. Like the size of a table." I listen to Lincoln's deep voice from my hiding place.

"I know. I still think you can do it on your own. Sewing isn't all that difficult," Dotty answers him. Is she his grandma?

"You know if I make it it's going to look like a kid's craft project." His voice smiles. I can tell he's being playful without even seeing him, and my heart just dissolves. I imagine his face, his little crooked smile creeping up one of his round cheeks. He must tower over Dotty. I bet he has to lean down for her to hear him.

"I just don't have the fingers for it anymore, Link."

"Look at these big stubby things! I never had the fingers for it," Lincoln jokes.

"Would you get that box down for me?" Dotty changes the subject.

"Of course. Anything else?"

Lincoln and Dotty chat about her pet bird and the weather and how things are going for him at U of O. Standing there, hidden between the rainbow of embroidery thread and notions, I realize I want to know everything there is to know about Lincoln.

All I know now is that he's easy on the eyes and can weave one heck of a tale off the top of his head.

"I don't know, things are . . ." I can hear him take a deep breath. He sighs it out and switches tone. "Fine, things are fine." I feel a little guilty listening in, so I make myself busy and tiptoe around the aisle to finally get my supplies. Thankfully, they're nowhere near the register.

The needles are all lined up together; Dotty keeps an amazing selection that takes up an entire wall. I grab a pack of four blue universal needles and a pack of teal quilting needles. Might as well have the right ones if I want to keep quilting that green piece. I like shopping to the sound of their chatter. Dotty complaining about something and Lincoln teasing, then the reverse. They have rapport; it's snappy, musical. There's a spring in my step, the song of their conversation in my heart. I pick up some more thimbles and debate a new spool of gold embroidery thread.

"You should have that cute girl help you," Dotty says, and I fumble, trying not to spill everything on the ground. "The girl, you know, she comes in all the time lately. I think she just moved here."

"No. I don't know," Lincoln scoffs. "Stop trying to fix me up, Nan."

"Who said fix you up? I said she should help you. She's a fine sewer. Great fingers." She has got to be talking about me. I have no idea who else it could be.

"Sure, Nan, tell her to call me. Love you. See you at dinner."

"I will! Bring home some of that bread I like, would you?"

"You got it."

The jingle signals his exit, but I'm not ready to come out of hiding. *Sure, Nan.* You could hear the eye roll from space. He isn't serious; he doesn't want me to call him. He was appeasing her. I *could* teach him to sew. I'd teach him how to make a quilt the size of a king-sized bed if he wanted, and we could celebrate a job well done underneath it.

"Is that all?" Dotty asks while ringing me up. She's dressed in a sleeveless black turtleneck, with a silk scarf draped around her shoulders. It's dyed deep purple with lighter purple batik patterns. I wonder if she made it herself.

"For today, yep!" I answer, trying to sound cheerful. She studies me over her thick tortoiseshell frames.

"Oh! I didn't recognize you. You don't look like yourself in that . . . *outfit*. Laundry day?"

"Something like that." I look down at my wrinkled clothes and remember I didn't even comb my hair.

"Quilting needles?" She raises a penciled-in brow. "Maybe you can help my grandson with a project. You just missed him! He must be your age, you know."

"He wants to make a quilt?"

"Something like that—you'd like him. He's handsome," she lilts. I want to tell her that I know just how handsome he is, but actually your darling Link thinks I'm a geek who rolls dice and drinks Mountain Dew. And is, you know, a boy.

"Maybe. I've been really busy this summer."

"Here." Dotty pens his phone number on my receipt in the adorable, shaky script that all old people write with. I wonder when my own mother's handwriting will start looking like that. Hopefully, not anytime soon. "You could teach him how. It wouldn't take long; he's very smart."

I thank Dotty for her meddling and supplies after gently folding the receipt and sliding it into my back pocket. It's a thin scrap of paper, but, I swear, I can feel it there the whole way home.

...

Mom must have been up in the studio while I was gone. Everything is just as I left it except the portfolio requirement letter is now prominently displayed up on my corkboard. I'm about to rip it down when my phone rings. It's Why. I consider not answering, but his dorky grin on the screen reminds me of our bad jokes last night, and I hit accept.

"Cameron! You answered!"

"Yep." Still feeling a bit messed up, I go deeper with my voice than usual.

"Are you busy? Not, like, now. Maybe later?"

"I don't know."

"Right, I um, I feel kind of bad? I had such a rad time at the game, you know?" Why speaks in quick, sharp sentences. Most of them sound like questions, even when they aren't.

"And you feel bad?"

"Well, Brody kind of, like, made stuff all awkward. He does that. You should know. It's not meant to be personal?"

"You sure about that?" I fire back.

"I don't know. Heh, neither does he. He's not really . . ."

"He's a bro."

"Exactly."

"And you're not?" It's not like Why stepped up to the plate when Brody was throwing his fit. Then again, it's not like he knew there was a girl present. But why should a girl have to be present for someone to stand up for her?

"Psh! I'm probably the least bro dude in the universe."

"Wanna bet?" I counter. Why certainly was quiet when Brody

was throwing girls under the bus last night. He's probably more of a bro than he even realizes.

"I've never watched a single football game. Televised or otherwise."

"I think beer is the most disgusting liquid a human could ever drink."

"I own twelve pairs of pink socks," he boasts.

"My closest friend here is an eighty-year-old lady, and we just met."

"Okay, you win." Why gives in.

"What do I win?" I relax and laugh. Okay, maybe Why's not so bad after all. The conversation reminds me of the ones Liv and I used to have. Full of quick comebacks and snappy jokes. And for a brief moment I feel less homesick.

"Dunno, pad thai?" He says the magic words.

"Tonight?"

"Five?"

"Lucky Noodle?" I suggest.

"See you then."

"Peace."

...

The portfolio requirements glare at me from the corkboard. Sun beams in through the skylight and highlights the paper so that it's barely legible. I know what I need to make, but for the first time ever, I'm afraid to make it. The pressure is on. All my other costumes and cosplays have been for me or Cooper or my friends. Seattle Comic Con was the first time I entered a competition, and that turned out to be a disaster. This is supposed to be the dream, my first step toward silver-screen status, and, dear lord of lost buttons, I can't fuck it up.

I've decided to outfit our entire ragtag D&D crew. There are plenty of characters to work with. If Why can be my friend, no questions asked, things might not be as bad as they seem. Why deserves his wizard robes; Cooper deserves his tunic. So Brody is still a jerk. It's not fair for me to lump Why in with him. I make my own list and pin it next to the letter.

Five original characters:

Wizzy
Jade
Clover
Brody's character can get eaten by an orc for all I care.
Something for Lincoln?

There's still the reimagined costume to make on top of these, but I have to start somewhere. I review the sketch for Jade, Cooper's wood elf. It looks good, but not complete. I'm not aiming for good; I'm aiming for greatest portfolio of all time. I'm very reasonable like that.

The costume is missing all those extra little details that make it feel real and not like a Halloween costume. Stuff like Luke Skywalker's lightsaber holster. All the pouches and belts and jackets that Samwise Gamgee totes around. The undergarments Viola wears in *Shakespeare in Love.* Luna Lovegood's Spectrespecs.

His clothes look like Generic Elf™ from any universe. There's nothing really original. It's because I don't know anything about Jade Everwood, but a few more hours playing D&D should help. I doubt Coop will let me interrogate him, and I realize I learn more from watching scenes play out in front of me than I do pulling ideas out of thin air.

I know a lot about Wizzy, Why's halfling wizard. I can picture him in my mind after playing with him, hearing how he talks, seeing how he acts. I flip to a new page but change my mind and immediately close the book. I don't want to sketch it out, I just want to make it.

The black scraps from last night are all twisted up in their bin; it takes me a while to untangle them. My fingertips turn red, then purple as the thread winds around them. I wedge my seam ripper into the impossible knots and pry the fabric apart from itself. If only I knew magic. I'd roll a d10 for a spell of unraveling and cross my fingers for a high number. Once I've separated out enough pieces, I lay them across the floor in piles according to size. I take the biggest strips over to the machine, replace the broken needle, thread it up, and get to work.

Even though the edges are still frayed and torn, I push them slowly and deliberately through the machine. Nothing snags, nothing tangles, and Wizzy's little hat starts coming together. Every few minutes I try it on and check it out in the mirror.

Wizzy, like Why, is funny, so I make it smaller than a traditional wizard cap. That way his ears will stick out a bit. Lincoln says that practicing magic is forbidden for us halflings, and Wizzy does it anyway. So he's brave. Black is brave, and dark, and mischievous.

My phone buzzes next to me on the table. New mail. I give my fingers a break from sewing so they can go on a deleting spree. But it's not from an anon. Right on top of all the junk mail is a message from the Quentin client.

Subject: I CAN'T THANK YOU ENOUGH.

My Quentin cosplay went over like—Mother-FLIPPIN—
Gangbusters. So many people stopped me to take
pictures at the con. It was amazing. I can't believe how
detailed you got with it. I told everyone who asked
about your blog. I hope you get some more customers
out of it. I sent the rest of your $ to your PayPal and
attached some pictures for you!

You rock.

—QQ

My hands are trembling so much my phone almost slips from my grasp. Attached is a photo of the client looking good as all getout in my cosplay . . . standing next to Gillian flipping Grayson. Gillian Grayson saw my costume. She posed for a picture with it. She put her arm around it and touched it. I imagine what she said when she saw it, if she recognized Quentin. She did design that amazing Wolverine costume in the tenth reboot. Did she ask him about it? Did he tell her my name, and did she instantly recognize it from the National Portfolio Review roster? Am I accepted already?

I want to write back and ask him all these questions and then some, but it's too scary. She might not have said anything at all. I'll find out what she thinks of my work soon enough. This right here is why I haven't closed my blog yet. If I take it down, who knows what opportunities I might miss. I'm about to cancel my plans with Why—I have to keep working—but Cooper clambering up to the loft interrupts me.

"I'm sorry, but I need, like, a whole damn hour to vent about what happened at work today." Coop collapses into the beanbag chair, his arms and legs all splayed out. "I don't even care that you're still in my clothes. That's how frustrating it was." I push out from the table, and my chair rolls across the floor to him.

"Poor Snap." I pet his shoulder with my foot.

"Ew, excuse your nasty, bare feet." He pushes them aside.

"Thank you."

"So?"

"So, who would you never, ever expect to be shopping in a Eugene mall, let alone in a Banana?"

"A lot of people. Jack Black? Mark Ruffalo?" I guess.

"Stop listing your crushes. Try again. Try the one person I was more than happy to leave behind in Portland."

"Not Farrin. Please tell me it wasn't Farrin."

"I hate my life," Cooper groans, and shuts his eyes. He's right. I would never have guessed, not in a gajillion years, that Farrin would be down here in Eugene. He's Coop's one and only ex. And therefore worst. His name isn't even Farrin. It's Brian, but apparently that wasn't *fartsy* enough for him.

"What's he doing south of Sellwood?" I ask, bile in my throat.

"He came to brag about the stupid summer program."

"NYU? He applied?"

"Of course. And apparently, he's the one who beat me. Took my spot."

"So, what? He came all the way down here just to gloat?" I sink into the beanbag next to him.

"Pretty much. Though he framed it like some sort of tearful goodbye."

"I can't even with him, Cooper."

"Me either."

"Is he staying down here? What did he say? When does the

program start?" I have a million more questions, but Cooper cuts me off.

"I don't know, Snip, okay?"

"Screw him, and screw NYU. If they chose him over you, they can go sit on a pancake. You know he can't write. You know his *films* might as well be crappy home movies."

"Yeah, well, he brought his script with him."

"*Exsqueeze moi?* Please tell me you framed him for shoplifting and got him arrested."

"Ughhhhh." Cooper rolls over on the beanbag and reaches into his messenger bag. He produces a thick stack of papers and holds it out. "He wants me to read it before he takes it to New York next week."

"Fireplace or fire pit?" I take the stack from him and hold it over an imaginary flame. "Shall I just chuck it out the window and let it compost in Dad's pile?" I stroll over to the window and hold it outside.

"Stop! Don't!" He scrambles to his feet to rescue the obviously overwritten script. No producer would glance at a stack of paper that thick. Even an intern would burn it.

"You're kidding me, right?"

"Look. I know he sucks, and the script probably sucks, but what, I'm just supposed to ignore him?" Cooper whines.

"Yes."

"You don't get it."

"Try me."

"You've never— I mean, I know you've, like, hooked up with guys, but you never . . ." Cooper trails off. He knows not to finish the thought. He doesn't need to. So I've never said I love you, never had a real boyfriend. Not one that stuck around for longer than a week before fizzling out because I happen to find perfecting my catch stitch to be a better use of my time. But why should that matter?

It's just never lined up; I can't seem to make a relationship click in all the right places. Every guy I've liked has been either too dense or too fast. I want to find someone it's just easy with. I think about Lincoln far too often, considering the size of the roadblock I've put between us. I mean, he's never even met me, only the guy I'm supposed to be now. How do you even begin a relationship from that kind of a starting point?

Cooper keeps running his fingers over the cover of the script. It's enough to make me want to rip it to shreds. He needs a new boyfriend, and even if things are complicated for me and Lincoln, they don't have to be for Cooper.

"You wanna come to Lucky Noodle? I'm meeting Why there."

"You are? For what?"

"For noodles."

. . .

Cooper caved and lent me another shirt to wear. This one is covered in little anchors. He says I can keep it, that it's *so last year.* I filled in my brows so they look thicker, untamed. On our way to Lucky Noodle I watch every boy who walks by us. I watch their sway, their step, their swagger. I lean back; I hook my thumbs into my belt loops, cock my head to the side. So unconcerned and casual. Cooper tries not to laugh.

There's never a wait at Lucky's, unlike Pok Pok in Portland, where you could end up waiting three hours on a sunny summer Saturday. And you can't even get pad thai there, so what's the point? If I could eat only one food for the rest of my life, it'd be those sweet and savory noodles. More lime, more tamarind, more bean sprouts. We sit at a table on the sidewalk and wait for Why. He's late.

"Two Thai iced teas." Coop orders for us both. I don't bother looking at the menu. I know what I want. "He's coming, right?" he asks.

"My company isn't enough for you?" I poke him with a plastic chopstick.

"Can't I crush on a cute boy in peace?"

"I don't think he's gay, Snap," I say as we both watch Why cross the street. His gait is steady, with a little bounce out of the bottom. His hair moves with each step, an extension of his golden aura. He looks like the friendliest, happiest person on the planet. He beams when he sees us.

"He better be," Cooper sighs.

"Heyo!" Why plops down in the seat between Cooper and me.

"Coop's having a bad day. He needs some noodle nurturing." I catch my reflection in Why's sunglasses, and I barely recognize myself. I look more like a cheap cosplay version of my brother. I look like a liar, and I almost lose my appetite.

"Sure, sure, sure," Why says, flipping through the plastic-coated menu pages.

"Ex-boyfriend drama. I'm sure you know." Cooper fishes.

"Eh." Why shrugs his shoulders. "Who doesn't?" He doesn't take the bait.

The waiter brings us two tall glasses full of that lovely orange ombré liquid. Deep burnt umber at the bottom and creamy pale peach at the top. Cooper stirs his up and dives in. I dip my straw in and slowly swirl, letting the flavors mix together gradually. We all order, pad thai for me and Why, pad see ew for the traitor, Cooper. None of us bother with the Italian selections from the menu. Whoever thought to mix the two cuisines under the same roof must have been tripping on mushrooms they got from some stoner at Reed.

"You guys were great at D and D. Naturals." Why smiles at me.

"I felt so awkward. I don't know if I can keep it up," Cooper says, straw between his teeth.

"Are you kidding? Nah, man, no. You were so golden. I can tell you're gonna have a big part to play." This makes Cooper so goofy happy he just about spills his drink.

"Thanks."

"It'll only get better," Why assures him.

"Yeah, you write monologues and dialogue all the time. Think of it like that. Like improvising a scene," I remind Cooper.

"I'm a writer, not an actor," he corrects me for the millionth time.

"Whoa, hold up. You write scripts? Like, movies?" Why shifts back in his chair to look at Cooper.

"I want to. Indie stuff. Short films."

"I'm not normally into indie stuff, but I did like that one trippy Duplass flick. The one where this couple goes on vacation to . . . Oh, I don't want to spoil it for you."

"The one with the guesthouse? Yeah, it blew my mind!"

"Seriously. I think I watched it three times in a row. You wanna make movies like that?" Why asks, leaning on his elbows. I'm hoping right along with Coop that Why will catch some feelings for him. Cooper deserves someone like Why, someone chill and silly. Someone less self-obsessed. They'd make a cute couple, and I don't mind playing matchmaker. Anything, as long as Farrin stays far away from him.

"I'd love to. That's the goal, at least. I write the scripts; Cam makes the costumes." If Why weren't sitting between us, I'd have kicked Coop's shins purple. What kind of dude sews costumes? He's gonna blow this whole thing for me. Why's my first new friend in town, not to mention my in with Lincoln. And the minute he finds out I'm a girl, it's all over. I feel bad about the charade, but I've learned that boys don't want to be just friends with girls. Brody made that quite clear. I shoot a vicious scowl at Coop across the plates of noodles and limes and tofu.

"Y'all are like the wonder twins," Why says, his mouth stuffed. "Are you identical?"

"Not possible," I reply. It's a knee-jerk response. A question we have been asked again and again. No, boy-girl twins can't be identical. You know, he's got an outie and I've got an innie—that's a pretty huge nonidentical difference.

"Why not?" he asks. Crap. Now that Cooper and I are supposedly both on Team Outie, there's no real reason why we couldn't be identical.

"The whole in-vitro thing," Coop lies, and I hope Why is gullible enough to fall for it.

"Oh. Right." He looks confused, but it doesn't stop him from taking another huge mouthful of noodles.

"I love your character. He's so fun," I tell Why. Though I'm not about to tell him that I'm sizing him up so I can finish making Wizzy's outfit later.

"I love playing wizards." Why makes finger guns and pretends to shoot lightning at me. "Pew! Pew! Pew!" I deflate into the chair.

"Ahh! You got me."

"Dorks," Cooper groans.

"I wouldn't talk, Jade Everwood." Why elbows Coop. The waiter brings by the check and sighs when he has to split it three ways on three separate debit cards.

90

No! You listen to me, Tiffani. I've done everything you've asked of me. I led you here; I distracted the orcs. Everything!

If I knew, don't you think I'd tell you?

And yet, you still have the gall, nay, the impertinence, the nerve, to question me again about your stupid crown?

Especially since it would rid me of you and your incessant nagging. The crown may very well be at the bottom of Qiris Spring, but it may not. It was my very best guess; I assure you.

Like, okay, you don't have to get all snippy about it.

. . .

"That was epic." Why stares at Cooper. We *all* stare at him. He pulled that speech out of nowhere.

"Thanks." He sheepishly accepts the praise. But I can tell, because I know Coop like I know myself, that he's feeling high as hell.

"So," Lincoln jumps back in, "you follow Jade through the catacombs. Weaving through crevices, barely able to see by the light of his enchanted torch."

"Thanks again, Wiz." Cooper nods to Why.

"All of a sudden the cavern opens up, stalactites reaching down from twenty feet up above. You all stand at the edge of Qiris Spring. It's a deep, sparkling, midnight blue. If you didn't know any better, you might think you were looking down at the night sky. Cracks in the ceiling of the cave admit beams of light that dance across the water, reflecting stars and comets on its glassy surface." Goddamn, Lincoln can build worlds out of thin air. "Everyone roll a perception check for me."

We all grab our d20s and roll them around in our palms before casting them across the table. Mine lands on eighteen.

"Whose is that? Who rolled the eighteen?" Lincoln leans over the divider. I raise my hand. "Hm. Well, all right, then. Cam, can you go into the back for a few minutes?"

"Wait—what? What did I do?" I panic.

"The story is going to split off. Something is going to happen that only certain people can know about."

"So just . . . leave?"

"Just chill in the back; I'll come get you when he's done.

There's some rare Spideys back there if you get bored," Brody offers. I'm surprised by his somewhat kindness.

"It happens all the time," Why assures me. Cooper looks up at me and smiles. Like it wouldn't bother him to be kicked out of the room. I push open the door—STAFF ONLY—and wait.

I don't bother looking for the rare Spider-Man issues; I wait by the door and try to listen in. It's heavy, with a push bar that I pretend is red-hot. Can't touch it, can't let them know I'm eavesdropping. Or attempting to, anyway. Their voices are deep and muffled. Occasionally I hear Lincoln's laugh, and my heart beats faster.

The back room is much bigger than I had thought, and packed tight with cardboard boxes. I give up on trying to listen in and follow the path winding between the stacks. How is it that I still end up being the odd man out? Half the lights back here are busted, and it feels like I'm actually wandering through the cold, dark elven caverns, except I'm all on my own. No magic, no brother, no friends.

The last turn through the boxes is the darkest, and I forget to mask my voice, no time to consider who I'm pretending to be, when I scream my head off, leaping back from the silhouetted figure standing in the shadows of the storeroom.

I speed around the boxes and crash through the door. Everyone at the table stops and looks at me like my hair is on fire.

"There's someone back there," I pant.

"What?!" Brody stands up and blows past me into the storeroom. Everyone follows on his heels, and I bring up the rear, hands shaking.

"Dude, are you kidding me?" He emerges with a life-size

cutout of a comic character with a creepy goatee and cape. "You afraid of Dr. Strange?" Brody cracks up. Why groans. I'm embarrassed beyond belief. Like, pee-your-pants-at-a-sleepover embarrassed. It wasn't even photographic. I was scared by a literal cartoon character.

"You scream like a little bitch," Brody snarks, and goes back to the table. An invisible seam ripper tears three stitches from my heart when Why laughs along as Brody imitates my scream.

"Come on, it's your turn anyway." Lincoln calls me back into the storeroom. Once I realize it's just going to be Lincoln and me, all alone, I don't feel so bad about my little side quest.

. . .

"So, now what? I forgot my book; should I go grab it? Do I need to write anything down? I didn't even bring my dice, I'm sorry, I don't know what—" I ramble, patting my pockets down, looking for I don't even know what. I keep replaying my scream in my head; each time it's shriller and more humiliating than the last.

"I got you." Lincoln holds up his stack of supplies. "You okay?" he asks, skeptical.

"Yeah, sure." I slump back down into the cold folding chair. "I don't know what I'm doing."

"You know this is just a game, right? It's supposed to be fun."

"Yeah, obviously. I mean. I just—I want to be good at it," I tell him. Lincoln leans back in his chair and sighs. He looks right at me, his eyebrows inching closer together. He's not judging like Brody did; he's just taking it all in. There's no harshness in his gaze. It's all softness. Everything about Lincoln is soft. Normally, the awkwardness of the silence would make my skin crawl, but Lincoln is comfortable. He scribbles something down in his notebook and circles it.

"You're gonna be great," he reassures me.

"If you say so."

"Now." Lincoln flips back a page or two in his book. "There was some debate—well, an argument—about who was going to dive into Qiris Spring. Tiffani didn't want to get her hair wet—" Lincoln rolls his eyes at this and takes a breath. I snicker. He snickers. We both bust up laughing at the sheer stupidity of Brody's character.

"Sorry, it's just so . . . cliché," I say, getting my breath back.

"Seriously, he's not fooling anyone. Brina wasn't that bad. Her character was a little strange, but she was a beginner too."

"She used to play with you guys?" I ask a little too quickly. They played with a girl? I wonder how long she lasted before Brody ran her off.

"Yeah. She was our *token* girl for a little while. But she quit, and Brody got all . . ."

"Ah." She was just a girl, just trying to play a game. At least she had the ovaries to show up as herself and not some low-rent Amanda Bynes, *She's the Man* version.

"Yeah." Lincoln angles his notebook away from me, ready to continue the campaign, but I want to talk more; I don't need to jump back into the game. I want to ask him about Dotty and what his major is and if he likes pad thai and everything. "Anyway. While everyone in your band of travelers argues, you hear something. A laugh."

"A laugh?"

"A giggle, to be more precise. It's coming from behind you."

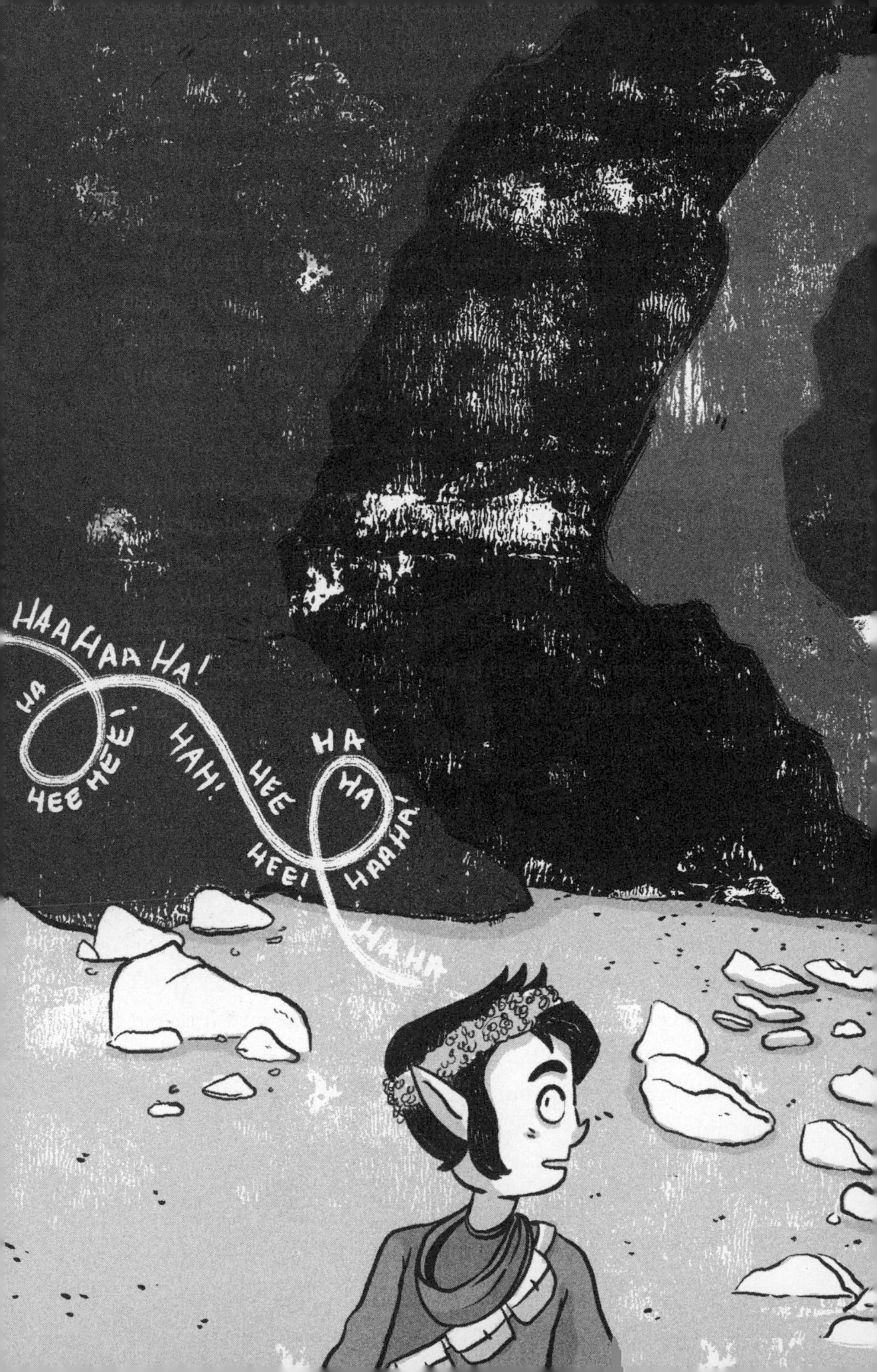
HAAHAAHA!
HA
HEE HEE!
HAH!
HEE
HA
HA
HEE!
HAAHA!
HAHA

UP HEREEE!

Wh-who goes there?

I know what you're looking for, and it ain't here.

Who are you?

A friend, you ninny. You better watch out who ends up with that crown.

Or else what?

Whoa there. No one said or else.

Lincoln leans forward on the edge of the metal folding chair. He closes his notebook with a satisfied sigh. I'm so impressed by the story he's weaving. How he's just making up dialogue on the spot. I want to impress him too, but I feel like I keep coming up short.

"Well then, I, uh, how much is it, um . . . I mean, we'll just see if I decide to—" *Cameron, you dummy.* It's hard for me to keep in character. Lincoln is sitting a little too close, and the storeroom is a little too private, with the exception of Dr. Strange, who looks down his nose at us, grinning wickedly through his creepy goatee. I'm tongue-tied, Lincoln's smiling, and I'm suddenly very aware of just how much of a girl I am.

"Bindi retreats back into her hideaway just in time for you to notice a very mad and very wet Tiffani emerge, empty-handed, from the spring."

"Back to the table?"

"Back to the table," Lincoln echoes, but he pauses at the door. "Be nice to Why, okay?" he asks before turning back around.

"Are you kidding? Of course. Why wouldn't I be nice to him?"

"Just don't play games with him—he's been through a lot lately, and I feel like he's finally getting back to normal."

"So have I." Lincoln doesn't even know the half of it. Dressed up as one of the bros, ignoring the hate pile in my inbox. Why would he be asking me to play nice? I am nice.

"I'm—I'm sorry. This is coming out all wrong," Lincoln stammers.

"Why is my friend; I think he's great."

"But do you like him?" He looks me over, not really judging, but like he's trying to tell if I'm about to lie. I don't understand what he's so nervous about. I wouldn't be here if I didn't think Why was cool, if I didn't plan on being friends with him. "Of course I like him; I like all of you guys," I lie a little. Lincoln should be asking me if I like Brody; he's the only guy here I have an issue with.

"Look, I don't mean to be a busybody," he explains. I can't help but smile at the phrase. I'm sure he picked it up from Dotty. "But we haven't played in so long. I've missed it." Lincoln smiles too, his eyebrows arching, like a puppy dog.

"No worries. Why's great, you're great, everything is great. I really needed some friends down here." I try to reassure him.

"You might want to tell Why that. Just be clear. You know, things get messy, get weird." He nervously brushes his hair behind his ears. My eyes follow the path of his fingertips, and I wish mine could do the same.

"No kidding." He doesn't know the half of it. "S'all good," I say, imitating so many boys I've heard say the same. "It's D and D—what could go wrong?" Lincoln laughs, and I unravel at the sound. He pushes the door and holds it open for me. "Thanks, Link." I try not to smile as I pass in front of him, but I've never had a decent poker face. He looks puzzled and I feel giddy. He has no idea I have his phone number tucked into my pocket.

•••

"Cam! Wait up!" Why calls from the entrance of Atomix. "Can I talk to you for a minute?" Why shoots the quickest glance in Cooper's direction. "Alone?" I look over at Coop; he gives me a nod of approval, or indifference—it's hard to say.

"What's up?" I ask as we walk, slowly, down to the corner. Why turns around and stares at me, right into my eyes, biting his lip. Oh God, he knows. He figured out I'm a girl. He's going to call me out for being yet another fake-geek-girl and tell me to never come back. Then he'll tell Lincoln, who'll be majorly pissed at me for breaking up the group, and he'll never touch me with those hands of his, much less let me teach him how to sew. What was I thinking? Why did I ever do this?

"You wanna go out sometime? Just, like, you-and-me style?" Why asks, and the relief is so extreme I don't know whether to laugh or cry.

"Sure, but I don't know what's fun around here. I bet Cooper knows. We could all—"

"No. I mean, go out. *Go out?* You know, I pick you up and we sit in a movie theater and maybe, like, you know? A date?" I wonder if my face is as red as it feels. As soon as he says the word, everything shifts. It catches me off guard, knocks the wind out of me. And I realize this is what Lincoln was talking about. He could tell Why was crushing.

I thought for *once* I was going to have a purely platonic friendship with a guy. But Why's ruined all that now; all it took was the d-word. I tap my toe against the pavement, my eyes darting back and forth, searching for the right words in the cracks in the sidewalk. Words that, like a spell, could somehow undo this, save our friendship. But the best I can come up with is,

"I'm not . . . I'm not gay. Sorry."

"Shhhhhhhhhiiiiiiiiiiiiiit." Why hangs his head, mortified. "I just thought, you know? You're just so . . ."

"No, I'm not. You wouldn't want to date me. Trust me."

"Damn it!" Why curses under his breath and turns away from me.

"Hey, don't worry about it. It's fine." I try to comfort him. It sounds weird masked in my tenor voice. I want to be real, be honest. But that's not an option.

"It's just . . . so embarrassing. I'm sorry. I . . . I'm an idiot." He doesn't turn around. I pray that he's not crying. This is horrible. I've never turned down a date before, and Why is the last person I'd want to hurt.

"You're not an idiot. You're awesome. I'm sure there's a ton of guys who would—"

"Right."

"Really. Why. Dude. We can still be friends, right? Please?" I practically beg. He sighs and finally turns around.

"Yeah. Sure." He curls his lips inward. A fake smile.

"Because I just moved here, and we just met—"

"Oh, of course." He shakes off a bit of his embarrassment and straightens up. "Have you been to the ABP yet?" he asks the ground.

"The what?"

"Alton Baker Park? It's nice in the summer."

"Uh, sure. Sounds fun."

"Wednesday?" He perks up.

"Should be okay." Gives me a few days to really buckle down and get back to work. There's not much time left and I've barely scratched the surface of what I need to finish.

"See you then. . . . And I'm sorry . . . about . . ."

"Don't be."

Girl crush.

"You should have told him," Cooper snipes from the little platform in our studio.

"*You* should tell him," I say, and *accidentally* poke him with a pin. He yelps and swats me away. The fabric around his legs flaps about as he moves. "Stay still!"

"Just tell him *I'm* into him. No. Tell him you *think* I *might* like him. And then you'll really be off the hook."

"Don't be so high school about it, Snap." I attach two bits of fabric around his thigh with one pin, then another.

"Snip, we *are* in high school."

"Point taken." I step back to check my work. I've been working on Jade Everwood's costume for two days, and it's still not quite right. "What if I drop the crotch?"

"Absolutely not. It'll look like I'm wearing a diaper."

"But it's different! I don't want to do the same ol' tights look."

I'm just playing around with the silhouette for as long as Coop will let me.

"No."

"Fine." I poke him again.

"Farrin keeps texting me, wants to know what I think of his stupid script. I thought if I waited long enough he would just forget about it. He's already in New York."

"You didn't actually read it, did you?" I make Cooper spin around so I can work on the back. I think I'm going to do a dropped crotch anyway. I think they're weird and cool, and a wood elf would totally wear one.

"I started to. It's about us. Our whole relationship."

"But told through some metaphor or something?"

"Sort of . . . We're all these stop-motion animals. You're a rat."

"Lovely."

"There's nothing interesting about it. It's just our story. He's so lazy." Cooper goes quiet as I work out the rest of the seams on his pants. My stomach is in knots, and I know it's because his is too. I wonder if Farrin included the part where he ripped Cooper's heart out for some other boy.

They hated each other when they first met. Always trying to out-cool each other, trying to be the bigger movie snob. Who knew more from which commentary on which director's cut of whatever indie darling was playing at Living Room that week. Which of course led to them making out at some film fest. Then they were inseparable for two whole years. I liked Farrin at first. It felt like Cooper had found someone who loved all the things he loved, but it became obvious—to me, at least—that Farrin never stopped competing. Cooper just didn't mind coming in second place anymore. Farrin became the authority on everything. "You shouldn't wear that . . . see that . . . do that . . . go there." It got really annoying, but Cooper never saw it that way. He was in love. Right up until he caught Farrin tongue-deep in Noah Baker, the lead in our school production of *Fiddler on the Roof.* Cooper said he was wearing the beard and everything. I hope Farrin choked on it.

"I'll tell him. I'll tell Wyatt."

"I love you."

"I love you more."

...

I run my fingers over the softest jersey-knit fabric I've ever felt at Kozy Corner. It's white, but I can dye it the burnt-orange color I came in here for. White might be even better. I can fold the fabric, tie-dye it, and get some natural-looking rusty patterns instead of solid color. Jade Everwood should look like all of his clothes were made from natural materials. I tuck the bolt under my arm and grab a box of dye. I was dreading running into Lincoln, and yet here I am, dressed in my most flowy sundress, hoping to get caught. He's not here.

"Now that's a dress!" Dotty grins from behind the counter. "Perfect for this weather. Do a twirl!" she demands. I oblige. I turn on my toe, and the dress floats around my knees. The colors swirl together and form new kaleidoscopic patterns. I stop spinning; the dress tries to keep going and wraps itself around my legs once more before settling back into place.

"I sewed it right before we moved here. I thought it would be my lucky dress."

"I love it," she declares, crossing her arms over her chest.

"Thank you." I blush, looking down. I check over the supplies in my arms and remember I'm still a bit short. "Hey, you're out of that rose-colored crushed velvet," I tell Dotty, hoping she has some more stashed somewhere so I can finish Jade's costume today.

"And *you* didn't call my Link." Dotty frowns as I approach the counter. Reading my mind.

"No. Not yet." I've tucked his phone number into my bra. I never leave home without it.

"Give him a call, would you? He's getting on my last nerve around the house. He's so young and vibrant! He should be going out, not spending every night playing Hegemon Scrabble with me. I'm old; the last thing I need is a teenaged babysitter." She rings me up, and I giggle at the thought of Lincoln playing games and letting Dotty win. The two of them puttering around her house, probably all shag carpet and plastic furniture, cracks me up.

"Maybe."

"And maybe your velvet will be here on Tuesday." She hands me a paper bag. Her fingernails are long and pointy, painted a deep glittering green that matches the emerald on her claddagh ring. The heart faces inward.

"Thanks, Dots."

"And listen"—Dotty leans over the counter, her voice soft and serious—"you have to make your own luck. Just like you made that dress."

. . .

"What happened!" Liv shouts through the phone. "Can't I go off to Mount Hood for a hot sec without everything blowing up?"

"I thought Jen told you." I was surprised to see Liv's face pop up on my phone screen today. I didn't expect to hear from her any time soon.

"Not the whole deal, no! I've been scrolling through the drama for, like, hours. I feel like it's all my fault."

"Please don't say that. It's not true." The last thing I want is for her to feel so guilty that she gives me time or space or whatever. I just want my friend back.

"It was my idea, the whole Final Fantasy thing. That's what started all of this, right?"

"A bunch of randos started it. Not you," I reassure her.

"What're you gonna do?" I picture her bouncing in her seat like she always does when she's on the phone.

"I dunno. Nothing? Wait it out?"

"Fuck that with a million bananas, Cam. You should say something. I'm gonna say something!"

"Don't!" I beg.

"Why the heck not?" She's getting fired up. Liv is like that. Fierce in ways I can't be. She would never disguise herself to fit in. She'd march right into Atomix and force Brody to dismantle his *girl section* piece by piece. Still, if she speaks up, I know exactly what will happen.

"It's not worth it."

"Of course it is!"

"They came after Jen; they'll come after you next," I warn her.

"You know Jen has always been shy. I can handle some puny trolls. Bring 'em on."

"I would have said the same thing myself, but you don't know what it's like, not until it's your inbox and feed and everything full of the grossest shit, Liv. Please don't."

"If I don't say anything, you have to. Don't wilt. Don't waffle."

"Don't waver—I know." Liv and her mottos. She's printed out a thousand quotes from various blogs and websites and hung them all over her room. A new mantra for every week.

"I got you, girl. And you got this." She hangs up and I log in.

Two hundred sixty notes. Three hundred forty-eight notes. Five hundred and two notes. My blog is blowing up. The Quentin cosplay brought me a bunch of new followers, but they're not all fans. I can't wrap my head around it, people who started following my posts, combing through the archive just to hurl insults. Why waste your time? If you hate me so much, why follow me at all?

When I'm dressed as Poison Ivy, I'm a noncanonical whore. When I'm dressed as Agent Carter, I'm a frigid bitch who can't sew. When I'm dressed as Zelda, my dark-ass eyebrows completely ruin the look. The posts of Cooper dressed as Nightwing, Nathan Drake, Shay from Broken Age don't get nearly as many comments. Do the trolls not realize I made those costumes too? They're in *my* blog. There are plenty of nice comments, but the nasty ones always seem louder. They dominate my inbox.

And how dare they? They don't know what goes into making something like a Samus suit by hand. They've never picked up a thimble that wasn't on a Monopoly board. I have. I put my blood, sweat, and now tears into my work. That's why I'll have a career, and they'll be stuck on the other side of the moon, never bothering to come out from behind their screens. Liv is right. I don't want to be a wilting waffle.

Hey everyone. Pinz+Needlez here. I'm kinda thrilled
and stunned that so many of you like my work. I
wanted to tell everyone that every cosplay you see

on my page was made by me with my own two hands. Sometimes lovingly, sometimes after hours and hours of bashing my thumbs and jabbing my fingers. But there isn't a thimble big enough to protect me from some of these nasty comments! So yeah, please consider that before you go and say something harsh or mean or rude. That a real person made all this and is here and can read what you write. If you don't like what I make, you can unfollow me, or just, you know, lay off.

I stare at the dress form with the half-finished Jade Everwood costume, proud that I'm finally working on my own designs. Anons can't scream at me for being "inaccurate" when I've designed everything myself. It's canon if I say it is, bitch. I snap a picture of the work in progress and attach it to the post.

I have some cool new projects in the works, so all of the randos can show themselves out. Thx.
—Pinz

I put the Internet drama behind me and get back to stitching up Jade's vest. I'll pick up the velvet lining on Tuesday. I'm going for impressive, couture, so I hand-sew every seam with metallic-green thread. I'm not going to give Gillian Grayson a single thing to criticize in my portfolio. Every detail, every stitch is considered and deliberate.

"Hey, thimble girl!" Dad calls up to me from the garage. My hand slips, and I jab my finger with the needle. He's never called me that before. Did Cooper figure out my password? And why would he tell Dad? "Dinner!" I rush down the stairs, but Dad's standing at the bottom, grinning, with his hand held out. A bright, shining thimble sits upright on his palm. It's beautiful, with butterflies carved all around the rim. "For your collection." He beams. I love the way his eyes sparkle when he's happy. Little brown gems set in half a lifetime's laugh lines. Dad's eyes smile all on their own.

"Where did you find it?" I take the thimble and place it on my finger.

"In the garden, would you believe it?" He wraps his arm around my shoulder and walks me out of the garage. "You've been busy. Haven't seen you much lately."

"You see me every night at dinner."

"Yeah, but you're actually off on the moon somewhere designing costumes in your head."

"No. Not the moon, never the moon," I assure him. The moon is the last place I like to think about with its army of anons and assholes.

"Don't forget to have a summer. You shouldn't spend every minute holed up in there."

"I'll see what I can do." The kitchen smells like garlic and basil. Mom spoons the green pesto-coated penne onto our plates. Cooper shaves a mountain of Parmesan onto his before even bothering to sit down.

"Do you need to take your plate to the loft?" Mom holds the dish above my place at the table.

"Lori," Dad scolds her. "Give her a break."

"She can take a break if she wants to. Do you want to take a break?" Mom turns back to me, still hovering. Cooper is already stuffing his face.

"I can eat here, it's fine." I appreciate what she's trying to do, let me off the hook for family dinner so I can keep working. It's a fight we've had before, but usually with me on the other side of it. I would beg to work through dinner, but family time was more important. Now that college is on the radar, Mom has pulled a complete one-eighty.

"Okay, whatever you think is best," Mom says skeptically, taking her seat and laying a napkin on her lap.

"She's going to be fine. My little Snip." Dad is in a sentimental mood tonight. He's picked up on our nicknames and uses them like he invented them sometimes.

"I know she's going to be fine. But I want her to know she can work whenever she needs to. It's important."

"She knows. She'll work when her muse decides to—"

"Ben. Cameron doesn't need a muse." She glares at Dad, who giggles. He loves to egg her on. It's this little game they play. Sometimes it's funny; sometimes it's just plain gross. "She can—"

"She's right here." I slam on the brakes before it gets heated, which always leads to them kissing right at the table. And nobody needs to see that.

"So is her brother, your *son,* who you also love just as much as her," Cooper snipes.

"Don't worry, my little Snap," I tease. "They will be on your case when you're writing your spec scripts or whatever."

"They wouldn't. They know I can handle it."

"Did you have to write another script?" Mom butts in. "Can I read it? Where are you sending it? Is there a deadline?"

"Told you. They'll get on your case anyway," I assure him, and Mom grumbles.

"Okay, okay, *they* get the picture."

···

I'm sweating through the oversized Hawaiian shirt that I got at Goodwill yesterday. I picked out some shirts for boy-Cam to wear to D&D and, now, for hanging out with Why. It's way too hot for the two-mile walk to Alton Baker Park, and way too hot to be wearing this stupid beanie, but here I am, trekking over the De-Fazio Bridge, wishing I could just jump into the river and swim the rest of the way.

The bridge has been the nicest part of the walk, no cars to worry about, just me and the cyclists making our way to and from the park under the weird, tweezer-like support beams. I brainstorm a costume idea for my halfling character, Clover, on my way to the pond where we're supposed to meet.

I keep imagining Clover as a girl, though. I guess it's because she's me, and as much as I'm trying to be *just one of the dudes,* deep down I know I'm not. I do know that Clover will wear a crown of his namesake around his head. Dutch white and crimson blooms.

Someone bumps into me as they pass by to cross the bridge. A man in a tracksuit slows down the minute he's in front of me. I try to copy the way he's walking: like he owns the place. Not a care in the world. Anyone in his way is just an obstacle to overcome. I square my shoulders, lift my jaw. I pretend that everything the light touches is mine. Arrogant.

"Smile, wouldja!" he brightly calls out to a girl walking past us, and I slump back to my normal posture. Her eyes dart to the ground, and she tightens her fingers around her phone. Something I've done when I've walked alone dozens of times. I recognize it right away. Usually I'll pick up a fake phone call so I don't have to respond to the catcaller. "Hey, I'm almost home, so get ready," I always say. But *he* doesn't recognize any of the signs. He doesn't have to. He's too busy turning to watch her backside walk away from him.

I want to trip him. But I don't. I feel oddly guilty in my guy getup. I could stand up for her; I could say something without worrying he'll hit on me next. But it's too late; she's gone, and I settle for jogging past him. I have more important places to be.

Why isn't late. I spot his blond halo-hair from across the water. He's scrolling through something on his phone, glancing up to check for me every now and then. I guess he doesn't see me. I need a minute to get myself back to that place. The boy place. I pace back and forth until I find my stride. Leaning back, shuffling my feet, nodding my head to some imaginary beat.

"Yo! Why!" I call out to him and wave once. He stuffs his phone into his pocket and waves, like a maniac, back at me.

"You're, like, sweating gallons. You know that?" he says.

"I'm fully aware. Is there some shade? Lemonade? Anything?"

"We'll figure something out." Why starts walking the path around the pond. The opposite side looks like it has more trees, and I'm looking forward to the shade. I keep wiping my forehead on my arm, but my arm is just as sweaty as my face, and I'm a girl—I'm not supposed to sweat this much, right?

"I wanted to say, you know, I'm sorry again because, like—" Why stops and starts.

"Dude, I told you. It's really okay. Stop beating yourself up about it." Maybe I should bring up Cooper now, get it over with. Get it all out in the open.

"Didn't you say you make costumes and stuff?" Why asks, slowing down to walk next to me. I had just about forgotten that conversation over pad thai when he called Cooper and me the wonder twins.

"Yeah, I do," I say, trying to take it an octave lower.

"And you're sure you aren't . . . ?" He looks me up and down; I can't tell if Why is joking or not. I want to move on from this. I'm not a prospect—I'm a friend. Remember?

"Yes, I am. Sure. I am sure. I can sew and be straight."

"Of course! Ugh—yes—totally," he stammers. I can tell he feels bad for making the assumption. But I'm the one lying, so why should I make him feel guilty?

"Please don't worry about it. I totally get it." I elbow him, trying to lighten the mood.

"Well . . . tell me about it," he asks.

"What part?"

"Costumes. When did you start?"

"Jeez, hmmm." I search for the right words and try to remember when all of the madness began. If I'm being honest, it probably started when I would make outfits for my Barbies. The clothes they came with were always so boring. I liked adding pom-poms and fringe and sequins and tassels all on one outfit. I remember spending all day on this one look: it was messy and weird with fake flower petals glued together to make a wild hat, and I just had to match her. I had to make the outfit for myself. That's when Mom taught me how to sew. But I can't tell Why that story. I can't tell him about Barbies and silk flowers and glue guns.

I think harder and follow a different thread back to a Halloween. Perfect. How else would you get interested in costumes when you're a kid? "I really, *really* wanted to be a robot for Halloween when I was ten." We finally hit the opposite side of the pond, and I'm already feeling better in the shade of the Doug firs.

"So we looked for robot costumes everywhere—Target, Freddies, you know."

"Sure." Why listens intently, grinning and bopping to the sounds of the birds in the branches overhead.

"None of them were right. Silver foam and fabric, everything looked soft and wrinkled and not robotic at all. I complained for two whole weeks, really dragged it out. I would print out pictures of robots and slide them under my parents' bedroom door. My mom finally had enough and suggested I make my own."

"Let me guess, classic cardboard box and accordion tube arms." Why makes a wave from one arm to the other and back again. He moves like liquid; it's mesmerizing.

"What do you take me for, an amateur? Please. I got a white motorcycle helmet and bent sheets of white plastic. I looked just like ASIMO. Scared the crap out of my mom for a week pretending the suit was empty and then moving when she least expected it. After that, I was sold."

"I'm waiting for that." Why digs his hands into his pockets. "It's there; I know it is. I just don't know what *it* is yet."

"Your thing?"

"Yeah."

"Have you tried classical French horn?" I joke.

"Maybe I should join a traveling circus. I could train a flock of peacocks to sing *Carmina Burana,*" he counters.

"Or study nineteenth-century fine artists."

"More like figure out how to steal the *Mona Lisa* from the Louvre." He pushes down an arm of his glasses, making the frames wiggle up on his nose.

"Hey, at least that one involves a trip to Paris," I offer.

"I can use my two years of high school French."

"Can you say: 'Run! It's the cops!'"

"*Merde.* I'm screwed."

We leave the pond and start walking around the perimeter of the park. It's big, but it's no Forest Park. It makes me miss Portland. We stop in front of the off-leash dog park to watch the doggies chase each other across the dry, golden grass.

"That one is Cooper." Why points to a little spaniel with glossy ears, preening in the shade of a plum tree. Not bothering with any of the other dogs, it really does seem like Coop.

"Ha! True, but Cooper is friendlier than that."

"Really? He's kind of . . . intimidating."

"Cooper?!"

"Yeah, man. Both of you got good genes, or whatever."

"Please." I roll my eyes.

"You both make me nervous. That's all."

"No way, you're cooler than both of us combined," I reassure him.

"See, then you have to go and say something like that. It's nervous making!" The spaniel gets up and walks around the tree. It settles back down in the exact same place.

"Thanks for inviting me to D and D. I really like the game."

"Hey, it's not every day a guy walks into Atomix wearing a shirt as legit as yours."

"Sure it is." I bet it would be more of an anomaly if a girl did.

"Okay, well, not one like you."

"That one's Brody." I point out a stubby pit-mix, trying to dodge the compliment. If it were growling, it would look vicious, but it's rolling on its back in a patch of dandelions. Harmless and scary at the same time.

"Yeah, right down to the lack of nuts." We can't help but crack up. I double over, head between my knees on the park bench where we've sprawled out. I keep my laughs in, mouth closed. I'm getting used to it.

"Lincoln is the yellow lab," I sigh.

"Totally," Why sighs back.

"Which one am I?" I ask Why, and he scans over the park, squinting through his glasses.

"That one." He grins, pointing to a tricolored dachshund. It's scrambling around the dog park, trying to run in ten different directions at once, its tongue hanging out of its mouth. It's derpy and manic, and he pretty much nailed it.

"And that's you." I point out a black-and-white collie. It prances around, happy, smiling, and wagging its tail as it bounds after a butterfly.

"Too true," he says. "Always chasing something I can't have."

"Listen, about that."

"I know. I'm sorry. I shouldn't have said—"

"Well, I think I know someone who might not, you know, mind being chased." I figure now is the best time to bring it up. It's my first time being a wingman, and I have no idea what I'm doing.

"Right." Why shifts away from me and switches from his red-framed prescription glasses to his mirrored shades. "I get it. And I'm sure they're really, you know, cool, if you know them. But. Not yet? Not from you. Not yet."

"Oh. Okay. Sure. You just—" I stammer.

"I'll let you know."

"Wanna hit up the shop?" I offer as the world's worst consolation prize.

"Sure. Why not."

. . .

There's no bell on the door at Atomix Comix. No happy jingle to welcome you, just the metallic screech of the hinges.

"Dude, it's dead in here," Why scoffs as the door closes behind us. Brody, stationed behind the glass counter, silently motions to us. *Knock it off.* He holds up his palm and shields a pointing finger. Why and I both turn in unison, and there she is. A girl in the shop.

She's tall, with shoulder-length curly orange hair. The thin buzz of an undercut peeks out above one ear. She has the most amazing enamel-pin collection I've ever seen. Her messenger bag glitters in the fluorescent lights, every inch covered in pins.

"Brina," Why whispers to me.

"Oh . . . ," I mouth. Brody waves his arms, beckoning us behind the counter. He wants to huddle up.

"What do I do?" he asks through clenched teeth.

"I'm out." Why throws his hands up. "I'll catch you at the game, right, Cam?" he asks.

"You know it." I nod, and we bump fists.

"C'mon, man. Help me out here. Please?" Brody begs. He looks at me like he lost his mommy in the supermarket. Brina browses the graphic novel section, seemingly unaware of his presence. I can't believe Brody is asking me for help. With a girl. I take it as a sign. Maybe I can actually help him, not just as a guy but as a person. Step up and show him how to interact with people without being a total creep.

"Have you tried saying hello?"

"I'm not an idiot." He bristles. But I beg to differ. "She just said hi and that's it. Nothing else. Like she doesn't even know me."

"Maybe she just wants to shop."

"So, what? I ignore her?"

"Just wait. Don't be so thirsty," I scold him. It feels good. Finally I'm this powerful person, able to let it fly and say what I actually want to say. Unafraid of Brody's reactions. I lean against the counter and try not to watch Brina.

Brina looks like I do when I'm in cosplay. Confident, at ease, happy. Turning pages, smiling, shifting her weight from one hip to the other. Unafraid. I don't know her, but I want to be like her. She tucks two books under her arm before walking over to the counter. I covet her Wonder Woman Chuck Taylors.

"Hey." She slides the books across the glass.

"Hi. Did you see?" Brody points over to the graphic novel shelf again. "I stocked more of them."

"Yeah, not bad. Still pretty light, though." She folds her arms in front of her chest. I don't know too much about graphic novels, but the section is kinda puny. Brody pounds the keys on the register, taking her comment personally.

"I'm sure you'll get more. Right, man?" I nudge. Trying to snap him back to reality. No reason for him to blow one tiny comment out of proportion.

"Yeah, sure. I still say you should get into some classic runs, though. I know you liked Dark Knight."

"It was all right." She shrugs.

"I'm telling you, there's some great stuff. Especially Marvel."

"What about the new X-Men movie?" Brina asks. "What should I read before I see it?"

"There's gonna be a new X-Men movie?" I cut in. I wonder if Gillian is working on it. I make a mental note to check up on it later.

"Do I know you?" Brina tilts her head and asks. "You look so familiar."

"Uh . . . I, uh, I don't think so," I spit out. Her comment catches me off guard. Should I know who she is? I've never seen her before. I'm pretty sure I'd remember that hair of hers.

"That reboot is going to be terrible. Don't waste your time. I hear Dazzler's gonna be in it." Brody rolls his eyes and smiles at me. I can't believe I actually smile back. It's infectious. I've made it. I'm part of the club. I'm in the inner circle. I'm so overcome with acceptance I almost don't recognize the sound of my own voice laughing at Brina when she says,

"Who?"

"See, this is why you need to read more than just graphic novels, Brina." Halfway through his sentence I start hating myself. Did I seriously just laugh at her? Brody smirks at me and elbows my arm. I open my stupid big mouth, but nothing comes out. "You got some bad taste," he adds.

"Yeah, yeah." Brina takes it all in stride; nothing he says fazes her in the slightest. "Mr. Tastemaker over here." She opens the glittering flap on her bag and tucks the comics safe inside. "See you round." She pivots on her heel, and we both watch her as she leaves. Both of us jealous for entirely different reasons.

"Are you sure I don't know you? Do you have a blog?" she calls back to me, foot propping open the door.

"A what? A blog? No. I don't, I don't have one. A blog. Sorry. No." I am as smooth as twenty-four-grit sandpaper. I pull my hat down and tilt my head away from her.

"Well, okay, then." And she's gone.

"See what I mean?" Brody asks, leaning against the wall.

"No, sorry. I don't."

"Come on—"

"I gotta go. See you later." I scramble toward the exit. I need to get out of here.

"Later days, man. See you on the battlefield."

■ ■ ■

My face is all over my blog. I scroll through post after post of photos of me and Cooper. Most of them don't really look like me, my features masked by layers of face paint and wigs. But every now and then there's a selfie, or a photo of me working on a build. If you've seen enough of them, you might recognize me. I never thought someone in Eugene would have stumbled across it. This town just keeps getting smaller and smaller.

There's been some pretty harsh backlash to my most recent post. My one attempt to stick up for myself. I've tried to avoid it, but the post keeps getting passed around, commented on, and torn apart. It's hard to ignore. I try to find the nicer comments, tucked in between the STFUs and the images of Cloud getting impaled. There are a few saying that the sword came out amazing, and how Jen's Aerith costume is gorgeous. I focus on those, because Jen's costume did turn out gorgeous: I took five yards of pink raw silk and some red denim and made magic. She looked perfect. I miss her.

A familiar avatar scrolls past, and my heart sinks. I told Liv not to say anything. I didn't waffle; I wrote that post! She shouldn't have chimed in. Now they're all going to come after her too. I click on her post, and there she is. Posing like a superhero in the most amazing shirt I've ever seen. PINZ HAS A POSSE is written in Sharpie across her chest.

LISTEN UP YOU PLEBS!! I have shit I gotta say on this matter. First off, I asked Pinz to make those costumes for Seattle. I've played enough FFVII for the both of us. So back the fuck up and think before you type. Nextly, y'all need to accept the fact that girls aren't going anywhere any time soon. We play games, we read comics, we like nerdy shit. Your attention has NOTHING TO DO WITH IT. Get over it. Because if you think we get off on your dick pics and death threats you're fools. FOOLS. And Imma bring it home with this: If you're not one of these wart-covered trolls, leave my girl some love. Show her what's up. Let her know she's not alone.

#pinzhasaposse

. . .

"Wait, wait, wait." I break character and stop the game. I can't believe what I'm hearing. It's our first big in-game battle. We are all kicking ass and having fun, and Brody pulls this? "This isn't what Tiffani would do. Is it?"

"Obviously," he scoffs.

"Why? How is this fun for you?" I ask. Everyone else is silent, no doubt wondering what the hell I'm doing. No matter how badly I might want to deny it, Brody and I sort of bonded the other day, and it doesn't feel as scary to call him out.

"It's hilarious! It's not like you guys can't handle it. It's just an orc."

"Wouldn't it be more fun to help?" I keep going.

"Yeah, if I was playing a ranger or paladin. But I'm playing a girl, so . . ."

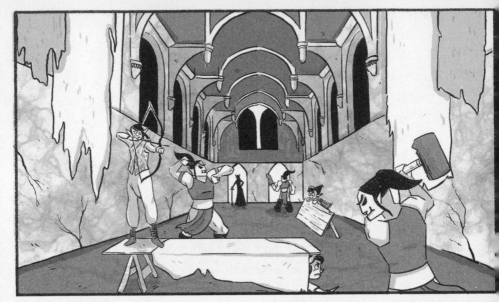

"But you chose fighter as her class!"

"I always choose fighter," he counters.

"I just don't understand why you're treating her like a joke instead of actually playing."

"Cam. What aren't you getting? She's a chick. She's a whiner." Brody isn't mad at me; he's dumbfounded that I can't seem to follow his logic. I glance at Cooper, who's covering his mouth to keep himself from laughing or giving something away. Why doesn't look up from his character sheet.

"You know," Lincoln chimes in, "I don't know a *single* girl like that. Now, are you passing on your turn? You're making me regret giving you that sword." Lincoln scowls at Brody from behind the partition. I want to reach over Brody's head to high-five the hell out of Lincoln's amazing hand.

"It's *my* character. I can play her however I want."

"You're telling me, if you were a chick, this is what you'd *want* to be like?" I prod.

"Can we just play? I'll take my turn. Fine." Brody rolls his d20, and it lands on eighteen. "Plus my strength bonus, and my sword's plus four against orcs, so, twenty-five." Undoubtedly a critical hit. We all look to Lincoln, who clears his throat.

"The orc reaches for you one last time, and you've had it. You smell the stale blood and muck on his leather armor. It turns your stomach. You look out into the room at your companions, who, unable to help you, seem pitiful. What were you thinking, asking two halflings and a wood elf for help? The orc snaps at you; black spit flies from his lips and spatters your cheek. Enough. You tighten your grip on your sword and raise it up above your head. Rage surges through you, and you come down hard, slicing into his skull like a coconut. Spent, and disappointed in your choice of companions, you can't help but think . . ." Lincoln pauses. He looks right at me; his light brown eyes sparkle. I feel flush; I want to bite my lip; I want to tuck my hair behind my ears; I want to flirt his face off. "Never send in boys to do a woman's job."

I want him.

•••

Cooper's phone won't stop ringing; he holds it in both hands and stares down at the screen. As the color drains from his face, I realize it must be Farrin who keeps calling him.

"You can take it—we're at a good stopping point," Lincoln tells him, but it barely registers.

"We can't pack it in now!" Brody begs, but Lincoln's already cleaning up. Coop's cell goes quiet for a few seconds and starts right back up again with his ringtone: *If you like it, then you should've put a ring on it.* The irony.

"Put it on silent; you can call him later," I offer.

"Who?" Why asks, picking up the empty cans of Mountain Dew and black-cherry cola. He pitches them, one by one, across the table and into the trash bin.

"No one." Coop and I both answer in unison. The phone rings one last time, and he answers.

"What. What do you want?" Cooper flings his bag over his shoulder and hurries out. Brody folds up our table and hauls it into the storeroom. The silence drags on, and I can tell Why must be feeling left out, watching Cooper pace back and forth in front of the shop.

"His ex," I explain, letting him in.

"Ah." Why nods, one quick small motion. He understands. Cooper slams his car door and starts the engine. Everyone gathers around the window as he drives off. He's so damn dramatic. He never should have answered. I pick up the rest of his things and add them to my backpack. I should be pissed that he left without me, but I can walk. I probably would have done the same exact thing if I could drive, and if I had an ex-boyfriend.

"I'd give you a ride, but I have to make curfew. I've got, like, the strictest mom in the universe, you know?" Why is rushing to lock away his stuff under the counter.

"It's all good. I live on Clark, not far."

"Word." Why reaches his fist out, and I bump it. We blow it up and laugh. Firmly in friend territory and feeling good. "Later!" he calls out to the rest of the shop.

"You're gonna walk all the way to Clark? Past the Butte?" Lincoln stops me before I leave.

"I take a different road, but it's just a mile or two. I got it."

"I'll walk with you," he suggests, and my throat knots up like a poorly wound skein of yarn.

"Dude. I thought you turned Why down," Brody says to Lincoln, stepping between us. He's holding a ring of keys, ready to lock up shop.

"Excuse me?" Lincoln scrunches his forehead. It's the first time I've seen him angry. Not that I blame him; I guess Brody gets on everyone's nerves. Gender doesn't have to enter into it.

"Gayyyyyy," he sings, shoving us out of the store.

"Don't be an idiot, Brody. I just figured—"

"He doesn't need a babysitter, Lincoln," Brody fires back. I want to deck him. Right in the face, lay Brody out flat right here in front of Atomix, not only because he is being the world's biggest douche, but because he's right. I don't need a babysitter. Guy or girl, I can walk home just fine on my own.

"Grow up." I slam into Brody's shoulder, remembering that jerk from the park. I want to leave them all in my wake. I start walking up the road, and I can barely catch my breath. My head is swimming, satisfied that I said anything at all. Even if it was just two words, I didn't mope away or wait for Lincoln to say something for me.

I turn back and call out to Lincoln, "You coming or what?" Because yeah, I don't need a babysitter, but maybe I want one.

• • •

"My whole damn life," Lincoln says as we pass under the last of the streetlamps downtown.

"We've only been here since June. It's . . ." I pause, trying to find the right words to describe the small college town that still has a bit of a wasteland vibe.

"It's Eugene." He laughs, pulling out his hair tie and wrapping it around his wrist. He ruffles his hair, and it falls around his face. Bits and pieces all sticking out and wild. I want to run my fingers through it, not to smooth it out, but to add to its madness. "I'm sure it's a huge letdown, coming from the city."

"Sometimes." I want to say more, but I wasted all my bravery on bodychecking Brody, and I feel myself locking up. It doesn't help that we somehow managed to take the path around Skinner Butte anyway, and the stars and the trees and the night all seem too sweet. "So you're at U of O?"

"Yeah. How'd you know?" Oh no. I really shouldn't have been eavesdropping at Kozy's. Not with my big mouth.

"Isn't everyone around here?" I try to save it.

"Good point. I'm just in a summer class. I'll be a freshman in the fall. Hang on a sec?" Lincoln stops at a bench and pulls a flannel shirt out of his bag. I don't want to leave yet. We're inching dangerously close to home, and it feels like we've only just started talking. Before he can put his bag back on, I sit on the bench. And wait.

"I'd get the heck out of here for college if I were you." He takes my cue and sits next to me while buttoning up his shirt. I can just barely feel the warmth of his thigh next to mine, and it creeps up my leg and into my chest.

"Why?"

"There's no one here. It's hard to feel like you fit in. Unless you like football or organic urban hemp farming. Which I don't. For a long time I fancied myself a loner. Now, I'm just . . . lonely." Lincoln leans back against the bench, looking up at the navy sky, like he's trying not to look at me.

"What about Why and Brody and all them?" I copy his posture and train my eyes on the handle of the Big Dipper.

"They're fine." He pauses. He searches the sky for the right words. "Sometimes I wonder if they're just friends out of convenience." He takes a breath and coughs out one little laugh. "Which is so rude. We're all in this geeky tribe together. I just feel like, like I want someone to know *me*. And they don't really. They've never even asked about my life outside D and D. You get me?"

"Yeah, I get you."

"You've got your brother, though. I'm sure you guys know each other inside and out."

"He doesn't know everything." I jump to correct him, a little defensively. Yes, Cooper knows me like I know myself. But he doesn't know about the anons right up there on the other side of the moon. Sitting in front of their screens, waiting for me to check my inbox, waiting to cut me down at any chance they get. "So why'd you stay? You could have gone to college anywhere."

"My nan. She isn't *anywhere*—she's here. And she needs me. I live with her."

"She's great," I reply, without thinking.

"What?"

"I bet she's great." I try to cover.

"She is. She's taken care of me ever since I was little. Raised me, you know? I can't just up and leave her now."

"I think about that sometimes; my parents are older. I want to leave, but every now and then I really worry that I'll miss them. Is that stupid?"

"Not at all." Lincoln folds his hands behind his head, and I'm ready to call a truce with the moon for all the wonders it's working. Casting its silvery glow on his skin, his hair. I want to put his face in my hands and press our mouths together and not come up for air until the sun rises.

"What does your nan think about all of it?"

"She wants me gone! She says I'm a pest. Lovingly, of course. She keeps trying to hook me up with girls."

"Ha!" I blurt out, nervous. His phone number in my pocket burns a hole straight into my thigh.

"But they never call," he shoots back fast, like he's accusing me, like I've personally wronged him. There's no way he could know. Unless he found my blog, but wouldn't he have said something? If he knows, he must think I'm the biggest weirdo ever. Who does something like this?

I look down at my outfit. My perfectly crafted boy costume:

the Hawaiian shirt, the slouchy jeans; none of it's mine. I want him to know the real me. Or at least give him the chance to. I wonder if he would have liked me if we had met the way Dotty had planned. If I had just called him up out of the blue. I reach out for him, but before I make contact, he stands up and starts walking. I catch up to him, and we meander past the butte, past the trees, all the way up to my driveway in silence.

"Snip!" Cooper yells as we approach the loft. He's sobbing, eyes red and puffy, covered in tears and sad-slime.

"What happened?!" I rush to him, taking him into my arms. He whimpers into my shirt.

"I hate him, I hate him so much." I look over Coop's shoulder at Lincoln, frozen in our driveway. He looks surprised and concerned, his hand covering his mouth.

"I've got it. Thanks for the walk," I call back to him. But Lincoln doesn't leave. He takes the hair tie off his wrist and pulls his hair back into a ponytail. He clears his throat.

"Jade! After the battle of the three orcs, you find a vest in a trunk. It's the most beautiful piece of fabric you've ever seen in your life. Intricate and delicate. It weighs almost nothing but feels substantial when you pick it up." Lincoln starts to smile as Cooper listens to him from his place in my arms. I feel his breathing slow. We're both entranced. "You put it on, and you can instantly feel its protection. Its buttons fasten perfectly, like it was tailor-made for you. It feels like another limb. Like something you've been searching for your whole life has now made its way back to you and you dare not part with it. It gives you plus four to your constitution, plus three charisma, and plus motherfucking eighteen against asshole exes." Lincoln doesn't say another word.

He gives us a little salute and pivots away, leaving Cooper and me frozen and amazed.

...

"I'm sorry I left you." Cooper is laid out on the studio floor, recovering. Normally, I would lie right next to him so we could stare into the void together. But after Lincoln's incredibly nerdy and lovely speech, all I want to do is make Jade's vest. And I know exactly what to make it from.

"You did me a favor." I retrieve the sheet of green ombré quilt from a cubby. It's perfect. Well, it will be perfect, once I sew it back together in the right shape, and line it with some rose-colored crushed velvet.

"He doesn't even want my notes on his stupid-ass script! I sent them back to him, trying to be nice. Civil. Ugh. Screw him." He pounds the floor with his fists.

"Help me with this." I motion to the fabric. Coop holds up one end to keep it from dragging on the floor as it goes through the machine. But mostly I ask for help to distract him. "That's it? He pouted about your notes?" I ask as we pass the fabric back and forth.

"He knows me, so he knows just what to say to get to me. He said I'd never cut it there."

"He's just nervous you'll show up and knock him down a peg or two."

"It's bullshit! Farrin goes off to NYU for *one* week and is acting like he's Charlie Kaufman or something. Said my scripts aren't *deep* enough."

"You and I both know that's bull." My sewing machine hums along, keeping time with the pace of our conversation. My hatred for Farrin only grows stronger. He needs to get a life and leave my brother alone.

"He met someone. Someone else. Again."

"I'm sure he's a real charmer." I gently lay out the soon-to-be vest on the floor and grab my heavy silver scissors from their spot on the wall. I trim off the frayed threads and extra fabric from the hems. I save every scrap.

"He says he's in love."

"Sure he is."

"I was supposed to be the one who wins, Snip. He destroyed me! Ripped my heart out for fun and now he's moved right on. He's all happy and in love like I should be. He doesn't deserve any of it!" Cooper starts monologuing.

"Do I need to set the timer?" I look up at him from the floor.

"No. Sorry." I get him to crack a smile. "What is that for? It's beautiful." He leans down and runs his fingers across the fabric. "It looks like a landscape. You know, when you look down from an airplane?" We both stand over it and squint.

"Kind of. It's your vest, look . . ." I whip the fabric up off the floor and wave it around his shoulders with a flourish. He sticks his arms through the holes.

"You're so gonna get into CalArts. It's stupid good." He looks like himself again. I run my hands down his shoulders.

"Don't let Farrin get to you like that. You don't have to let him win."

"Did you tell Why? He barely looked at me tonight." He takes off the vest and adds it to the dress form with the rest of his costume. I'm just about ready to move on to the halfling outfits.

There's still a lot of work left. Maybe I *should* have taken dinner upstairs the other night.

"I tried, he wasn't really ready to—"

"What do you mean, wasn't ready? Cam. You can't keep doing this." He pulls on the hem of my oversized men's shirt. "You don't need it."

"Sure. I know. Right."

"I'm serious—you're leading Why on."

"No I'm not! I'm his friend."

"That's what you think."

"Because it's true. I'm allowed to have a friend that isn't you."

"Easy there, Snip. I just think it's time to nip all this madness in the bud." He's right, but he doesn't get to make that decision for me. I rummage through the cubbies, looking for suitable buttons for Jade's vest.

"I gotta keep working, okay?" My voice breaks a bit, and I turn away from him. This happens with us sometimes. I'll get sad or pissed and vent it to Coop, and he'll end up absorbing it as soon as I feel better. This time he feels better, and now I'm bummed.

"Got it." He taps my shoulder and leaves me to it.

I dump out my tin of stray buttons, and it reminds me of Why spilling the dice across the counter at Atomix. I'm not leading him on; I made it clear that I just want a friend. But I don't know why I'm so afraid of telling him the truth. Once I do, there's no going back. And even if he wouldn't care that I am, in fact, a girl, he probably *would* care that I've been lying since day one. I need a better exit strategy; the only outcome I can see now is scorched earth.

I find four mismatched buttons, but for some reason they feel like they belong together. I start stitching them on, and I fall into a rhythm. My mood evens out. I run through Link's little narrative about the vest over and over as I put on the finishing touches. Hearing Lincoln's voice in my head makes me feel even better.

Ignoring the fact that it doesn't have a lining yet, I point a lamp at the vest. The metallic stitching and the quilted material take my breath away. This is mine, from top to bottom, my very own design, and it's glorious. I take some pictures on my phone and immediately post them.

There are fifty-two messages in my inbox. All ranting and raving and angry after Liv's reply. I don't bother reading them, not tonight. Tonight I'm going to work straight through until morning, sewing robes for my wizard best friend, and thinking about the boy who takes care of his nan and weaves stories out of thin air.

...

I look even more exhausted than I feel, wearing the long black wizard robes I finished at seven a.m. The dark circles under my eyes and my tumbleweed of hair actually fit the part. I look like I could conjure up something dark and sinister. I twirl in front of the mirror, and the black strips swing out and expand, as if floating. Each piece sewn carefully together with invisible fishing line. I look like a tornado.

With every spin my exhaustion is whisked away and replaced with excitement. I'll go to Kozy Corner today and pick up my velvet, then I'll have two costumes finished and ready to photograph for my portfolio. I doubt anyone else will have considered what their designs will look like in motion. It's a new level for me, and I'm proud. Goodbye, Eugene; hello, Hollywood.

I shrug out of the robes and hang them up next to Jade's costume. They look even better next to each other. My head is screaming for a cup of coffee, but I want to finish the hem on Wizzy's robe before I take a real break. I thread a needle and lie on the floor as I hand-stitch along the bottom edge. My phone starts ringing.

It's not a number I recognize. I run around the loft, phone ringing in my hand, looking for the pants I wore last night. What if it's Lincoln? I want to cross-reference the phone numbers. I don't know how he would have gotten my number, but something tells me it's him. I give up on my search and hit accept.

"Hello?" I try not to sound too eager. No one responds. "Um . . . is anyone there?" I plug up my left ear and listen closely. And I hear it. Deep, labored breathing. "Who is this?!" I demand, but the caller doesn't say anything; their breathing just gets heavier and faster. Freaked out, I hang up, hitting the end button on the screen about a thousand times. I spot my jeans and dig out Lincoln's number. It doesn't match.

I get a chill, and I'm suddenly painfully aware of my state of undress. I wiggle back into yesterday's jeans and oversized Hawaiian shirt. I crack open my laptop. My inbox is a mess. It exploded overnight. I start deleting notifications, but there are too many to manage. I scroll through some of the posts. There's a surprising number of hashtag supporters. The Quentin client even posted wearing his own Sharpie-scrawled #PINZHASAPOSSE shirt. But the anons are out in full force, and way, way worse than before.

There are long wall-of-text posts; I shy away from the tl;drs. I don't want to know. There are posts that try to analyze my blog, pointing out my laptop, my phone, whatever they can see in the backgrounds of photos to prove I'm spoiled or entitled. There are pictures of my face photoshopped onto porn. There are death threats.

Kill yourself.

I wipe the tears off the keyboard and slam my laptop shut. I fall into the beanbag and stare at all the work I finished last night. Even without the hem, Wizzy's robe might be the most interesting and satisfying costume I've ever made. And I designed the whole thing myself. I breathe, long and deep breaths. This will get me out of Eugene. This will get me into design school. This will get me up on the big screen. A screen that the randos can't harass me on.

Lincoln's number on its increasingly worn scrap of paper lies on the floor, begging me to pick it up. Dotty's perfect handwriting nagging me to call him. I need a break, time away from Wi-Fi and work. I slip on my sneakers and grab my wallet. I'll walk to coffee and buy my fabric. I tap his number into my phone. Halfway into town I hit call.

It's ringing.

A girl and a boy.

"Hello?" His voice sounds even better through the speaker of my phone, soft and deep like the crushed velvet I'm about to buy.

"Hey. Hi. Hello. Is this Lincoln?" It's a struggle not to slip into the tenor voice I use when I normally talk to him.

"That's right. Who's this?"

"Oh, I, ah, your grandmother, she told me you needed, um, help with a sewing project?" I take the long way into town, walking past the butte just like we did last night.

"Did she now? It's okay—you didn't have to call. I've got it."

"But I wanted to call?"

"Oh." He laughs the smallest laugh, barely audible over the sounds of scrub jays squawking from the pine trees.

"I'm actually pretty good at the sewing thing. What are you trying to make?" I ask.

"A map, but you know, out of fabric."

"What kind of map?" I ask, and he pauses. The early-morning sun shines through the tops of the trees and casts a glow over the park. It's just as beautiful in the morning as it was last night. I sit down on the bench, right where he was sitting hours ago, and lean against the cold wood. I tip my head back and let the sun warm my face.

"I have to warn you, kind miss, that it's for something very, *very* nerdy."

"I can get down with nerdy. Everything I've ever made has had some pretty decent nerd cred."

"Like what?" he probes. I kick at the ground. Of course he needs me to clarify. I'm a girl, so I must not like nerdy things. I can't just say I'm down with geeks; I always have to prove myself. I picture him in his bedroom, leaning back in his desk chair. I imagine he's surrounded by *X-Files* and *Doctor Who* posters. His desk cluttered with papers and dice.

"Girls can be geeky too, you know." I get up and follow the trail around the butte into town.

"Of course! I know quite a few. But I've never known a geeky seamstress." I can hear him pacing as he talks.

"Once, I watched my brother play through all of Portal. So naturally I wanted to dress up as Chell, but who has the money for a Portal gun?"

"No one I know."

"Right? So I sat down and made my own out of PVC, card stock, and Bondo. Oh, and some glow sticks." The pause is palpable. It lasts just long enough for me to reach Wandering Goat Coffee and push open the door. "Hello? Are you still there?"

"How have I never met you?" he finally asks. "It seems impossible."

"I'm new in town—hang on, I gotta place my order."

"What're you getting?"

"Caffeine. Preferably iced caffeine."

"Well then, a dirty chai is in order."

"What's in it?" I ask him, loitering in the back of the shop, trying not to annoy other customers with our conversation. But it's not like I'm gonna hang up.

"You're kidding, right? You can make a Portal gun, but you don't know about the magical elixir—nay, nectar of the gods—that is a dirty chai?"

"And your nan works in a fabric store and you can't sew two pieces of cloth together?"

"Touché. It's chai with espresso, and it's—"

"Otherworldly. Got it. Hang on a sec?" I press mute and order one sixteen-ounce iced dirty chai. The cashier writes my name on the clear plastic cup, and spells it right for once. I don't know why every barista is convinced it's spelled Camron or Cameran. Sometimes they mess up altogether and write Carmen. "Back," I say after getting my drink from the counter.

"And?" he asks. I take a sip. My mouth fills up with sweet cinnamon and cardamom cream, with the slightest nutty note of coffee. It reminds me of fall.

"It makes me want to carve a pumpkin."

"Right? So good."

"It may just be my new favorite." I play coy because of course it's my new favorite. Everything about today is my new favorite. My phone beeps, and I check the screen. Another unknown caller.

141

I don't even bother hitting ignore, I just go straight back to talking to Lincoln. They can wait. Everyone can wait. "So . . . ," I start.

"So."

"When do you need to finish this ubernerdy project of yours?"

"Good question. A few weeks? No big rush or anything. When are you free?" he asks, and I want to tell him *right now*. I'll hit up Kozy Corner, buy my fabric, and walk straight to his house.

"Whenever" is what actually comes out.

"Look. It's okay—you don't have to. I know my nan can be very persuasive." He doesn't fool me, not for one second. He wants my help. He wants to meet me.

"Just pick a time and I'll be there, wherever there is." I cross the street; the neon sign in Kozy Corner flashes OPEN. I imagine Dotty yelling at me for not calling her precious Link while he's actually on the phone with me at that very moment. Maybe I'll hand my cell over to her and let her embarrass him for a few minutes.

"I don't know . . . um, how about . . ." Lincoln pauses, perhaps trying to think of an open date in his schedule, and I'm on the edge of the phone like, *Just say now, dude*. The bell jingles inside the shop. The bell jingles through the phone. Startled, I spill dirty chai all over myself. Lincoln and I stare at each other, phones to our ears, jaws on the floor. "How about right now?"

...

He's putting down his phone. He's leaving the counter. He's walking toward me. The loose knit of his henley shirt looks well worn and stretches across his soft tummy. An obvious favorite. He's bending down. His hair falling forward in a sandy curtain. He's picking up the cup. He's reading the name scrawled across it in permanent marker. He's looking up at me. He's smiling.

"I knew it."

...

"I'm so sorry I . . ." I pat my pockets, searching for a napkin I know won't be there. I look up, over the spill, to the counter. No paper towels in sight. "I'm a mess." I can't bring myself to look him in the eyes.

"Nah, you just made one." He rummages through a cabinet underneath the counter and produces two rags and some Windex. "Here."

"Isn't this for windows?" I ask, sopping up the beverage.

"Beggars and choosers and all that." Lincoln sprays the floor, and we make fast work of the spill, neither of us saying a word. There's no radio or other customers to break the awkward silence. I try to think up an excuse, a lie, anything I can tell him to make this situation seem the least bit understandable. But nothing is coming. He takes the rag from me and stuffs it back under the counter. He doesn't look mad, but he does look like he's trying to keep himself from laughing in my face. I don't know which is worse.

"As I was saying." Lincoln folds his arms and leans forward on the counter between us. "I knew it."

I kneel on the floor, unable to move. "There's no way you knew," I say to the white linoleum floor.

"I totally did." I can hear him smiling. The same way he does when he talks to Dotty, and when he talked to me on the phone.

"I mean, you know right *now*. You *just* realized that—" I poke the floor for emphasis.

"I may have pieced it together at some point between Skinner Butte and your house. I was pretty certain by the time I got home last night."

"Oh, God." I cover my face with my hands.

"If it makes you feel any better, I didn't know for sure it was you on the phone," he offers, but I'm mortified. "I'm glad it was, though." I peek at him through my fingers.

"You must think I'm so weird. Like, who even does something like this? It's straight-up banana-pants behavior."

"Who says weird is a bad thing? Plus, I think I know you better than that. So . . . out with it." He hops up onto the counter and hangs his legs over the edge. I don't know how to explain myself. There's nothing I can say to fix this. No matter what, Lincoln will forever know me as the girl who pretended to be a boy because she was too scared to be herself. And that's not who I really am. Or at least, it's not who I want to be.

"But you *don't* know me," I sigh.

"Of course I know you. I see you every week. I walked you home last night. I know you." He pats the counter, an invitation to sit next to him. I'm too nervous to take him up on it, but I do pick myself up off the floor.

"I *want* you to know me. But you don't. Not yet," I explain. Everything he is saying is kind and understanding and just right. But if he really knew the kind of coward I am, he'd stop acting so forgiving.

"What are you hiding from?" His fingers curl around the lip of the counter. I can tell he's getting anxious. I realize that the only way Lincoln will ever get to know me is if I let him. I start pacing back and forth in front of him.

"I couldn't shop there," I start. "At Atomix. I know that every time I go there as myself, Brody will be there. With nothing better to do than follow me around and question my presence in the store. Quizzing me, making all these patronizing comments. But I need to be able to buy comics, and I thought it might be easier, you know, if I were a guy."

"So dressing in drag, changing your voice, pretending to be a whole different person, that's easier?" I didn't expect him to fully understand. But explaining my perspective is proving difficult.

"When you've been making cosplay for the past eight years, yes. And I wasn't a whole different person. Just me, with a wang. A pretend wang?" I try to break the tension, but Lincoln remains skeptical. "It was never supposed to go on this long. I wanted to win Brody over. Then I would do this grand reveal. You know—" I hop up on the counter, stand triumphantly, and point down at Lincoln. "Ha! You've been friends with a *girl*! We're not monsters! Cut us some slaaaack!" I yell toward the sky, arms held over my head.

Lincoln finally breaks, laughing from his spot on the counter. The sound of it is such a relief I can't help but join in. My first unguarded burst of girlish laughter since we met, and it feels so good I barely hear my phone beeping. Someone's left me a voice mail. No one ever leaves me voice mail.

"Hang on a sec?" I ask Lincoln, and he nods. I type in my passcode and wait.

"I hope you fucking die, cunt," a voice growls into my ear and down deep into my stomach. I hang up before I hear anything else.

"Everything okay? Cooper okay?" Lincoln hops off the counter and offers me his hand. I don't take it. I don't want him to know mine are shaking. I'm dizzy; the room is spinning. "You're white as a sheet—come down." I slowly crouch and slide my feet off the edge of the counter. "What happened?"

"I keep getting these calls. I don't understand." I frantically open my inbox to find that there are more messages than ever before.

"What the hell is going on?" I ask no one in particular. My eyes sting as I scroll through filthy subject lines for pages; finally I make it back to the last time I posted. Everything is in response to that, the one time I spoke up to defend myself.

> **SJWHunter0 left a comment on your post:**
> JESUS CHRIST. Cosplayers are so stuck up their own asses! Get another fucking hobby. They're all so OBSESSED. This "girl" should pack it in and give it up already. Trying to come off like some "rare breed" like she's conquered stereotypes or some bullshit. Maybe like, ten years ago guys would be worshipping her or whatever. But now it's fucking pathetic. Just look through her posts, she's gotten so many details wrong on a shitton of costumes. Not that any of them are doing her any favors with that busted-ass face of hers. Honestly she'd look better with my dick in her mouth.
> Yo, if you're tired of this shit, call this fake bitch and tell her and her fucking #pussyposse to kill themselves already:
> 503-555-0219

I'm going to be sick. The room is spinning, and the dusty smell I used to love overwhelms me. My stomach feels like a well-used pincushion. It's hard to breathe. I want to get up, to run home and hide in my bedroom. Throw my phone into the toilet and flush. But I can't because I'm frozen stiff. It feels like if I move one inch, I'll throw up all over Lincoln, and there's not enough Windex in the world to wipe that image from his mind.

"C'mon." He takes my hand and helps me off the counter. "Let's get out of here. You can explain as long as you'd like." Slowly he leads me to the front of the shop and takes a wad of keys out of his bag. He flicks off each row of lights, and as the store gets darker, I feel my grip on the situation loosen. Panic sets in. Everything in my body is screaming *RUN*. Go home and get safe.

"Don't," I tell him before he has a chance to lock up the store. "You shouldn't."

"But—"

"I have to go. Please don't, don't tell any—"

"I won't. I promise." He makes an X across his whole chest with his finger. He doesn't want me to leave, but he didn't have to hear what I just did. I can't look at him with that anonymous voice repeating in my ear. I can't have the sweet expression on his face and those foul words stitched together in my memory of this moment. The bell jingles, and I don't look back. I just focus on putting one foot in front of the other, staring straight ahead, the whole way home.

Kiss the girl.

Did Gillian Grayson ever go through this? I try to picture her as a teen, sewing in her bedroom without blogs or feeds or anons, and I envy her. I try to forget the Internet exists. I stack my laptop and phone on the worktable. After a moment of thought, I unplug the router and add it to the pile.

I curse Liv for writing that post. All it did was egg on the randos, and they came at me with a vengeance. Lincoln wonders why dressing as a guy is easier than existing as a girl. Being boy-Cam is easy, a cakewalk compared to the comments section. There's no way he'll ever see that. Weeping, I change out of yesterday's boy clothes and put on my hand-sewn trapeze dress. I want to feel like myself, top to bottom, inside and out.

I stare down at the table cluttered with tech. I know all the things I probably should do: switch my phone number, delete my blog, make a new email address. But the dead electronics will make good fabric weights, and the only thing that will really make me feel better is creating in the wake of all their destruction.

It's time for Clover and his—no, *her*—costume. I've decided. Wizzy, the secret mage, has to hide his identity, and Clover has to do the same. Maybe halflings have it tough in general. Clover is a girl. A girl who, to flee the trappings of the fairer sex, had to become a boy. She wanted a life of adventure, and she stole it for herself.

The design comes so easily, like I've been planning it forever. She wears a multitude of layers, hiding secret pockets and compartments. Each one is stuffed with coins and gems and trinkets from her travels. She's got a deep purple robe that she wraps over everything when she needs to vanish into the shadows. And of course, her crown of clovers.

I get all my fabric ready; I clear off the dress form; I have Dad crank his Motown from the boom box in the garden. I'm going to finish another costume today if it kills me. This is it; this is all there is. This is the only thing that matters.

•••

Mom was thrilled when I took my dinner up to the loft. I'm so close to actually finishing. If I were on *Project Runway,* I'd be killing it. One: I have two weeks left to finish the greatest portfolio Gillian Grayson's ever seen. Two: every assface on the Internet wants me dead for the stupidest reason imaginable. Three: I'm lying to my new friends about my gender. Oh, and four: I ran out on the boy I like. That's the challenge I've been handed, and it's time to *make it work.*

"Another one?" Cooper asks, halfway up the stairs.

"I need five total."

"Clover?" He holds one of the sleeves and considers it.

"You got it," I tell him, not looking up from stitching.

"Snip, are you mad at me?" Coop sits at his desk. He hasn't used it much this summer, but I'm sure once the school year kicks in he'll be hunkering down as usual.

"Of course not." I sew on another button. Each pocket will close with a button and a loop. Clover protects everything that matters to her.

"You ignored my texts, all day." I miss the fabric; the needle slides off the thread and onto the floor. I had forgotten about my phone, and what happened, for hours now.

"My phone died." I search around for the lost needle, knowing I probably won't find it until I'm barefoot and not paying attention. "I forgot to plug it in with all my work and stuff. What happened?" Cooper picks up a packet of extra needles from my desk and tosses it to me.

"I saw Why at the mall."

"You didn't tell him, did you?" I panic and drop the packet.

"Calm down. No, I didn't rat you out. Not yet, anyway."

"I'm sorry, it's just—"

"Yeah, yeah, I know. But listen. This isn't about you and your shenanigans," he scolds me, and sits in the rolling chair.

"Right. Listening." I go back to sewing on buttons while Coop talks.

"He noticed me and came into the store and, like, I know I've said this a bunch of times, but he's really cute, Cam. No joke." Cooper is positively glowing, and I can tell he's fallen. Hard. "Okay, so anyway, he stuck around and grabbed lunch with me, and we were talking about movies."

"Of course you were." I sew on a tiny silver button without even looking down.

"Right, but get this: he doesn't like them."

"What." I stare at Cooper. Deadpan.

"Okay, he likes them, but he only likes the awful ones."

"What do you mean?" I fish around my button tin and grab a pink flower-shaped one and attach it to another pocket.

"He has terrible, *terrible* taste in movies. He hates everything I love. He likes disaster movies and corny sci-fi and those movies about car racing or whatever."

"So why are you smiling?"

"Because it was the best conversation I've ever had. It was fun and funny, and I could have sat there and fake-argued with him until the mall closed."

"That's kind of amazing." I smile at him.

"So if you could just . . ."

"Not yet."

"Well, why the hell not? You know what I've been through with Farrin and everything. Just do it already."

"What *you've* been through?" The voice from the phone floods back into my head, snarling, calling me pathetic, a coward.

"You have no idea what it's *really* like," he accuses me. "You're just playing pretend! You've never had to deal with anything close to what I went through."

"But—"

"But nothing. I love you, Cam. I really love you. And I'm asking you to please not fuck everything up with this stupid scheme of yours." He motions to the pile of boy clothes in the corner. I want to tell him he's wrong, that now I *do* know what it's like to be tormented. But it's not a competition. Just because I can sympathize doesn't mean his troubles are less real, less important.

If I'm honest, I've created most of my own problems. Cooper can't help his. I can turn off my phone and ignore the randos all day. He can't turn off his feelings. He doesn't need to know about any of my issues.

"Soon, Snap. I just need to find the right moment."

"One week. I'm giving you a week. Then all bets are off."

. . .

I can feel Clover coming to life on the dress form, smiling at me, or at least she would be if the dress form had a head. The three costumes look like a family next to each other, though equally unfinished. Each one is missing some detail or another. Nothing that can't come together after another late night in the loft.

There's a soft knock on the studio door. I'm sure it's Dad coming to remind me that summer will be over soon and I shouldn't be this pale and this tired. I look over the railing to shoo him away, but it's not him. It's Lincoln. He waves, holding a Scrabble box and the crushed velvet I was supposed to buy up to the window.

What on earth is Link doing here, at my loft, at my door?

"Thought you could use some cheering up?" he says through the glass. I hold up a finger, asking for just a second. I sprint around the loft, stashing my dirty boy clothes, trying to fluff my hair into an acceptable shape in the mirror. No time for shoes or straightening anything else, because Lincoln is here and I don't want him to wait.

"Hey. Come on in." Lincoln walks past me and up the stairs

while I peek back at the house, making sure no one saw him come in. It's not that they would be mad that I have a boy over; I just don't want to answer any questions, not when I don't know the answers myself.

"I met your dad," he tells me as we walk up the stairs.

"He didn't embarrass me too badly, I hope?"

"Nah, I just told him I liked his first-edition handbook and that we should all play D and D sometime."

"You're joking."

"Why not?"

I want to change the subject. My dad is the last thing I want to be discussing when Lincoln is actually here, in my studio, right in front of me. Here to cheer me up. I hop up off the top step and try to affix everything about this moment in my mind.

"Wow, this is marvelous." He looks around the messy workroom, mouth wide open. I scoff at his word choice.

"Recognize anyone?" I motion to the lineup of costumes hanging next to the dress form.

"No way! It can't be. Jade and Wizzy?" He figures it out without missing a beat.

"They're for my portfolio review. I'm trying to get into CalArts."

Lincoln whistles, impressed. "CalArts should be trying to get you, not the other way around." He slides the Scrabble box next to my sewing machine and places a stuffed, ratty notebook on top of it. The cover has *HEGEMON DICTIONARY* written on it in Dotty's slanted handwriting. He goes straight back to looking at the costumes.

"May I?" He motions to the sleeve, asking if he can touch it.

"Sure." I let him. His thumbs feel the fabric; he inspects every stitch. He opens one of Clover's pockets and pulls out the silver thimble I've hidden inside. "She collects them."

"Oh, does *she*?" He smirks over the dress form's shoulder. "Very interesting." He studies the drawing of Clover's costume that's pinned up behind her. He moves on to Wizzy's costume, gently running his fingers through the black scraps.

"I'm pretty bad at Scrabble. You'll have to take it easy on me," I tell him.

"You'll do fine—it's Hegemon Scrabble." Lincoln doesn't turn around. He's still mesmerized by the fishing wire on Wizzy's robes. I love that he is interested in what I do; even so, I'd rather he look at *me* right now.

"I don't know what that is." And then it happens: he looks at me like it's the first time he's ever seen me. And maybe it is. He's never seen me in my own clothes, my own skin before. His ears flush red, and his eyes dart to the Scrabble box. He takes it and the notebook and sits cross-legged on the floor. I sit across from him, folding my legs to the side.

"Dotty and I invented it when I was a kid. Before I could really play, like when I was seven or something." He takes his time scrambling and flipping over all the little wooden tiles in the lid of the box. "I wasn't good at reading, and I took the losses pretty hard. So we just started using made-up words."

"What do you mean, like gibberish?" I join him, flipping over letter after letter, hoping his hand brushes mine by accident.

"Well, not just any combination of letters. Words that could be real, but aren't. And when you play a word you make up, the definition goes in the book." He taps the Hegemon dictionary.

"What's 'hegemon' mean?"

"I dunno—I think she was reading *Ender's Game* to me at the time." He picks seven tiles and lines them up on his rack, making a big show of hiding them from me. I take my own, though I have no idea how this is supposed to work.

"I'll go first." He plays the word SNIKEL. "'Snikel.' A secret nickel that you have hidden away for a rainy day." He takes the notebook and finds the *S* section. He adds his new word on one of the crammed pages before tallying up his points. His handwriting is neat and straight; he writes in all caps underneath Dotty's signature slanted script. "Your turn." He beams.

"Uh, how about 'yolker'?" I play my tiles off the *K* in his word.

"Sure, what does it mean?" He flips the dictionary open to the *Y* words and slides it to me.

"It's when, um, you get double yolks in an egg?"

"Perfect. Thirteen points!" He hands me the pen to write it in and mark my score. We both pick out new tiles from the box. He takes his time, pondering his next move. I flip through the dictionary, years of imaginary words filling up hundreds of pages, and as far as I can see, mine is the only other handwriting in the whole book. He finally plays ROZEZ, a robotic bouquet, off my *R* tile. I play SLUBBIN off the *S*.

"Ha! What's that one?" Lincoln leans on his elbows, giddy with the game. Happy and at ease, despite the fact that I haven't offered an explanation for what happened this morning. He hasn't even asked.

"It's that feeling when everything should be great, but you keep thinking about that one bad thing and it ruins it." He looks up from the dictionary; his eyes land on mine.

"You didn't ruin anything."

I take out my phone from the cubby and turn it on. Lincoln is the last person I want to see what's written in my comments section, but if he's going to understand, he has to.

"This is why. This is why it's easier for me to dress and act and be that guy from D and D." I hand him my phone and let him scroll. I never thought it would get this bad. It's just a stupid blog about cosplay. Time passes as he goes through my phone, brow furrowed. I fidget, crack my knuckles, chew my lip, hoping that he'll still be able to treat me the same way after reading all that poison.

"Dear lord. How are you still standing?" He looks at me with a mixture of admiration and pity.

"Am I? I feel like I'm falling."

"Wait, are all of these costumes yours? You made them?" He must be scrolling through the posts now. He swipes up the screen over and over.

"Yep."

"What are you doing in Eugene? You're, like, the most talented person I've ever met. This is incredible."

"They don't seem to think so." I point to my phone.

"It's the Internet—what did you expect?" It's a kick in the gut. My perfect image of Lincoln now has a frayed edge. What did I expect? I expected to post some photos and get stupid reaction GIFs from my friends. Not hundreds of pages of abuse, not death threats growled at me through my phone.

"Do you have a blog?" I ask. Lincoln is still scrolling through the archive.

"I used to; I always forgot to update it."

"So, how many death threats have you gotten? When some jerk released your phone number to the masses, how many disgusting calls did you have to answer? Did you switch your number when it happened? Or did you weather it out?"

"But I didn't—"

"It's the Internet, after all, so I assume you've gotten some, no?" I need to think about something else before I lose it. I lean out the window. Dad's garden is really coming along. He has all the paths lit with glass solar globes; they change colors every few seconds. A rave for ladybugs and squirrels. I take a breath.

"Hey, I'm sorry. You're right. If someone called my phone, someone from the Internet, I'd pee my pants." Lincoln stands up and I can feel him get closer to me, but he stops before joining me at the window. He waits for me to give him the go-ahead. "I really am sorry. I wasn't thinking." I move aside and leave a space for him to stand at the window. We both lean out, look up. "I'm listening."

"I just want to feel like myself again. But if I do that, things go back to the way they've been all along at Atomix. And it's not like jerks will just stop posting crap online. I wish there was an easy answer, but I know there isn't."

"There never is." He leans in the slightest bit; his arm is touching my arm, and it's warm, and it's there, and I don't want to move.

"If I ignore it, they win. If I yell at them, they win. They win, they win, they win."

"No. You can't think of it like that. Because no matter what you do, they're still gonna be anonymous losers with nothing better to do, while you're making costumes for the next Spidey reboot."

"But what should I do?"

He thinks it over for a moment. "Whatever it is that you need to do to get yourself through this is the right decision. If you feel safer being dude-Cameron, do it. If you want to change your phone number, go for it. If you want to tell them all to screw themselves, I will make a hundred accounts to fight off each and every commenter. You know, if you want me to. Because in the end, you will have a life and—" Lincoln motions around the studio, his cheeks rosy pink with fire. "And a whole career that they could only dream of. You just need to get through it."

• • •

I am kissing Lincoln. I am pushing his hair out of the way of our mouths, even though the smell of it makes me want to pull him closer. I am pulling him closer. I am opening my mouth. I'm tasting him and he tastes like cherries and cinnamon and I can't figure out if he just drank a soda or a chai. He is very still, his thumbs in his belt loops. He leans in, but not too much. I feel his tummy press against mine. He is careful. He is patient. Too patient. He pulls away and lifts his arms, just so, pausing right at my waist. Hovering.

"May I?" he asks, just the same way as before. As if I'm the same sort of masterpiece my costumes are. And it's the first time anyone's ever asked instead of just grabbing, and I had no idea how much I'd like that. I want to say yes and please, and I do over and over again. And he lets me.

"May I?" Before he wraps his arms around me, pulling me closer, kissing deeper.

"May I?" Before running his hands up the front of my dress.

"May I?" Before kissing down my neck, his lips trading places

158

with his hands. Each time pausing, waiting for a yes, and each time we are both thrilled when I say it. We find ourselves back on the floor, and I climb into Lincoln's lap. I feel his hands tug on the edge of my dress.

"May I?" he asks again, and as much as I want to, I'm not sure I'm ready.

"Not yet." I wince a bit; he moves his hands back into mine. "I'm sorry."

"Don't apologize," he whispers into my neck.

"I just think that—"

"You don't need a reason." He pulls back, to make sure I know he means it. Our fingers interlock.

"May I?" I ask him this time, leaning in to kiss him again.

"Please." And he lets me. We spend the rest of the night scattering Scrabble tiles across the floor. Spelling out countless Hegemon words all on their own. We're far too busy to make up the definitions.

Girl friends and boy friends.

"Sixteen-ounce dirty chai, please." I order my new favorite drink at Wandering Goat. My cheeks hurt; I don't think I've stopped smiling since Lincoln left the studio last night. I walked him down the stairs; we parted ways in my driveway. He kissed me on the cheek. I bet I smiled in my sleep.

Why waits for me at one of the tables underneath the huge maple outside. He ordered a mocha with orange zest. I'm hoping the sugary sweetness of it will mask the bitter news I'm about to drop into his lap. Today is the day: I promised Cooper I would come clean, and I've never backed out of a promise to him. Never.

I balance the mug on its saucer and open the door with my hip. Why is taking a picture of his mocha. I'm dressed in my thrifted boy duds: another Hawaiian shirt, this one adorned with lobsters, and my hair tucked in place under my beanie. I don't want to shock him, so I swagger over to the table.

"Chai?" he asks, smelling the steam over my mug.

"Dirty chai."

"Heh, that's Lincoln's drink." He leans away from the cup. The mention of Link's name makes me blush, and I pray Why doesn't notice it through his tinted shades. I wonder if Lincoln dropped by the Goat this morning and ordered one for himself.

"I'm glad you wanted to hang," Why says after a long sip of his drink.

"Yeah, I wanted to . . ." I pause. How do I bring this up? Ease into it, or rip it off like a Band-Aid? Actually, I usually just pick at the edges or make Cooper rip it off for me.

"I'm glad you moved here, you know? Like, not glad that you *had* to move, but glad that it ended up working out?" Why rambles on in his Why way. Everything is a question, everything over-explained.

"Eugene's not so bad, I guess." I take a sip of my chai; it's the perfect temperature. I take another sip before it starts to get cold.

"It's not the best either, but, man, I didn't know how I was gonna get through senior year."

"What do you mean?"

"You're going to South next year, right?" Why asks.

"I think so? To be honest, I kind of totally forgot about high school." CalArts feels more important than senior year, so I haven't thought about going back to school at all this summer.

"Shit. I wish I could." He ducks his head and hides behind his mug. "I don't know what it's like in Portland, but everyone here is kind of . . . samey?" Why looks around at the other patrons and at the people walking by. I see what he means. No one looks like him. Everyone's white; everyone is in cargo shorts and hiking sandals. Why is the chicest geek I've ever met, in his wrinkle-free button-up and round-framed sunglasses. He's got too much style for this place, that's for sure.

"I feel like next year, though? With you and Cooper at South? It's not gonna be so bad."

"Coop used to get bullied a lot. But it calmed down after a while."

"Oh, it's not so much the haters. I was feeling lost. And then I met you, and you get me. Like really, you know?" Why smiles, and I want to crawl under the table and hide. Dig a hole straight to China and never tunnel back. What was I thinking, keeping my identity secret for so long? He trusts me and has no reason to.

"About that . . ."

"And your brother. He's hilarious. I want to do a podcast with him. Do you think he'd be into that sort of thing?" Why asks.

"Absolutely. Especially if it's with you." I ease into my explanation. "He really—"

"Looking schlubby as ever, Cam." Farrin's voice snaps me out of the trenches. I whip my head around, and, sure enough, there he is.

"What are you doing here?" I snipe at him through clenched teeth.

"Just visiting. Who's your boyfriend?" Farrin nods to Why.

"Friend . . . we're just friends." I try to keep my voice deep. Farrin looks at me like I have two heads.

"I'm Wyatt."

"Nice to meet you, just-a-friend Wyatt. I'm sure I'll see you round, Cam." And with a wave, he's inside the coffee shop, about to order the snobbiest thing on the menu, no doubt. Farrin makes my skin crawl. Even after he cheated, his breakup with Cooper lasted months. Farrin kept dragging it out. He would cast Coop off, and then slowly but surely reel him in again. There's no way I'm letting him keep this up any longer.

"Gimme a sec? I'm so sorry." I beg Why's forgiveness.

"Yeah, sure."

"I'll explain, I promise," I say as I push in my chair and chase after Farrin.

He's waiting for his order and tapping something into his phone. Smiling, smug, and slimy.

"Hey." I get his attention as I saunter over to him. My boy clothes still make me feel brave. It doesn't matter that Farrin knows what's going on underneath them. "Leave Cooper alone already, okay? Just leave. Period."

"How about no," Farrin yawns, not bothering to look up from his phone.

"Shouldn't you be in New York? Did you get kicked out of NYU already?" I jab, hoping to hit a soft spot.

"Shouldn't you be sewing some slutty catsuit, trying to get a boyfriend?" He hits one of mine instead.

"Please?" I ask, trying to be sincere. Cooper's been through enough. "Leave my brother alone."

"I came here to see him; I just want some closure. I'm entitled to that," he says over the hiss of milk being heated. "What's going on with you anyway? You look like the love child of Weird Al and Paul Bunyan."

"Low-fat, no whip, apple-graham, pumpkin iced latte? For Farrin?" the barista hollers. I love how they shout his order as if it's a question, as if they don't even know what the hell they just made. It's the most ridiculous order I've ever heard. It sounds like the cup would be full of just syrups and ice. Nothing else would fit.

"I asked for extra whip."

"It says no whip."

"Well, it's wrong then," Farrin spits. I lean back and look at Why out of the window. He flashes me a thumbs-up, followed by a thumbs-down. I hold up one finger and shrug. He nods.

"Here." The annoyed barista grabs a can of Reddi-wip and sprays on a tower of whipped cream so tall it starts to tip over. I give him a sympathetic glance, but he's already working on the next order.

"I'll tell Cooper you say hi," Farrin says, taking his "coffee" and pushing the door open with his hip.

"You better not!" I call after him as he walks to his car. He doesn't bother responding; he lazily rolls his eyes and slurps through his straw. "I'm serious!" My voice is deep and menacing.

"Yeah, okay."

"You drive your ass right back to New York. You're not here for closure. You're here for an opening."

...

"We're following him, right?" Why is already busing our mugs and saucers into the bin. He takes out his key fob and unlocks his car; his headlights flash nearby.

"I don't know, maybe we should—"

"Get in," Why demands happily. We both hustle into his car, worried we will lose sight of Farrin's obviously pre-owned Mercedes. Why's car is different. It's got four seats, but it's tiny. Really tiny.

"Sorry, it's smaller on the inside." He laughs.

He isn't wrong. The car feels like a toy, but the inside is spectacular. He's decorated every available inch. Rope lights border the ceiling, which is covered with those glow-in-the-dark star stickers. Why reaches into the backseat and takes a porkpie hat off a stack of board games and crime novels. He fixes the hat over his golden Afro, grins, and guns it.

Next to the board games, there's a pile of role-playing handbooks topped with unopened packages of silver miniature figurines. Sometimes Lincoln will use them in our D&D campaign to represent our characters or monsters. Why has enough back there to simulate a whole army.

He plugs his phone into the center console, and the speakers blast some weird podcast. A low voice warns us about going to a dog park. He quickly turns the volume down with a few taps on the screen.

"Your car is cool. Very high-tech-looking." I point to the second display behind the wheel. Green arrows animate over a picture of his engine.

"It's electric!"

"Seriously?" I ask, and he nods. We catch up to Farrin at a red light, but I don't think he notices us.

"He's going to the mall," I tell Why. It won't matter if we tail Farrin the whole way there; I know exactly where he's heading.

"What else is there in this neighborhood? So, you gonna fill me in, or what?" He adjusts his sunglasses in the rearview.

"Right. Sorry. He's Cooper's ex."

"Cooper dated *him*?" Why squints at Farrin's car. "Wow."

"I know, right?"

"He's hot as hell."

"Please tell me you're kidding," I sigh.

"I'd kill for a boyfriend that hot. But, you know, it makes sense."

"In what universe does it make sense?" I try to follow Why's logic, but I can't.

"Cooper's hotter. So, you know, they'd make a hot couple."

"First of all, ew. He's my brother. Secondly, Farrin is such a fake. You and Cooper could both do better than him."

"You think? Really? I don't know. I bet Cooper could. He's a writer! And smart, with the right taste in movies, and down for D and D. He's a catch."

"So are you."

"Nah, I have bad, bad luck. No game, no dating mojo whatsoever."

There is a pause, so thick, so awkward, you'd have to stitch it with a wedge-point needle. I wish I didn't like Why as much as I do. I wish he were more like Brody so I could at least try to ignore him, but he's not. He's hilarious and warm and exactly the kind of friend I was desperate for. The guilt is real; I don't want to be responsible for breaking his heart.

I have to come clean. Tell him I'm a girl, and then all this awkwardness will go away because he won't be into me anymore. Not in *that* way. And we can settle on just friends and pretend that none of this ever happened. Especially the part where I lied for weeks.

"Looks like you were right." Why nods his head as Farrin pulls into the mall's parking garage.

"I wish I wasn't."

"Heh, I hate the mall too."

"He's going to Banana," I say, trying to remind Why who works there.

"No. No, he can't just . . ." Why trails off as he parks his little electric car. We both race toward the entrance, hoping we'll beat Farrin to Banana Republic and spare Cooper the drama, or at least give him some backup.

Farrin casually meanders through Macy's. He stops in the shoe department, checking the prices on the soles of some shoes. Why and I duck behind a rack of button-down shirts and watch him browse.

"Maybe he's just here to shop?" Why whispers.

"At Macy's? In Eugene?"

"Point taken."

We dash from rack to rack, suppressing laughter and hiding between suit jackets and slacks. It feels like we are our characters, mischievous halflings on a mission to thwart an evil dark elf. If Farrin came to Eugene just to torture Cooper, he sure is taking his time. He even lets one of the salesmen spray him with a cloud of cologne.

"This is what I mean," Why chuckles. We hide behind a makeup display.

"What?"

"I seriously can't wait to have you guys around for the school year. Eugene needs more of us."

"Us dorks?"

"Exactly." He holds out his fist, and I tap it with mine. It's too much to take. I'm ending this.

"Why. Listen—"

"Wait, where did he go?"

"I just wanted to tell you—"

"Come on!" Why grabs my hand and pulls me out of the department store and into the mall. My palms are so sweaty he almost loses his grip. We run past kiosks, holding hands and our hats to our heads. By the time we reach Banana, we're gasping for air as Farrin saunters right by us and into the store, followed by the chemical stench of cheap cologne.

...

We're too late. If we barge in after Farrin, we're only going to cause even more of a scene. I feel awful. We shouldn't have goofed off in the department store. We should have come straight here and warned Cooper. I let him down.

"Hurry, text him!" Why must sense my guilt. I take my phone out: it's off. My hands tremble, remembering the last time it was on. How many more anons have tried calling me, left messages, since I turned it off? I don't want to know. I'm not sure I can handle it.

"It's dead," I tell him, and slide the phone back into my pocket.

"What's his number?" Why asks, taking his own phone out and unlocking it in a flash.

"I–I have no idea." Cooper has only told me his number once, when I was programming it into my phone. I had no reason to memorize it. I wonder if he knows mine.

"Oh, please!" I hear Cooper's voice ring out from the store. Why and I creep closer so we can watch through one of the windows. I can't see Cooper. Farrin is blocking my view. "You really think that's going to work? Now?" Cooper laughs.

"I don't think you understand what I'm saying." Farrin waves his arms in frustration. Cooper walks away from him and starts folding a messy pile of shirts.

"I understand perfectly," he says without looking up.

"Oh my God. He's wearing the vest," I blurt out.

"It suits him," Why says with wide eyes.

"I made it. For Jade," I explain.

"This is it, Cooper. Your last shot." Farrin stands behind Cooper, looking over his shoulder. Haunting him like a level 9 Soul Eater. But Cooper has his vest, and with it he's unstoppable. Even if he rolled a one, he'd slay.

"Oh, Farrin. You're adorable." Cooper finishes one pile and moves on to the next. Farrin's face shifts from pasty pale to deep pink, pissed that he isn't getting the reaction he wanted. "You came all the way to Oregon, down to Eugene, to give me one last shot? Really?"

"I thought that—"

"*I* thought that you were in that *super-exclusive* summer program. It's over already?"

"We had a—"

"And what about your new boy? I thought you were so in love or whatever."

"We weren't—"

"I don't care." Cooper rolls his eyes.

"You used to." Farrin spits back at him. He looks hurt. I wonder if Farrin really did want to get back together with Cooper.

"Has Cooper always been so . . . so . . ." Why trails off, captivated by the drama.

"I did care. I really, *really* did. And then you got bored. Just like you are now. Bored. So you came here to toy with me. And I'm done."

"Get over yourself."

"Nah. I'll just get over you, if that's okay."

"Oh shit!" Why and I cackle in unison. Farrin pushes over a pile of neatly folded sweaters and storms out. Cooper picks up after him without so much as a frown. My chest swells with pride. Seeing Cooper vanquish an enemy like that, it makes me feel like nothing is impossible. If he could be that strong, so can I.

"Wyatt—" I turn to him, but he's already walking into Banana, hands held high, cheering for Cooper.

...

"What in the hell was that?" I ask from the kitchen doorway. The lights are dimmed, and the table is littered with papers and pencils and dice. And there's Dad—my dad—rolling a handful of d6s across the clutter. Everyone around the table whoops at the results.

"*That* was epic," my dad says, and leans back in his chair. He's thrilled, surrounded by his friends. I only barely remember Dad's professor pals. They would stop by our old apartment in Portland some nights, where they would grade midterms and finals together. I remember that dude in the ugly paisley shirt was really harsh. Wouldn't let his students get away with anything, but expected them to take him seriously in those hideous shirts. This is the first time I've seen any of them in Eugene.

"Well, that takes care of the dragon. For now, at least," Lincoln says ominously from behind his Dungeon Master screen. I can't believe I didn't even notice him. He fits right in with the rest of the group. Geeking out and looking up at me over his laced fingers.

"You're—uh, um—gaming? With my dad?" I stammer, caught off guard.

"Actually, Cooper, we're doing my taxes," my dad's friend with terrible taste replies, to even more laughter.

"It's Cameron." I frown and pull off my beanie. I'm getting tired of pretending to be someone else. It's exhausting.

"Oh, sorry, buddy," he says. His nose flashes red with embarrassment.

I take it all in. My dad with his cronies, cracking jokes and rolling dice. His old cardboard box, the one I helped him get from the closet, sits on the countertop. He must have taken it back from the studio. And Lincoln—my Lincoln—is hanging out in my kitchen, without me? I don't think my kitchen has ever had so many dudes in it at once.

"Lincoln is the best DM we've ever had," Dad starts. "You don't mind if we—if we finish up? Do you?" I forget about feeling jealous and move right on to feeling proud. Of course Lincoln is the best Dungeon Master—Lincoln is the best. Period.

"Sure, Dad. Slay away. I have work to do anyway," I say, and head up to my bedroom.

"See you after?" Lincoln calls out, stopping me in my tracks.

"Second door on the left."

• • •

Cooper looked great in his vest today. It fit him like a glove; I could sew clothes for him with one hand tied behind my back. I've already made him countless costumes. He was so brilliant at the mall. Not only did he manage to run Farrin off, he got Why to stick around and grab lunch with him. All I did was walk home. Alone.

I need to feel productive. At anything. Today I failed at every single attempt. I wanted to tell Why the truth, to come clean and start our friendship off fresh and new, but Farrin had to come and ruin it. So then I wanted to save Cooper, and he went and saved himself. I hate feeling useless.

My room is a dump, but I don't want to work in the loft. I want to be under the same roof as Lincoln. I love hearing the muffled voices and laughter down in the kitchen. I'll have to make do with what I have here. Which isn't much.

All the costumes I've designed are in the studio: Jade, Clover, Wizzy. I still have three left to meet the portfolio requirements, and I haven't given those a second thought. I flip through my closet, hoping to be inspired by some cosplay I've already made. Something I could repurpose.

A white plastic bag from Kozy Corner hangs there like a ghost. It taunts me. I can hear it whispering in a crinkly plastic voice:

Tiffani.

No. No way. I'm not making a costume for Brody's character.

Tiffani.

He doesn't deserve it. Neither does his character, for that matter. All she does is whine. I hear Lincoln's voice murmuring downstairs, too low to hear what he's saying. He punctuates his speech by pounding on the table. Suddenly I'm reliving the moment Tiffani sliced open that orc in our own game.

Fine.

I shake the deep blue satin out of the bag and lay it on the floor. I creep around the edges. My room isn't as spacious as the studio, but I'm used to working in cramped quarters. Cooper would watch me puzzle out patterns from the top bunk in our old apartment. Now I tilt my head this way and that, alone, trying to picture the shapes of the dress all spread out flat.

It should be floor-length, but not too tight. Tiffani is former royalty, so the dress should look rich and intricate. The fabric itself is gorgeous; it won't need all that much adornment. I'm going to give her matching ballet flats, ones she can move around in. Nothing that would get wedged in cobblestone streets or rocky cliff sides.

Picturing her scrambling up rocks and jumping into Qiris Spring in a gown tickles me. And I unlock the key to designing her costume. Wear and tear. A rough and ripped hem. Dirt stains, scrapes, burns. She's a girl on a mission, and she's been through the ringer. But she's never looked more fabulous.

The only scissors I have in my room are ancient, orange-handled Fiskars. If I try to cut the satin with them, they'll ruin the fabric in an instant. Satin demands sharp scissors. But I know there's some aluminum foil stashed under my bed, so I don't have to creep back down through my old man's game.

I learned how to sharpen scissors with foil when my mom refused to buy me that fifty-dollar pair I ended up saving a jar full of quarters for. In a pinch, it works wonders. I pull out a shiny silver yard of the stuff and fold it over and over again until it's a nice square stack. Carefully I cut into it. Using the whole length of the blades, I snip, over and over, turning the aluminum into fringe. It gets easier each time, the blades becoming sharper with every cut.

Once the scissors are sufficiently sharpened, I turn the satin, pointing a corner straight at me. If I cut on the bias, diagonally across the weave of the fabric, it will fray less. I know I'm going to fray it myself later, but I want total control. I want it to fray on my terms. The scissors bite and slice into the fabric and make the most satisfying sound in the universe.

shiik shiik shiik

First, I will make Tiffani's bodice. Off the shoulder, but not too revealing. Pleats: many, many pleats. I want the satin to ripple like water. I fold in a few and pin them down; I'll sew later. I hold up the front half of the bodice to inspect. It's pretty, but missing something. A tough element. Tiffani is a badass when she actually wants to be.

I need some black leather. I can't remember the last time I bought any, because it's expensive as all get-out, and it's not like I have any new clients banging down my door. I accidentally jab my finger with one of the pins. The bodice falls to my feet, and I pray, with my finger in my mouth, that I didn't get any blood on the satin.

I wonder if I do have any new business. I can't avoid my inbox forever. I'll have to turn on my phone; I'll have to face them. But I don't know what else there is to say. *Hey, could you stop harassing me? Kthanxbye.* Yeah, that'll go over really well. I grab a thimble off my shelf and power up my phone.

I see all the texts I've missed from Cooper. Nothing all that urgent. Just typical stray observations and emojis. As soon as it picks up the Wi-Fi, it chimes and beeps and vibrates like crazy. My inbox is overflowing, my voice mail is full, and I have some texts from unknown numbers. I open one without thinking. It's a dick pic. I batch delete the rest without opening them. These jerks are relentless; if someone wanted to hire me, I would never know. Their message would be lost in the sea of hatred.

Who is this girl they think they're smearing? It's obvious

from their comments that they don't actually know anything about me. They just needed someone to hate. Someone to fill the endless hours of their empty lives. A villain to make them feel like heroes. I don't bother going through any more. I have better ways to fill up my time.

There's a seam ripper in my pencil cup, and I decide to put the thing to work on an old pair of pleather pants I bought back in my monthlong punk phase. There should be enough to work with here. My portfolio is more important than pants anyway. I tuck in strips of leather between the folds of satin, and I'm pleased with the way the different materials play off each other. They'll be a mega pain in the ass to sew, but worth it.

There is the slightest knock at my door, and I swivel around. Lincoln is standing outside my room; he sticks his hands in his pockets. Nervous.

"Oh no. I'm interrupting."

"Of course you aren't." I drop the bodice, studded with pins, onto my lap.

"If I didn't come up here"—he looks around my room—"you'd keep working. Wouldn't you?"

"Probably, but—"

"See. Interrupting. It looks beautiful." The blue of the fabric reflects in his brown eyes, making them look purple and enchanted.

"It's for Tiffani." I hold it back up for him to see. One of the strips of leather falls out from the folds.

"Ack!" He gasps and lunges for the scrap. "Is it going to be okay? I didn't screw it up, did I?" He looks so anxious, worried that he's set me back hours of work. It's so adorable it hurts.

"Calm down. Here." I have him hold up the bodice while I slip the leather back in place, pinning it more securely this time. "Crisis averted." I put my hands on his; they're white-hot. He hides behind his hair, still embarrassed about nothing. "Seriously. Look. All better."

"I should go."

"Don't make me jab you." I brandish a pin in his direction. "Sit. You can keep me company while I finish—how's that?"

"Better."

"Good." I take the bodice away from him and lay it out. I start making more pleats, slipping in some leather where it feels right.

"It's like magic," Lincoln whispers.

"Painstaking magic."

"I like your room," he says as he leans against the wall. "Good and messy."

"Are you a fellow slob?" I ask.

"Nope."

"Then why would you—"

"Dunno. The mess suits you. It feels like it's yours."

"I'm not a mess."

"I didn't say *you* were. You have priorities. Bigger dragons to slay. Obviously." He waves his arms at all of the fabric spread out around us. "Are those all dice?!" Lincoln shoots up to his feet and tiptoes over to my thimble collection. "Oh, they're those finger things."

"Thimbles."

"Right. I should know that."

"Why?"

"Nan. She's got a whole cookie tin full of them. Fools me every time."

"I bet she's got some beauties."

"I've never seen so many in one place. I like this one! So tiny." He picks up a thimble and holds it out to me, resting atop his pinky finger.

"That"—I take it from him and slip it over my own pinky—"is the first one I ever got."

"Wow," he marvels without a hint of sarcasm in his voice. I can hear my dad saying goodbye to his friends, and I realize just how open my bedroom door is.

"Can you help me bring all this to the studio?"

"Of course." Lincoln holds out his arms and waits for me to fill them. It takes all the strength I have not to wrap myself up in them. Instead, I carefully fold up the satin and drape it across his perfect, waiting arms.

• • •

The sun set hours ago, but it's still warm outside. Summer is my favorite season by far. If I could live in sundresses full-time, I would. I'm tired of oversized jeans, oversized shirts. Tired of hiding. Lincoln carries the fabric like it's precious cargo. Like it's worth a million dollars. So careful not to drag any of it on the ground.

"Hang on a minute," I ask him. He turns on his heel to face me. I walk him through Dad's garden. It looks enchanting at night, almost unreal. The artichokes are already taller than I am. His rosebushes are still new and small, but I can picture them, next year, when they'll wind up the arbor and shade a bench Dad has placed underneath. It truly is the garden of his dreams.

"Sit with me?" I sit and pat the bench. He obliges, and I feel the warmth of his leg against mine. Just like that night he walked me home. So much has changed since then, and yet so much is exactly the same. I look up at the moon. Link ever so carefully drapes Tiffani's dress over the back of the bench. I take out my phone.

"How are the trolls treating you these days?" Lincoln asks.

"You tell me. You're the Dungeon Master."

"No, I meant—"

"I know what you meant. I just wish—I wish people didn't call them that. Trolls." I swipe patterns into the grease on the screen.

"It's what they are, though."

"No it's not. They aren't mythical creatures. You can't look up how to defeat them in the *Monster Manual*. There are no critical hits, no saving rolls. They aren't make-believe. They're real. And they're assholes."

"Point taken."

"I'm so close to finished with my portfolio. I can feel it. And if I keep letting them get to me, I don't know how I'll ever—" And speaking of the devil himself, my phone lights up and starts ringing. Unknown caller.

"Don't answer it," Lincoln says.

"You know what. Screw this guy." I jump up and hit accept. "Hello? Who is this?" There's a pause on the line, and then, like thunder, the caller clears his throat.

"Uh, is this Cameron Birch?" his dry voice crackles.

"Yeah? What do you want?" I ask. My knees are shaking; my hands are shaking. Keep standing—you can keep standing.

"Did you know your phone number is, like, all over the Internet?"

"Yes. I'm aware."

"Um, well . . ."

"What do you want?" I repeat, not just to him but to every stupid rando that's decided I'm the target of the week.

"Sorry," he croaks out, and disconnects. I can't believe it. He just hangs up. No threats, no name-calling, just an apology. I can't stop looking at my phone. Is that all it takes, letting them know you're real? I feel more real standing here, standing up for myself, than I have in weeks.

"Are you okay?" Lincoln whispers.

"I think I am."

"I'm so sorry, Cam. You don't deserve it."

"No one does." My fingers curl around my phone. Tight. Tighter. It's not fair. I bet most of the anons haven't given me a second thought. To them, I'm just a name on a screen; the idea of the real Cameron isn't enough to keep them from harassing me. And here's Lincoln, apologizing for something he didn't even do. And here I am, obsessing, cross-dressing, letting them into my head. I have work to do; I have people to impress; I have a boy to kiss; I don't have time for second-guessing and their pathetic attempts to sabotage me. They don't get to win. Ever.

I lift my phone over my head and Hulk-fucking-smash it right into the ground. I can feel my skin turning green, my muscles ripping apart the seams of my boy outfit.

"Whoa!" Lincoln laughs. I pick up my phone; the screen is broken, but the rest is still intact. I wanted to smash it into a thousand pieces. The one spidery crack running across the front isn't doing it for me. I hold it out to Lincoln.

"Want a turn?"

"I think it's already dead."

"Then we should bury it." I kick over some dirt underneath one of Dad's tomato plants.

"You can't be serious!"

"Why not?" I smile up at him and nestle my phone in the mulch. Rest in pieces, anons.

I spread the dirt on top of it, feeling overjoyed, free. So happy that I pull Link right down in the dirt with me.

...

The ground is cold, but my skin warms with every touch of Lincoln's hands. We crawl, lips connected, behind the screen of plants. I worry, only for a moment, that Mom or Dad will spy us splayed out under the heirlooms, but the moment is over the minute Lincoln whispers my name into my ear. Everything else fades away, far away, as if we are the only two people left alive.

His heartbeat is everywhere. I can see it in his neck, feel it in his chest. A slow, sure, and steady beat. My own feels erratic, threads catching in my bobbin chamber. Jumpy. I breathe slowly, trying to find a rhythm, but my heart just thumps over and over. *More, more, more.*

I lie down and he follows, pressing my back into the dirt. Our legs weave together, alternating. His, mine, his, mine. His arms, my waist, his hair, my fingers. He pulls us closer together, just slightly at first. I push my hips into his; he pushes back. My entire body shivers; we lace our fingers together.

I open my eyes; Lincoln's skin changes colors with the solar lights. The stars, the smell of the tomato vines, the heat of his breath, surround me. A small brown leaf clings to his hair. My lips part and our teeth clink together. I have to stop smiling, but I can't. I'm overwhelmed. Dizzy and happy. I start laughing. The laughs turn into cackles; Link rolls off, giving me room to breathe, but I can't. I'm so happy I could burst. He joins in, small chuckles at first, but he too can't seem to stop himself. We lie there with our sides split, but I'm too busy cracking up to sew us back together.

• • •

"He's my soul mate, Cameron. I'm serious. Are you listening to me?" Cooper says in his singsong voice. He's talking about Why while I'm ripping up the hem of Tiffani's gown. Putting on the finishing touches. She came out even better than I had imagined. I'll sew on a few more seed beads, and she'll be complete. All four of them will be. I'm running low on time, but I know I can bust my ass and get the final two costumes in under the wire. I just need to figure out what they will be.

"We recorded a podcast together for two hours. Two whole hours and not one awkward pause. Even though he's not super into arty stuff—I don't know—he makes me feel like less of a snob. Like we can both just like what we like and have fun talking about it. I swear I could have made out with him right then and there."

"Maybe you should have."

"I'm nervous. He's dorky, but he makes me nervous."

"Shouldn't you be writing?" I ask Cooper. I stare down the back of his laptop. He may not have made it into the NYU summer program, but he still has his own work to do to prepare for applications next year.

"And, oh my God, his dimples. He's the one."

"I'm going to start the timer if you don't knock it off," I scold.

"Like you weren't tongue-deep in Lincoln last night. I saw you two in the garden."

"Gross."

"Girl, get yours," he says, and starts hammering away at his keyboard. We fall into a flow, no music, no talk. Just the sound of typing and thread pulling through satin. Working away. I take a step back and look over the collection. It's epic. Everything fits; all the pieces seem cohesive, like they're about to go out and storm some craggy, ancient castle together.

"It's your mother-flipping masterpiece. Take a picture!" My hands reach instinctively for my pocket, but my phone isn't there. It's outside. In the ground. This might be a problem. How am I going to afford a new phone, and how long can I survive without one? I can't tell Cooper I smashed it—he'll ask why. If he got through seventh grade without a mile-wide path of destruction, through all the taunting with his head held high, I should be able to handle this with the same decorum.

"I—I lost my phone." The lie comes out before I realize I thought of it.

"Shit, where? The mall?"

"I don't think so. I don't know." I feign annoyance and look around my workspace.

"You have to find it; Mom'll kill you."

"Right. Right."

"And how else are you gonna tell Why?"

"Tell Why what?"

"You're joking, right?" Cooper takes out his phone, sets the timer for thirty seconds, and goes off. "Enough is enough, Cameron! I don't understand why you're keeping up the charade at all anymore. You know for a fact that Wyatt isn't going to judge you. Lincoln is certainly smitten with girl-Cameron. And I hate to say it, but what you're doing is super selfish. You get to have your guy, and I don't get to have mine? Grow up."

I wonder if he practiced that speech; it's punctuated perfectly by the beeping of his timer. I snatch the phone straight back from him and set a half minute for myself.

"You have no idea what it's like to be a girl, Cooper. None. But I would have thought that if *any* boy on earth was going to understand . . . it would be you. My brother. My flipping twin! When you went through all that shit, did I tell you to just grow up? No! This isn't about Lincoln or crushes or boys. This is my life, and sometimes it's scary!" I get cut off. Cooper takes his phone back and retaliates.

"Oh, poor *girl*. Poor you. You're so naive, Snip. Sitting up here sewing your magical-fantasy-world clothes. Making cosplay outfits for video game characters? Damn right I'm telling you to grow up. You have an opportunity to make art, and you make wizard robes?"

"Snap!" I cut him off before the timer does. I can't listen to this anymore. "What the hell?"

"You think I'm kidding? Look, I love comics and video games and all of that. But it's a hobby, Cam. Not a career."

"What about—"

"Save it. I don't want to hear about superhero reboots, or Hollywood, or any of that garbage right now."

"Garbage? Seriously? You know who you sound like right now, don't you? Why did you and Farrin ever bother breaking up? You're perfect for each other. Snobs."

"Screw you."

"You too."

"Oh, I'm naive, huh? Poor girl has no problems at all, right?" I yell at the door below, even though I know Cooper can't hear me. I open my laptop; I may have smashed my phone, but there's more than one way to check out the vitriol that piles up in my inbox. I read five new messages just to prove him wrong.

Tonight, one post sticks out among all the others. A familiar face in an avatar next to a long rant.

> Oh my god I hate cosplay as much as the next guy but stop giving this chick the attention she's obviously after. Don't you see you're playing right into what she wants? Seriously. They keep doing this fake stuff because we keep giving them attention. Of course she didn't know who the fuck she was cosplaying as. That shit doesn't matter to these girls, as long as they get the attention and clicks and dick from whoever they want.
>
> They come into the store where I work sometimes and they look so damn lost. Of course they want my help learning about comics and shit, and I'm nice, I help them out. I try to be a gentleman and they seem to be into it right up to the point where I ask them out. Then they run for the goddamn hills giggling, looking to ride the next meathead asshole to cross their path. Shows me for being a nice guy right? Stop bitching about this chick and give her the ZERO attention she deserves.

Did Brody seriously not recognize me? I mean, I'm glad he didn't, but my picture was right there at the top of the thread. Did he see it at all, or did he just rant about me, thinking all of us "cosplay girls" are interchangeable? Cooper wants to believe there'd be no problems at all if I just came forward. Told everyone who I am. But he hasn't seen *this*.

I close the laptop and stare at my collection. Maybe Cooper is right. What if I blew it, my big chance to make an artistic statement, and I made stuff you'd wear to a ren faire. Clover's cloak has some extra thread hanging from the seams. I grab my scissors to trim them away.

"Shit!" I scream, and grab my foot. Certain that I stepped on the needle I lost. Except when I look down, I see it's a Scrabble tile. The letter *W.* Four points. A smile spreads across my face as I think about how the tile must have gotten there.

Who says wizard robes can't be art? I pick the *W* up off the floor and sneak it into one of Clover's many pockets. She could use the win. We both could.

• • •

"Lincoln, what the hell?!" Brody breaks character. He flips through some papers and finds his inventory. Carefully he goes through everything on the list. "What are these guys talking about? We haven't found it yet!" I try not to look directly at Brody. I don't need to jog his memory, just in case he did see that photo of me dressed as Cloud.

Lincoln shrugs his shoulders. He's not giving us any hints. And why would he? We've been looking for the crown the entire campaign. He isn't going to just hand it to us.

"I'm rolling a perception check," I tell Lincoln. Cradling the purple sparkling d20 in my hand, I shake it up before casting it across the gridded mat. On it, I can see the ghosts of erased marker lines from my dad's campaign. It's been well used and loved. I imagine all the worlds that have been played on this beige plastic sheet. Link deserves a better one, a beautiful one. I let the d20 fly, and it lands on a three.

"No luck." Link clicks his tongue.

"Ugh. Come on." I can feel Brody's frustration radiating out from his seat next to me. He jiggles his leg and chews his thumbnail. Fuming. Cooper stole my usual seat next to Why. I know he's the only reason Cooper even bothered showing up. He drove and I walked.

I've made up my mind. I'm coming clean to Why the minute we leave tonight. The second Brody is out of earshot. He's too angry about this battle, and I'm worried his excess anger will spill out onto me.

"This is your last chance, Tiffani," Lincoln coos in a soft voice. "The drow elves lift their staves; you see that each has a blade discreetly embedded in it. They're not going to let you go alive," he explains in his own voice.

"For the last time, I don't—"

"I attempt to take one down." Cooper steps in.

"With what?" Lincoln asks, getting ready for the inevitable battle ahead of us.

"My bow, which uses one-d-six for damage, plus my strength bonus," Cooper rattles off.

"No strength bonus for two-handed range weapons, remember?"

"Oh, right, sorry."

"You still get your dexterity modifier. So roll it." Lincoln invites Cooper to start.

"Use mine!" Why offers Cooper his own d6. "It's never failed me." Cooper tries to keep his cool taking the die from Why's hand. I can tell he's nervous as hell. He looks up and scowls at me. He doesn't know it's almost over. I'll come clean, but there's no way I'm going to play matchmaker for him. Not after last night. He can grow a pair of his own and tell Why about his crush himself.

"Hurry up and roll!" Brody shouts. His anger is putting me on edge. I hate that whenever he talks I second-guess myself. What if he freaks out? He wouldn't hit a girl, would he? Cooper tips the die out of his hand. Why was right. It lands on a six.

"Wow, all right, then." Lincoln scribbles something behind the screen. "Before Tiffani can finish her thought, the drow, right here"—he motions to one of the figurines on the mat—"is pierced in the thigh with an arrow. It comes so quickly it almost doesn't register, until the pain shoots through her leg. Now, roll for initiative."

We each roll our own twenty-sided die. Whoever rolls highest gets to attack first; we take turns in descending numerical order until everyone, including the enemies, have had their turn. Then it starts over again until the last baddie is vanquished. Why rolls the highest. A fifteen. He goes first.

"Magic missile. This one, right here." He taps the head of the injured drow figurine. It's a hit. Cooper goes again, firing another arrow into the same elf. They're aiming to take her down fast. Smart. The elves attack next.

"Filthy halflings!" Lincoln uses his drow voice. "How dare

you?" He rolls behind the screen. "Oof, I'm sorry, Wizzy. The drow to your left swipes at you with her staff. It makes contact with your left arm. You take four points of damage."

"Dang it." Why starts tallying his remaining hit points. The drow really have it out for halflings, so things are looking precarious for Clover and Wizzy. He takes two more points of damage, and I get hit for five.

"Brody, your turn," Cooper pipes in.

"I attack the wounded drow with my long blade. That's two-d-four piercing damage." He rolls without any hesitation. "Seven. Plus my strength mod, making it ten. Not great."

"Good enough!" Lincoln tips the figurine onto its back. "Two more to go."

"Cameron?"

"Perception check."

"What?!" Brody, Cooper, and Why say in unison.

"I want to do a perception check, for the crown."

"Interesting. Roll it." Lincoln seems amused with my tactic. I roll the purple die on my palm and let it go. Four.

"Sorry, not enough. Okay, Wizzy. Back to you!"

"I cast cone of cold. It should hit both of them from where my character is standing." Why rolls a sixteen, and the elves take their damage. It's not enough. They're tough. Cooper fires three arrows at once, Brody misses, and I do another perception check.

"Are you kidding? Take them out!" Brody looks pissed. "Stop being a little bitch." He pounds the table. The angrier he gets, the worse I feel about ditching my boy armor. I try to summon up the bravery I had in the garden. But it's different when the angry, possibly dangerous, jerk is sitting right there next to you. I can't just ignore him.

I roll my perception check and land on a reasonable ten.

"Sorry, Clover. All you see is your friends getting their butts kicked." Lincoln scratches something down behind his screen. The elves take their turns. One of them must roll some low numbers and doesn't deal any damage. The other takes twelve hit points off Tiffani.

"Are you kidding me?! I'm almost dead!" Brody isn't having it.

"Almost," Lincoln fires back.

"What happens if Tiffani dies?" Cooper asks.

"That's it for her. Brody has to start over," Why answers. "Take it easy, Lincoln! We're still pretty low level."

"She's not dead yet! Go ahead, Jade. It's your turn." Lincoln motions for Cooper to roll.

"I'm shooting again," Coop declares, and rolls a seventeen.

"Well, well," Lincoln starts. "That's more like it. Jade, you're sick of the fighting. The drow are keeping you from getting your payout from Tiffani. She hired you to help track down the crown, and that's just about all you are willing to do for her. You sure as hell didn't sign up to die for her cause. You pull back and focus. The rest of the room blurs around your target. You inhale, one deep breath. You aren't stressed, or frightened. You're at peace—this is what you were born to do. You let the arrow fly, and it pierces the drow right through her eye. She's out." Lincoln tips another mini-fig over. "Nicely done."

Wizzy uses magic missile again, and Tiffani doles out a few points of damage to the remaining drow. She must be on her last legs.

"How do you expect to leave Gelvvin castle alive? The crown belongs to us," Lincoln coughs in his drow voice. "The time is now."

"I want to . . . ," I start.

"Roll a perception check. Ugh!" Brody finishes for me. He's right, though. I've been on a bad streak with my purple die, and I remember Why's advice about switching it up, back when all of this started. I pick up the glow-in-the-dark die and roll it between my palms until the cold plastic is the same temperature as my hands. Until it feels like it's a part of me. Then I let it fly.

Twenty.

"Oh. Oh, okay. Well. Um." Lincoln flips through some papers; it's the first time he's looked disorganized since we started playing. "How about . . . Yeah, how about this?" He lifts up a massive die. It must be the size of a tennis ball.

"Oh shit. Large Marge?" Brody asks. "For a perception check?"

"Yep." Lincoln writes something else down behind the partition; I can tell he circles it.

"How many sides is that?" Cooper asks.

"A hundred." Why, Brody, and Lincoln all answer.

"What?!"

"Everyone roll a perception check except for Clover," Lincoln instructs. No one rolls anything remarkable. Lincoln seems pleased by this. He takes Large Marge and rolls it in front of the screen so we all get to see it tumble across the mat and slowly stop on a three.

"Well, fuck me. This is happening sooner than I thought." Lincoln laughs. "Clover, come with me, please." He gathers up a few papers and sticks some dice in his pockets. "Give us a minute, guys," Lincoln says as we vanish behind the staff door.

. . .

"The fight continues around you, Clover, but for some reason you can't bring yourself to ready your dagger. You know Tiffani doesn't have the crown, but the drow must know something about its location or else they wouldn't be here at Gelvvin castle. When you see the crystals on their staves illuminate, you are certain the crown is somewhere in the tower. You know your efforts would be better spent searching.

"But there is nowhere for it to be hidden! No trunks, no tapestries, no sconces. You are in the world's most sparsely decorated tower. Plain stone walls, windows without sills or boxes. You stomp on the floor—maybe a trapdoor? But it's solid. Wizzy takes a hit and snaps you back to reality. You know the drow have it out for your kind. You have to find the crown—you need it. You can use it. Bindi, from the lake, was right. If you kept the crown, you could end the magic embargo. Halflings could be wizards. Girl halflings could go on adventures; everything could change. Determined, you closely watch the staves of the drow as they fight. The crystals flashing some sort of pattern as they swing around and change directions."

Lincoln could weave stories for hours, and I would hang on to every word. I don't know how he does it. He's not reading from a piece of paper; he looks right at me as he describes the scene. Making up the details on the spot, never stumbling; it's remarkable. The room feels warmer than the last time I was back here. I don't feel lost or alone. I feel relief. This comic store, these guys, have become part of my life, my friends. This is the last night I'll have to wear Hawaiian shirts and Cooper's hand-me-downs. The last time I'll have to lower my voice and shuffle my feet. I can curl my hair and paint my nails and wear my hand-sewn summer dresses. I can roll dice and design costumes for heroes and flip through comic books. All as myself. *Finally.*

"So what do you want to do?" Lincoln asks, pencil poised and ready. I'm not sure what Clover wants to do, not yet. But I sure as hell know what Cameron wants to do.

"This."

I take Link's face into my hands and bring my lips to his. His notebook falls from his lap, sending flurries of papers to the floor. I feel his fingers run down my back. I straddle him in the folding chair.

"I'm a girl," I tell him, burying my face into his neck.

"No," he starts, and I pull away. His face is pink from the friction. "You're *the* girl." I sink back down into his arms. He tucks his fingers up under the edge of my hat, and I melt. He's touching my hair, my neck, but I feel his fingertips everywhere. It's wonderful and terrible and I want to tell him that he's *the* guy but I can't speak. Just kiss.

"Should we order a pizza?" The door swings open and slams into the wall. Startled, I jump off Lincoln and back away from him. "Wait, what?!" Why stands in the doorway, and I think I can hear his heart cracking in two. "How? How could you?" He looks right at Lincoln. Not at me. He doesn't spare me a single glance. All his shock and anger is laser-focused on Link. My eyes sting, and I can barely catch my breath. This is not how I wanted Why to find out. Cooper was right: How could I have been so selfish?

"Why, don't!" Lincoln calls out to Why. He chases after him, but Why isn't slowing down; he heads straight for the door.

"I thought you told him!" Lincoln turns on me, puzzled.

"I—I—I was going to!" My voice catches in my throat.

"I have to go." He chases after Why and doesn't look back.

Boy meets girl.

"You? You. You're a chick?" Brody asks. He won't stop staring, but I don't care. I'm watching the door, waiting.

"Yes," I say under my breath, and take off my beanie.

"I don't get it."

"I hope all of this was worth it, Cam!" Cooper shouts. I don't bother responding. He doesn't really want me to anyway. "Yeah. That's what I thought. See you at home." Cooper takes his stuff and leaves me behind.

"I should go," I say to Brody, without making eye contact.

"Wait, wait. Are you that chick from online? That Pinz girl with the cosplay?" Brody asks, staring at me, piecing it all together.

"Yes."

"That's fucked up."

"It's all fucked up," I sigh, and pack up my things.

"This whole time you just . . . But why?"

"You've seen my blog. And I saw what you said."

"Yeah, but it's not like I knew that it was you," he justifies.

"As if that makes any difference."

"Of course it makes a difference."

"Do you even hear yourself?" I ask.

"So they all knew? They knew you were a chick this whole time?"

"Except for you and Why."

"And what, you didn't tell me because I'm just some jerk?"

"Why would I tell you anything? You scare the shit out of me sometimes."

"What the fuck did I ever do to you?" He raises his voice, incredulous, and I know I have to leave before it gets worse.

"Nothing, forget it." I make a break for the door.

"So that's it? The game's just over, then?" I don't answer him. I feel lost. And I have no one to blame but myself. That's the worst part. Just as I thought I was getting brave, I'm reminded that I'm anything but. I leave without uttering another word and drag myself through the longest walk home ever.

Why did I think this would be a good idea? Why didn't I call it quits the minute Wyatt started confiding in me? Why didn't I stop when Cooper asked me to? Why did I smash my stupid phone? I walk by the Wandering Goat, and all I want to do is order a dirty chai and call Lincoln and Why so I can apologize and explain myself.

I hang my head. I know when I get home I'll be faced with my portfolio, and Cooper, and the reality of this whole damn mess. As long as I'm walking home, I'm in that hazy in-between place.

Yeah, I fucked up and everyone is pissed, but I'm not ready to face the fallout. Not yet.

The Willamette is beautiful at night. There are no stars in the sky, but the flickering reflections of streetlights in the river make up for their absence. No one could possibly hear me crying over the sound of the frogs and crickets. Maybe they're crying too.

The silhouette of the DeFazio Bridge threatens to pluck the moon right out of the sky for me. I walk along the bike path to the center of the bridge.

"I'm such a coward!" I cry, leaning over the railing. I'm glad I can't see my reflection in the water, because I don't know if I could stand the sight of myself. My face is cold and wet; if I stay here long enough, I might just flood the river. The water will rise up, and a new salty stream will carry me far away from all the people I've misled. And maybe next summer, on a warm day, they will all go swimming there, happy and carefree without me.

I turn back the way I came. Finally ready to go home. I'll go up to my room and try to sleep it off. Tomorrow I can start my apology tour of Eugene. The collar of my Hawaiian shirt is soaked through after using it like a handkerchief. It doesn't matter, because I'll never have to wear it again. It's better off as a snot-rag.

"'Sup." Two stoners nod at me as I leave the park. I nod back and keep walking. Normally, I'd be a little worried. Worried that they might follow me, or that they might have bad intentions. But I don't feel nervous walking alone in my boy clothes, and I realize this is why I kept it up so long. This feeling of invisibility, of unquestioned acceptance. It was addicting. Comfortable. Easy. At least I thought it was.

I'm raw and drowsy by the time I reach my driveway. I

stumble across the gravel like a zombie. I've rehearsed my apologies so many times my brain is overworked and useless. I imagine how good it will feel to slide under my covers and surrender to the darkness.

"Hey."

My hand is frozen on the doorknob. I know when I turn around Lincoln will be there, waiting by the studio. Waiting for me. I don't want him to see me like this. Wrecked. A mess. He was right: mess suits me. My room's a mess; my life's a mess. I'm a mess.

"Hey," I say, just above a whisper.

"We need to talk."

* * *

Nothing good ever follows those four words. Those are the prep words. The words that Mom used when I failed gym for the third time. The words that Dad used when he found out Cooper and I had snuck out late one night to get Voodoo Doughnuts because I was enamored with the tattooed late-night doughnut slinger. The words that Farrin used when he dumped Cooper. They mean bitter, ominous business. Brace for impact; *we need to talk*.

"I know," I say, and lean against the garage door. If he's going to use those four words, he doesn't get to come inside. I don't care if it's my fault that he used them.

"So." He clears his throat.

"I'm sorry. Can I start with that? I'm *so* sorry—you have to know that."

He tips his head back against the wall, chin pointing at the sky, eyes closed.

"You don't need to apologize to me."

"Really?" I take his hand, but he flinches and steps away from me. I drop it.

"Why didn't you tell him? Why would you tell me but not Wyatt?"

"I was worried."

"Seriously? Why's harmless."

"I know; it's not that I thought he would . . . I just liked that we could . . ."

"You liked what? Toying with him? I told you at the outset not to play with him like that. And now you're saying you liked it?" He gets angrier as he goes. But he's got it all wrong.

"Of course not! I didn't mean to lead him on. I just wanted to fit in or something."

"Or something," he mocks, unconvinced.

"Sorry." I don't know what else to say, even though my rehearsed speech must have gone on a full ten minutes.

"Why and Brody, they're all I've got right now." Lincoln's voice cracks. "You know that. Aside from Nan, they're the only two people who give kind of a shit about me."

"I give a shit about you."

"But you lied."

"No I didn't! Not to you." I start tearing up. I thought I had set the record straight with Why, when I told him I just wanted to be friends. I didn't want my gender to matter.

"But you lied. I hate lying."

"Is there any—" I try to reason with him, but he cuts me off.

"I don't know if we can keep doing this. I don't see a way we can be together after all—"

"Of course we can. Look, I'm going to talk to Why tomorrow;

I'll explain everything. I'll apologize. It sucks right now, but we can get over it. . . . Right?"

"Why liked me. When I first met Why, he really, *really* liked me. And I was flattered, but it would never—I'm not—"

"Oh no."

"Yeah. Oh no."

We both stand there, the static of the crickets showing me some mercy in the longest, most awkward silence of my life. Why liked both of us, and for him to have walked in on what he walked in on . . . I'd never forgive either of us.

"I don't see it ending well. Do you?" Lincoln looks at me, pained. His eyes are glassy and red.

"I guess not." I'm trying to keep it together. None of this is his fault. But I can't help feeling sad and sorry. Sorry for what I did to him. Sorry for what I put Why through. Sorry for myself. My body betrays me, and I let out a wet hiccup.

"Don't, please don't," he begs, but it only makes it worse. I can't stop myself from sobbing—I'm too far gone.

The floodlights on the garage flicker on and shine a spotlight directly on us. Cooper pulls into the driveway. I can't see him behind the headlights, but I know he's still pissed. I can feel it.

"I should go," Lincoln says, already on his way back to the street. He doesn't wait for Cooper to get out of his car. One moment he was right there next to me, and the next he's gone. The floodlights and headlights go dark, and, for a moment, I'm blind.

I hear Coop slam his car door. I rub my eyes, trying to get them to adjust to the light. The door slams again. He's not alone? Squinting, I finally can make out what's going on.

"Wyatt! Let me explain!" I rush over to him.

"Don't," he growls, not looking at me.

"But—"

"You've done enough for tonight, thank you." Cooper cuts me off.

"I have to explain, Cooper! I didn't mean for—"

"Save it. You waited this long. You can wait a little longer." His voice is full of venom.

"Coop. Please," I whimper. I feel saliva collecting in the corners of my mouth. Everything is covered in spit and tears and snot. I've never felt more pathetic.

"Pull yourself together. Boys don't cry."

...

I want to wallow. Just lie on the studio floor and whine and cry and feel worthless. Torture myself by replaying the moment Why walked in on us over and over. Think about how I will never kiss Lincoln again. How I've managed to screw up every single friendship I have. Why should Link and Why be friends with me? Cooper has every right to be as pissed as he is. I didn't even do anything to Jen, and she dumped me too, when she got hit with my spillover online abuse. Everything the anons have ever said turned out to be right. I'm disgusting. I'm a hack. I'm nothing.

But I don't wallow. I pull out all the bins and bags with leftover fabric and scraps. I dump them all over the floor and throw the empty containers down into the garage. I'm going to need all of it: all of the space, all of the fabric. Every last scrap. I have three days to finish my portfolio, and if I don't, if I blow it, this entire summer will have been for nothing. And I can't have that.

This is what it's really about, I remind myself as I organize the fabric by color and size on the floor. The only thing that really matters is that this will be the most beautiful piece of clothing I've ever made. It doesn't matter that it's meant for Lincoln. Not at all.

It doesn't matter if he sees it and forgets just how badly I screwed up. It doesn't matter if he lays it out on a table and tells stories and runs games and remembers when everything was fun and good and easy. And when he wraps it around his shoulders, it won't matter if he falls in love with it and me again at the same time. None of that matters.

Those are just the details.

Lincoln's cloak will double as a map. It will be floor-length, with elaborate closures that hide what he's wearing underneath. He has to be so many characters during the game, there's no point in trying to nail them all down. The cloak is all-encompassing.

I gather up the remaining fabric from all of the costumes I've finished. The blue satin, the crushed velvet, Wizzy's frayed black scraps. I'll sew all of it into the cloak. We're all woven into Lincoln's story. I rearrange the pieces again. Not by size this time, but by shape. I join the scraps with pins when they look like they belong together.

Pools of blue fabric come together first. Puddles turn into lakes, then oceans and seas that split apart landmasses and islands. I thread up the sewing machine and start stitching waves into each scrap. Little silver crests rise and fall as the collage of fabric twists in the light. One patch of cerulean corduroy gets a hand-embroidered serpent that takes two hours and punctures two of my fingers.

I sew through the night. I sew mountains while the sky fades to predawn light. I sew deserts and farmlands while the sun rises, casting bright orange rays through the skylight. I sew a compass rose into the corner while the scrub jays screech and the neighbor's chickens lay their daily eggs. Sewing and stitching. Threading and beading. Mending.

I don't remember hearing Cooper's car leave last night. Which means there's a chance Why is still in our house. Maybe he stayed over and slept it off. He might be willing to hear me out over some of Dad's famous pancakes and a mug of coffee. Coffee.

I stare at Coop's car. Trying to determine if it moved an inch or two from last night, but there's really no telling. The cloak is just about finished; the last thing is to line it with gridded fabric. Just like the mat we use on the table when we play D&D. One side is the elaborate map, and the other side you can actually play the game on. It takes another hour to sew every last bead and button in place before I finally make my way to the house.

...

"Is there any coffee left?" I croak, voice raw from crying and dry from a silent night in the studio. Mom smiles and pours me a mugful. I dump in sugar and cream; the first sip is bliss. Warm and comforting.

"You sure look like you could use it," Cooper snipes.

"Is Why here?" I ask, looking right through him.

"No. So you can stop dressing like Raggedy friggin' Andy."

"Shut up," I snip.

"No, you shut up," he snaps.

"Be nice." Mom mediates without looking up from her book. "Are you ready for the big day on Friday?"

"Almost. Can you drive me?" I don't want to ask her, but there's no way I'm asking Cooper.

"All the way into Portland? Cooper, can't you—"

"No. Nope. I'm busy."

"All day?" Mom finally looks up at him.

"All year," he hisses back.

"Cameron, oh no. What are we going to do? I can't take you either. It's orientation week at the college, and you know what a mess that is."

"What about Dad?" I ask, starting to panic.

"He's helping me at work," she shoots back.

"What am I going to do? Walk?!" Coffee splashes out of my mug and onto the counter.

"Learn how to drive yourself," Cooper scowls.

"Oh! You can take the train! I'll buy you a ticket." Mom puts down her book and opens her laptop. "All is not lost. You'll get there, I promise."

"I guess."

"It's fine. It'll be nice; you can relax before all the interviews." Mom tries to flip the bad situation into a fun adventure. I still feel like crap. But I really do like riding the train. I refill my mug on my way to get changed. "Hey, missy!" Mom stops me. "You have to start answering my calls. I need to know I can reach you if I need you."

"Oh. I, um . . . I can't find my phone."

"Find it."

"Okay."

"I'm serious."

"Okay, I'm outta here. Bye, Mommy." Cooper kisses Mom on the forehead. "Later, *bro*." He flips me off, and I return the gesture. If my own brother wants to be pissed at me, let him. It's not like he knows the full extent of my story anyway. He hasn't been in my inbox or blog; he doesn't have a clue about the crap that's kept me in these oversized jeans so long.

"I'll find my phone. I'll take the train. Don't worry about it, Mom." And I don't know if it's a reaction to Cooper's antagonizing or the fact that I'm more proud of my collection than anything I've made in my life, but I feel fired up. I take my coffee straight up to my bedroom to put on my doughnut dress. If I can handle randos on the Internet calling me a whore day in and day out, I can handle Cooper and his shitty attitude. I can handle anything. I crack open my laptop and post a picture of me in my boy outfit.

Can everyone take a break from the death threats for a hot second? Cuz I'm only gonna post this once. That up there. That was me. Before I decided enough is enough with all of your comments and threats and phone calls. For weeks I decided I would be better off dressing like a guy, and living like one of you so I could fit in. So I could catch a break. I was the fakest geek-guy on the planet.

But I was lying every damn day to people I like. People I love. And for what? To try and hide who I really am? To hide from people I know in real life who I assumed were like you? Shitty, right?

Totally. Because you guys don't even know me. You like to pretend you do because you've seen my photos, and you've called my phone. But none of you pathetic babies actually know one real thing about me. Which is probably why you feel like it's okay to call me a cunt on my voice mail. Or send your deformed dick pics to my inbox. So let me introduce myself.

My name is Cameron Birch. I'm a level 17 Chaotic Good human being. I'm not going to stop making cosplay or sewing and designing costumes no matter how loud you yell. No matter what you call me. My veins are red thread, my heart a bobbin. Every stitch sustains me, so bring it on.

Wish I could say it's nice to meet you.

—Cam

I take a picture of the collection I created for my portfolio with the webcam on my laptop. Each costume displayed hanging from a beam. I upload the picture underneath the post and click publish. I fluff up my doughnut dress; I curl my hair; I slip on my gold ballet flats. It's time for everyone in Eugene to see me this way. Gently, I fold up Lincoln's cloak and tuck it under my arm. Let the apology tour begin.

The grandest girl.

There is no sweeter sound in the world than the jingle of the bell at Kozy Corner. I scan the shop for Lincoln, but he's not here. Dotty looks fabulous, intently hooking away at an afghan. I don't even think she heard me come in. Her violet hair is tucked neatly under a turban adorned with a brooch that looks like a bird's nest.

"Hey, Dots." I greet her and place the cloak on the counter. "Is Lincoln around?"

"'Fraid not. He isn't feeling too well today. I told him to stay home, but he insisted on going to class."

"Oh."

"You wouldn't happen to know anything about that, would you?" she asks as she loops a length of white yarn through her fingers and around the crochet hook. She doesn't need to look at her hands as she works; she knows every stitch by feel.

"I . . ."

"It's all right. It'll work out."

"I'm not so sure." I swallow. "But I did want to show him this."
I hand her the folded-up mosaic.

"You did this?" Dotty unfolds the cloak and lays it across her
lap with a flourish. She switches her thick tortoiseshell glasses
for the rectangular ones that hang around her neck and studies
my work. "My word." She inhales.

"Thanks."

"It needs lining!" she declares, flipping it over. "And we
should iron all those seams flat, don't you think?"

"I know, I know."

Dotty hops off her stool and wraps the cloak around my
shoulders. She cracks her knuckles and pulls me into the display
room. Her hands are so soft and cold.

"Now, it should be something sturdy, but it needs to move
well." Dotty taps her finger to the corner of her mouth.

"I want something with a grid pattern. Do you have anything
like that?"

"Oh, sure. How big should the squares be? One inch? Two?"

"I don't know yet."

"Come, come." She pulls me again, moving quickly past the
wool and the chiffon. "I have these four—what do you think?" She
starts reaching, pulling bolts of fabric down off a high shelf.

"Let me help—"

"I've got it." She slaps me away and grabs the last bolt. She
must have a sixth sense when it comes to sewing. The four choices
are each perfect in their own way. The first is an olive-color cotton with very fine white lines. The grid is tight; I'm not sure the
squares are the right size. But the feel of the fabric itself is supple
and delicate. It would make an excellent lining.

There are two dark brown options. One is more red, less machine-made. The grid looks as if it was hand-brushed on: the lines aren't perfectly straight, but they're striking. The other is the color of wet earth with even darker grid lines. They're very subtle, and slightly camouflaged.

The last is off-white; the horizontal lines are green, and the vertical lines are red. Where they overlap they make even smaller brown squares. It reminds me too much of Christmas, so I cross that one off first.

"Green and brown, my Link's favorite colors," Dotty coos. I'm sure Lincoln told her what happened. Or at least the highlights.

"This one is the winner." I point to the reddish brown bolt. I think the hand-painted look really fits with the way Lincoln weaves stories.

"Come on, let's get the iron."

Dotty flips the sign on the door to CLOSED and locks it. I follow her through the shop again, all the way to the back. She unlocks another door with a single key on a keychain that says I LOVE MY NANA on it. The door opens to a skinny staircase, just wide enough for one person. Dotty flicks on the lights with her green glittery fingernail and heads upstairs.

"You live up here? It's amazing!" I blurt at the sight of her apartment. It's not what I had pictured at all. Each wall is painted a different color. A pink one butts up against a deep turquoise. Every inch is covered in playbills, paintings, and photographs. A feather boa is draped across a window; the lampshades are trimmed with beaded fringe. In the corner is a dress form with a large floppy hat and velvet gown. I can't help but run my fingers along its silky surface.

"That's Gertie."

"Nice to meet you." I shake the air where her hand might be if she had one. Dotty pulls down a flap on the wall and reveals a built-in ironing board. I walk around the living room, taking it all in. A tiny canary whistles as I walk by its cage.

"And that's Birdie." Dotty laughs.

"Is that you?" I ask, probably sounding a little too amazed at a photograph of a young woman hanging on the wall. Even though it's black-and-white, the woman in the picture radiates warmth. She's wrapped up a young man in a long measuring tape, and her eyes are crinkled and laughing. He looks at her like Lincoln looks at me. Used to look at me.

"Long, long time ago." Dotty takes the cloak from my shoulders and lays it on the ironing board. Then I realize she's in *all* of these pictures; pinning and measuring. Fitting beautiful costumes on even more beautiful people.

"You used to design costumes for the theater? That's my dream. Well, I guess mine is for the movies."

"There are no costumes better than those in the theater," she says.

"But a smaller audience."

"I'd say Broadway is pretty big."

"You worked on Broadway?!"

"Like I said, it was a long, long time ago. Now, come help me with this." She waves me over, iron in hand.

"Tell me about it! What are you even doing here? Why did you leave New York?" I take the iron from her and start pressing down seams.

"A little boy needed me to make him Halloween costumes. Tea?" she offers, dashing through a door I didn't even notice into a tiny kitchenette. I've never thought about Lincoln's parents, where they are. Link and Dotty seem like such a natural pair, I didn't even question it. No wonder he feels like he can't leave her. I'd never be able to.

"Sure," I reply. "Thank you."

Without asking, Dotty unrolls the lining onto her parquet floor, cutting with abandon. She doesn't need to measure. Her eyes are sharp and impeccable. She uses the same silver scissors I use, and I feel connected to her.

"Want to finish it?" she asks from the floor.

"Now?"

"I don't see why not!" Dotty sweeps the cloak off the ironing board and into the kitchen, where her sewing machine is nestled in a corner. With another glittery-green flick she turns on a brass lamp; the shade looks like a seashell. Before I can even ask if she has any pins, Dotty runs one side of the cloak and the lining fabric through her machine. I barely have time to blink before she's almost finished the whole damn thing. I want to be that good. I need to be that good.

"Now, shall we do the hem together?" She hands me the cloak.

"Yes, of course."

Dotty sits down on her overstuffed sofa, and I drape the cloak over our laps. She picks up a cookie tin from a side table and opens it. It's stuffed with supplies. My heart aches, remembering Lincoln telling me about this exact tin, and how it fools him every time. Dotty threads each of us a needle. We sew from the outside edges until we meet in the middle.

"You've got some pretty good techniques there." She holds the stitching up to her glasses. "But I bet I could still teach you a thing or two, if you'd be interested."

"Dotty, I'd be honored." All the photographs of her work are proof of her impeccable skill. I'd be lucky to learn from her. I'd be lucky to live a life like hers. Even if it meant ending up back in Eugene.

"Voila." She holds it out for me. Finished.

"Dotty. It's perfect."

"You did all the hard work." She winks over her glasses. I fold the cloak back up and have a few more sips of tea. We sit in silence, admiring our handiwork and enjoying a moment of peace. Everything in Dotty's life is adorned with so much love. All of it so incredibly girly, womanly. She wears her womanhood like a badge of honor. Now, I want to sew that badge on myself.

"I think I have a few more things I need to buy. You don't mind, do you?"

"Never."

...

"Where are you going?! Hey, stop!" Brody shouts at me from the doorway of Atomix. I tried to pass by on the way from Kozy's as quickly as I could. Not wanting to accidentally bump into Why. I'm feeling okay after my sewing session with Dotty, and I'm not ready to have the conversation we need to have. Especially since I know he isn't going to forgive me.

"I have to go!" I holler back.

"Dude, he isn't even here yet!"

"Then what is it? What do you want from me?!" I turn around and yell in the middle of the sidewalk.

"Chill. I just . . ."

"Wanted to call me a fake-geek-girl? A fraud? A bitch?"

"Jesus, Cameron." He looks around, embarrassed, but I don't care. He said all of those things. Not to my face, of course, but I might as well make him face me now. "Come on." He disappears into Atomix. When it looks like I'm not following him, he pops out of the door again and waves. "Seriously, just come in. It'll only take a second."

Atomix is dead at this hour. It's just me and Brody and that good ol' cutout of Dr. Strange. The gaming table is folded up and leaning against the back wall. It's hard to take my eyes off it.

"So . . . What?" I'm already angry.

"Do you think we're gonna get to play again?"

"Is that really all you're worried about?"

"I was having a good time. Weren't you?" Brody pretends to organize a stack of paperbacks.

"Yeah. I was."

"I still don't get why you did all that."

"I know you don't."

"So that's it, then? Game over?"

"Probably."

"Fuck. No, no, there's gotta be a way. I'm sure you can work it out."

"I really don't think so." I start to pace around the shop; my feet don't want to stay in one place for too long. I spot exactly what I need to finish my last portfolio piece. I pull four back is-sues out of their box.

"Just work your girl magic on Lincoln or something."

"Please tell me that's a joke."

"It's half a joke. You can take half a joke, can't you?"

"I can take a whole joke, if it's a good one." He doesn't scare me anymore. I slam the comics down on the counter. Brody looks at them and winces.

"Now *you're* joking, right?"

"Not even a little. Ring me up," I demand. He obliges and slides the comics into a plastic bag.

"Look. I'm sorry, okay? If I knew you were a chick—"

"What? You would have waited for me to leave before acting like a jerk? Sat me down in the girl section while the big boys got to have their fun?"

"I just don't know how to act around girls. I'm a nice guy!" Brody hangs his head. I'm sure he believes what he's saying. But it's not true.

"You're not a nice guy. Not to girls, at least. You wrote that whole post talking about how you hate us."

"No, I said all you girls hate me. I only hate the fake ones."

"How can you tell who's fake and who's real?" I ask him, leaning in.

"I just can."

"Was boy-Cam a faker?" I drum my freshly painted nails on the counter.

"No."

"Why not?"

"Because you actually played. You came in and proved that you weren't just trying to get attention."

"You would never have given me, dressed like I am now, the same benefit of the doubt. Girls pick up on that. It's rude. It's the opposite of nice."

"What do you know?" he whines. I can tell he might be rethinking what I'm saying, though.

"Dude! A whole damn lot! We both know that when I came

in here with my beanie and baggy shorts, you treated me differently."

"So what? You were a different person."

"No. I wasn't. I'm the same exact person. In the dress or in the jeans. Treat me the same; treat us the same!" I can see the light go off above his head.

"But I don't mean—"

"I'm sure you don't mean to. But you need to try harder. Not every girl has some secret agenda. Not every girl who actually wants to be your friend is going to want to date you. Some girls are just gonna be your bros."

"Or stab you in the back." Cooper seems to be my nagging shadow today.

"Are you following me now?" I spin around and ask. Why is standing right next to him. "Oh damn it. I'm sorry, Why, I didn't know you were—"

"Sure," he says before taking his place behind the register.

"I gotta get . . . something from the back." Brody practically sprints to the storeroom.

"Can we talk?" I ask Why, hoping he's had enough time to calm down.

"I already explained for you," Cooper chimes in. Why nods, not making eye contact.

"Well, he didn't explain all of it." I plead with Why, trying to get him to look at me. "I want you to hear it from me, hear my side."

"I don't know," he mumbles.

"Why, please. If you still hate me, I can drop it. I'll never bother you again."

"I . . . I don't know," he repeats himself.

"I told him everything, Snip. Leave him alone, for crying out loud. He wants some space." Cooper flips through an issue of *Catwoman*. He's not looking at me either.

"No, you didn't tell him everything, because you don't know everything." My voice cracks; I swallow, trying to keep from crying. "I don't tell you every little thing that goes on in my life, you know. You have no idea what I've been through this summer. Neither of you do." I slam the door so hard on my way out it almost shatters.

■ ■ ■

One more design. One more day. I dump out the comics and fabric I bought. Two yards of dark wine-colored pleather, another yard of silver holographic spandex. Pink denim. Pink cotton. Everything is pink or glittering.

I start sewing the pants first. Ripped-up mauve skinny jeans. They fit like a glove. The top comes together quickly. Nowhere near as fast as Dotty can sew, but I'm proud of the progress. It's spandex but oversized; the wrinkles ripple and pick up the light as I move around the studio.

The fake-leather jacket takes the most time and effort. Weeks ago I thought about making Jubilee's signature yellow jacket. But that was before I knew who Dazzler was, and she needs a seriously bomb-ass bomber jacket.

"I have something for you!" Dad calls from the bottom of the stairs.

"Another thimble?" I answer, not getting up. I'm sewing a zipper into the breast pocket, and I don't want to move.

"Nope." He huffs up the stairs. "Cameron. Rose. Birch."

"You okay?"

"This is what you've been doing all summer? All of this?" He walks around the studio, looking at each costume.

"Yep."

"When . . . How did you learn how to do all of this? Your mother can barely sew a button on a shirt."

"YouTube."

"This is something else. Truly."

"Thanks, Dad." He has to love it. He's my dad. If he were reviewing my portfolio, I'd be a shoo-in. But he isn't; Gillian Grayson is. She's taking time off from working on *X-Men: No Time like the Present* to review portfolios, and I'm not going to waste it.

"Did you ever find your phone?"

"'Fraid not," I answer as quickly as I can. I don't like lying to him. I want to be done with lying for a while.

"Take this for now." He holds out his own phone.

"Dad, I don't need your phone."

"You're going into Portland all on your own tomorrow—you need a phone." He thrusts it at me until I take it from him. "How are you going to get all of this there?"

"Crap. I hadn't thought about that."

"I'll leave the rolling suitcase for you, the big one, in the kitchen."

"Yeah, that'll work."

"I'm so proud of you, little Snip. What a summer."

"Yeah. You can say that again." I finish sewing in the zipper as Dad looks around again. He leans in close to inspect the details. Every now and then he mutters something under his breath.

"Oh, Mom wanted me to tell you she ordered your train ticket. Check your email and make sure you got it, okay?"

"Sure."

"You're gonna knock their socks off. And then you can knit them new socks. And that will impress them even more, so, you know, you'll need more socks."

"Oookay, weirdo," I groan.

"Love you."

"Love you."

...

The last place in the world I want to be is the six-thirty a.m. train to Portland. The costumes came together; everything fit in Dad's giant rolling suitcase; I was ready. Then I checked my email. There were more messages in my inbox than I've ever had in my life.

They took my post as a challenge, and one of the creeps found my address and put it up online. But it's not my new address, thank Yondalla, goddess of halflings—it's our old apartment. In Portland. The city I'm headed to faster than a speeding bullet. Alone.

The college where the reviews are being held isn't close to the apartment, but it's not exactly far away either. The angry mob having my phone number was one thing; an address, the area where I used to hang out every day, sends shivers down my spine.

It doesn't help that I'm wearing my Dazzler getup. But I tailored it to wear; it looks better on me than hanging up, and I think Gillian would appreciate the effort. I'll stick out like a sore thumb the entire way from the train station to the school, but I don't think anyone is actually going to be on the lookout for me. At least I hope not. Plus, it's Portland.

I zip up the bomber jacket to hide the holographic shirt underneath and roll the enormous suitcase down off the platform. I've missed Portland. Big Pink standing tall and proud, our one and only skyscraper. The arch of the Fremont Bridge smiles at the sky behind me. Someone is playing the harmonica.

"Excuse me." There's a tap on my shoulder, and I jump straight up. How could they have found me already? "Where's Voodoo Doughnuts?" I take a second, exhaling all my pent-up anxiety before pointing him in the right direction.

"I'd get Blue Star instead," I offer. "Voodoo can be overrated." The tourist nods, but I know he's not going to take my suggestion. He came to Portland to take a selfie with that pink box, and he's gonna get it.

"There she is! Cam! Hey!" Liv and Jen rush up to me. "Wooooo!" Jen waves a sign with my name spelled out in glitter. Liv is holding two floating Mylar balloons. One of them says IT'S A GIRL!

"Ha. Ha." I point to the balloon.

"You look incredible!" Liv throws her arms around me.

"I missed you so much." Jen grabs my hand. Her voice is barely above a whisper.

"How did you even know I'd be here?" I ask, amazed that they showed up for me.

"We looked up the date online!" Jen boasts.

"And I called your mom," Liv snickers mischievously.

"You didn't need to—" I start.

"We couldn't let you come to Portland without a visit!" A wave of relief washes over me. It feels so good to be back in my old city with my old friends. To know that I won't have to walk around alone after that post went up. It's a small miracle, and I cling to it.

"How much time do you have before the review?" Liv asks. I check the time on Dad's cell phone.

"A few hours. Got here early."

"Good. Come on, let's get out of here." Liv leads the way, and Jen and I follow.

"Where are we going?" Jen asks.

"Shopping."

■ ■ ■

Books with Pictures is nothing like Atomix Comix. COMICS FOR EVERYONE! their logo boasts proudly. The inside is bright and cheerful, with zines up front and dozens of shelves of graphic novels. Even the weekly single issues look inviting.

"Hey, Katie, just dropping by." Liv nods to the girl behind the counter. God, I miss Portland. I wonder how many other girls work at this comic shop.

"Gurl, your outfit!" Katie points at me. "I love it."

"She flippin' made it! Can you believe it?" Liv brags for me.

"You know who you look like?" Katie smiles. "Dazzler." I start laughing, and I can't stop. How different would my life be if I had never moved to Eugene?

"What? What is it?" she asks.

"That's exactly who I'm supposed to be."

"Come on, we've gotta take your picture with the X-Men wall." She grabs her phone, and we all follow her to the back of the store. There's a huge X-Men sign hanging up. It looks like a wanted poster with rows and rows of characters. Each with their name and wanted status over their picture. Some say SLAIN, some APPREHENDED. The whole thing looks very cool.

"Okay, go stand over there." She motions to the wall. Jen and Liv look on, excited. I unzip the jacket and untuck the holographic top. I do my best superhero pose with my hands on my hips.

"Fuckin' epic," Katie says, and takes a few pictures.

"Get in here!" I wave for my friends to join me. Liv bounces over and loops her arm through mine. Jen hesitates.

"I won't post it online, I promise. It's just for me," I assure her.

"You know what? If you want to post it, post it." She skips over to us and strikes her own heroic pose. Katie promises to email me the photos. I can't wait to have my friends' faces populate my inbox again.

"How'd you do it?" I ask Katie as we get ready to leave.

"Do what?"

"The comic shop where I live, it's . . . not like this. I wish it was. How'd you do it?"

"You have to show up and put in the work if you want to make any kind of change anywhere. You can't be afraid."

"That's a tough one."

"You should work there," she suggests.

"What? Why?"

"It might be a good way to get more girls through the door if they see one behind the counter. Just a thought."

"Heh. Maybe."

"If anyone could do it, it'd be Dazzler."

• • •

Jen and Liv head home, and I pull the suitcase up the street, my other hand crammed in my pocket with my keys snug between each finger in makeshift brass knuckles. I feel better after spending the morning with my friends, but the minute I'm alone, it's impossible to forget that someone out there found my old address. And that anyone out there could use it. Thankfully, I make it to the school without incident.

"Last name?" the girl behind the registration desk grunts. She's obviously here for class credit or some sort of punishment.

"Birch. B-I-R-C-H," I spell for her.

"You're here to see someone from CalArts?"

"That's right."

"Here's your tag—take a seat over there." She points to rows of benches lining the hall before the auditorium. I join a group of other hopefuls. No one else is wearing a costume, and I feel a little foolish. Then again, the girl to my right must be a professional goth, right down to the Mohawk and black lipstick. I guess I fit in after all.

I try to peek at everyone else's work, but there's nothing to see. I'm the only one here dumb enough to actually show up in costume. Every now and then the auditorium door swings open and someone exits. If they're lucky, they leave the room with a smile, though there haven't been many of those. Too many people leave the double doors and make a beeline for the bathroom, eyes red and puffy. Some leave pale and quivering, looking like they're going to be sick. I wonder what I'll look like after I meet Gillian.

Time drags on. I bounce my leg up and down, trying to relieve some tension, but it doesn't work. I want to pace, but I can't risk leaving my suitcase unattended. I fiddle with the zippers on my jacket and snip off a loose thread with my teeth. I spit the thread into my hands, and *that's* when they finally call my name.

The wheels of my suitcase squeak, disrupting the reverent silence of the auditorium. College reps look up midsentence from the students they're judging to watch me roll down the aisle. It would embarrass anyone, but dressed like Dazzler, I'm mortified.

"Hi, I'm Cameron. I'm here for Gillian Grayson," I tell the lanky man behind the CalArts table, putting on my best impression of confidence.

"She couldn't make it. I'm Bill. Let's see what you have." He points to the table and crosses his arms.

"Um, what do you mean?"

"She's busy."

"But I thought—"

"She's not the only costume designer in the school, you know. You do want to have your work reviewed for CalArts, don't you?"

"Yes, of course."

"Let's see what you have."

His abrasiveness throws me for a loop. Should he be talking to students like that? I want to find out what happened. Why Gillian blew off the biggest day of my life. But this Bill guy isn't going to tell me. And Gillian or not, it's still what I've been working for all summer. I heave the suitcase up on the table.

"I made all the costumes with—"

"You were supposed to bring photographs."

"Oh, I thought it was an either-or situation." I swallow.

"You need to make sure you pay closer attention to instructions," he grumbles.

"Right. I'm sorry." I unzip the suitcase and reveal the costumes. "My original designs are based off of a—"

"Lay them out here," he instructs. "One at a time." I do as I'm told. I start with Jade, then Wizzy, Clover, and Tiffani. I leave the cloak for last. He inspects each one quickly, flipping over sleeves and hems to check my seam work. "This one moves when you wear it." I run my hands through the frayed fringe of Wizzy's robes.

"I can see that" is all he says.

"This is my last piece from the series." I drape the cloak over the table and flip up a corner so he can see the lining.

"Cute." His comment slices my heart. Cute? That's all he has to say? Hours of painstaking quilting and embroidery and he boils it down to *cute*?

"Where is your redesign?" he asks, and I unzip my jacket and tie on my headband.

"Right here." I put my hands on my hips. "I reimagined Dazzler."

"From the X-Men?"

"That's the one."

"Mmm, I see. Have a seat, Ms. Birch." We sit down opposite each other. All the summer's work splayed out between us.

"I can see you've worked very hard. Your skills are apparent." He looks over Tiffani's gown again, flipping the fabric. We may have had a rough start, but this is it: I'm going to be one of the smiling people when I leave the room. I inch closer to the edge of my chair. "But, the designs. They're very feminine, a little old-fashioned. I'm not sure you were really pushing yourself."

"I—I—"

"I think that you would make a fine seamstress. But you have a ways to go in the creativity department. I know you chose Dazzler because she's in Gillian's movie, but Gillian isn't here. In my opinion, you've made her too pink; no one would take her seriously. People want grit; they want drama."

"Oh. Okay."

"I'm sure you will find success with one of the other schools here. But I have to wonder if you're ready for our program."

"I know I'm ready. I know I can work hard and prove that I can—"

The timer on his watch beeps and cuts me off.

"That's all the time we have for now. Good luck." He shakes my hand and watches me pack up my designs in silence. Thankfully, the wheels squeak the whole way out; he doesn't get to hear me crying.

•••

"You're sure?" I beg the girl behind the registration desk.

"There's no time whatsoever. You should have registered for more than one time slot."

"But I have to see another school—I have to."

"You can submit your portfolio by mail like everyone else."

"Great. Thanks," I snarl, and wheel my suitcase into the bathroom.

How dare he say my Dazzler is too girly to be taken seriously. She's Dazzler! She's a disco singer, for crying out loud. I wipe some of the runny mascara from my eyes and take a deep breath. If he's a teacher at CalArts, I don't want to go there. Screw him. Screw Gillian Grayson for sending that ass here to replace her. Screw Cooper for steamrolling my apology and screw every last doxing shithead on the Internet. I look badass. Actually, I am badass.

I don't have the photos Katie took at Books with Pictures, but

Dad's phone has a crummy camera. It'll work. I take a step back, hold up his phone, and point it at the full-length mirror. I flip CalArts the bird and take the shot. Dad doesn't have my blogging app, but he's got a data plan. I log on via the site and start another post. This time, under the photo, I do my best to quote the hero herself.

> "I didn't ask for this. But I wanted something more. I wanted to amaze. I got way more than I bargained for, though. I thought I had to be one or the other. I gave it that power. I made some bad decisions. I lost myself. I let myself be the label. The mutant. The has-been. The joke. But the greatest realization I made in all of this is that it doesn't matter how everyone sees me. I'm not just a mutant. Or a singer. Or any one thing . . . All of this is me."
> —Dazzler

More than just a girl.

I make it out of Portland without trouble from anons, at least not in person. I feel silly about being paranoid, but I was legitimately scared. I spend most of the ride back down to Eugene trying to figure out how I'm going to break the news to Mom. She's going to be so upset. I'll tell her we can mail in the portfolio, just like the girl said. But it won't be this one. This one is going in the trash. I'm starting over.

Dad's phone starts quacking. I dig through my bag searching for it. It's a text. From Lincoln. Dad has his name plugged in as Lincoln the DM.

Lincoln the DM
I'm really sorry. Maybe another time.

I open the thread and read the chain between my dad and my would-be ex-boyfriend, if we had ever bothered to make it official.

Ben
That was great! Thanks again.

Lincoln the DM
I had a lot of fun too!

Ben
You've got a gift, my friend.

Lincoln the DM
Nah, that's Cameron.

Ben
You free for a game next week?

Lincoln the DM
I think I'm busy.
Sorry.

Ben
No problem! Maybe next month.

Lincoln the DM
Not sure.

Ben
You okay?

Lincoln the DM
I'm really sorry.
Maybe another time.

My thumbs hover over the screen, ready to reply. From my dad's phone, so he will actually pick up. But Lincoln made himself pretty clear: we're over. Over before we even got the hang of it. If I call him now, from another number, it'll only make it worse.

My bobbin of a heart is barely spinning. I ruined both of Link's campaigns. I'm not getting into CalArts. I'm heading to South High this year utterly friendless. Even Cooper is done with me. Maybe I'll just stay on the train. Hide out in the bathroom and ride this beast as far as it will go. The phone quacks again.

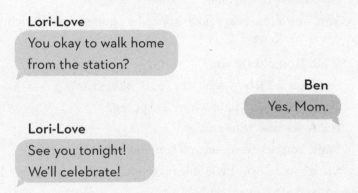

Lori-Love
You okay to walk home from the station?

Ben
Yes, Mom.

Lori-Love
See you tonight!
We'll celebrate!

"Oh my God! It *is* you!" A girl appears from behind and plops down in the seat across from me. "Pinz and Needlez, right?"

"Uh . . . yeah," I manage. I don't recognize her until she pulls her curly hair over her ear and I see her undercut. It's Brina. Brody's crush. As if I wasn't feeling bad enough, I'm reminded of the last time I saw her. When I laughed at her.

"You look amazing! I really love your blog." Thankfully, she doesn't seem to recognize me from that day.

"You can have it," I scoff.

"Brina." She sticks out her hand, and I take it.

"Cameron."

"Did you just get back from a con or something? I was up in Portland for an indie game jam."

"What?"

"Sometimes I like to program games, and once or twice a year there's this challenge where you try to make a whole game in forty-eight hours."

"Jeez. That sounds tough."

"It is, but it's also a lot of fun."

"Do you live in Eugene?" I ask her.

"Yep. For a few years now. My folks opened up a doughnut shop."

"Wait. How old are you?"

"Seventeen. I'll be a senior at South next year."

"You're kidding. That's where I'm going."

"Ha! Awesome." She smiles.

"Wait. You're seventeen and you make video games?"

"Oh, it's just dorky little side projects, but it can be tough. It's the best, and also the worst."

"I feel you."

"I was thinking about going to Rose City Comic Con in September. We should go."

"Yeah, maybe. I don't really know how I feel about cons lately."

"I think we'd have a great time. You should dress up. I mean, look at you! You're so cute!" I try to hide my grimace at the use of the word "cute." I tell her I'll think it over, and she grabs her shimmering pin-covered bag before joining up with her friends. It's for the best. Brina seems nice and all, but I'm not in a nice mood. The last thing I need is for someone to call me cute right now.

■ ■ ■

I don't remember the suitcase weighing this much. Every pull of the handle moves the luggage an inch. I get it up the gravel driveway, but it's a struggle. It's holding me back. I kick it to the ground and unzip it. I pull out each costume, one by one, and chuck it into the trash bin. The only one I can't bring myself to throw out is Lincoln's *cute* cloak.

I have no idea how I'm going to start over, or what I'll even make this time around, but Bill seemed to hate them enough. They'll never see the light of day again—that's for sure. I leave the suitcase where it fell and head up to my bedroom and crash. Using Link's cloak as a blanket, I close my eyes and finally sleep.

"Cameron!" Cooper is shouting and shaking me. "Cam, get up!"

"What do you want now?" I rub my eyes; everything is dark. I must have been sleeping for hours. I'm thrown off balance. "What time is it?"

"Have you checked your notifications today, thimble girl?!"

"Snap, no. You didn't. Please tell me you didn't—"

"Good things happen when I check it!"

"There is nothing good in my inbox. Nothing."

"Almost nothing." Cooper climbs under the cloak and puts his head on my shoulder. "Why didn't you tell me? You tell me everything else, and you're not going to tell me the Internet is raining a shit storm down on you?"

"I felt bad. It's my drama. You went through so much on your own, and I didn't want to—"

"That's just it—I wasn't on my own. You helped me so much, through all that shit, and Farrin! You didn't think I could help you?"

"I didn't want to bother—"

"I'm your brother!" He shoves me a little. "That's why you kept the boy thing up for so long?"

"I wanted to tell Wyatt; things just kept coming up and getting in the way, and I liked not having to be myself for a little while."

"I should have checked your blog sooner. I should have asked you what was wrong. I was being selfish. Not you."

"Maybe both of us."

"Your dreams aren't garbage. They're the greatest."

"You're not a snob. At least, not in a bad way."

"You know I didn't mean . . . I just got carried away."

"We both did."

"Well, you kicked fucking ass today."

"I wish." I bury my face in his shoulder. "She wasn't even there. It was some other jerkwad, who hated everything I made. Every last piece."

"But your post!"

"What post?"

"The 'fuck yeah I'm a badass' post? You put it up today."

"That was more of a 'fuck you—I am what I am' post."

"But that Gillian woman tweeted it!"

"Excuse me, *what?*"

"Here." Cooper sits up and grabs my laptop from my desk

and hands it to me. And there it is. In between all the hate is one little tweet.

Consider me Dazzled—may have to take a few notes from this one.

I ignore every other message and comment. I click the little heart and favorite her tweet.

"You should message her!" Cooper urges.

"Maybe. I think this was enough. For now. I'm sorry for everything, Snap. All of it."

"Me too. And please. This was nowhere near as dramatic as that time we both wanted to play Cinderella in fifth grade."

"Actors," I scoff. "Glad we gave up on that dream."

"No kidding. Plus, you ended up doing me a favor anyway."

"Ruining your horrible out-of-season button-downs?"

"I got to give Wyatt a shoulder to cry his very cute tears onto." Cooper pats the shoulder in question.

"I hope I didn't screw that up too badly."

"We'll see," he says with a knowing grin. "Maybe at the next game I'll make a move."

"There's not going to be another game. It got way too complicated for that. Why and Lincoln aren't you. They're not going to just forgive me."

"I think you're blowing all of this way out of proportion."

"Can we drop it?"

"It's dropped." We doze off, crammed together in my twin bed. Only waking up every now and then to make sure that tweet from Gillian was real, and that we're still okay.

"Are you gonna write me a movie soon, or what? I need five new characters to outfit."

"What happened to the D and D ones?"

"Garbage."

"They aren't garbage."

"Yes, they are literally garbage. Just promise me you'll write something."

"Promise me you'll stop keeping huge secrets from me." We drift off to sleep, connected by our pinkies.

. . .

"Cameron Rose Birch!" Mom howls from the kitchen over my alarm. "Enough's enough! Get up!" I roll out of bed. Cooper must've left for work a few hours ago. I slept through it. I lumber down the short set of stairs into the kitchen still in Dazzler's shirt.

"We need to talk," Mom says. My heart drops into my stomach when I hear those four words again. She's sitting at the kitchen table, next to Dad, my smashed phone between them.

"I found this when I was weeding the garden yesterday," Dad explains, and gestures for me to join them.

"I'm sorry, I just—"

"No excuses, have a seat." Mom cuts me off.

"But coffee?"

"Sit."

I do as I'm told and attempt to steel myself for whatever's to come. I know she's mad that the phone is broken. But God knows why they're turning it into some sort of family meeting.

"Why didn't you tell us?" Dad asks, his eyes wet.

"Because I should have been more responsible. I'll earn the money and buy a new one; you don't have to—"

"Not about the phone," he continues, "about this." He presses a button, and the phone turns on. The screen is cracked and dirty, but it still works.

"All those messages." Mom shakes her head. "Degenerates."

"You went through my stuff?"

"I just turned it on to see if it was still working, and all of these . . . comments kept popping up."

"Oh God."

"You should have told us," he sighs.

"We could have helped you," Mom adds.

"How? What, were you going to get online and make a post and say this is Cameron's mommy how dare you?" I understand why they were hurt and that they want to help, but there isn't really anything they can do. Nothing I haven't already tried.

"No, but we could have helped *you*. Supported *you*. We want to be there for you," she argues. "No more of this sneaking around stuff. I don't like it. If someone gets on your case, I wanna hear about it."

"All right." I give in.

"You have a lot of work ahead of you today, missy." Mom puts a new phone on the table. It's not as cool as my old one, but I'm not about to complain over a gift.

"You need to change all your passwords, and here's a list of everywhere you need to check to make sure our new address isn't online. I already did it for your father and me. Make sure your brother checks all his accounts too."

"Mom, this is overboard."

"No, it's not. You'll feel safer once we do this. And so will I."

"Dad?"

"You better do what she says on this one."

"And no more responding to these little rat finks. You focus on your work and everything you need to do for school."

"Fine."

"Speaking of school—"

"Can I please, *please* have coffee first? We can talk about any schools you want later. As many as you want. I just need the coffee," I beg.

"You're your mother's daughter." She kisses me on the forehead and drags Dad off into the garden. I check over my list of instructions. She's right. This feels like taking the slightest bit of control back, and I need it.

● ● ●

Cooper left a note in my coffee mug. He went off to work but wants me to meet up with him and Why at Atomix later. I pour myself one last mugful, and, after finishing it, I figure I shouldn't stand them up. If Cooper is right, and Why can forgive me, maybe I can get Lincoln to come around. Hell, Gillian Grayson tweeted me. I can do anything.

I flip through my closet; I need something that says *I'm sorry and I feel awful, but don't I look nice? Let's make out.* I flip through it three times before settling on my only green dress. It's got long sheer sleeves and is embroidered with little gold Saturns. It'll have to do.

"Two sixteen-ounce iced dirty chais, please." I practice in the mirror, combing the nest out of my hair. I'll go to the Goat and grab us some drinks to make my apology that much sweeter. I just hope he's home.

Why is in line at the coffee shop, looking up at the menu and trying to decide what to order. He cracks some joke, and the barista
starts laughing. I feel ashamed. I spent all morning getting ready
to apologize to Lincoln, and I didn't give Why a second thought.
What kind of friend does that? I don't deserve him.

"Whatever he wants is on me," I chime in at the register.

"Oh dang, Cam." He takes a step back. "I didn't recognize
you!"

"Heh. Yeah. Two iced dirty chais and a . . ." I pause, waiting
for Why to order his choice.

"Make it three." He holds up three fingers, and I hand my
debit card to the cashier.

"You don't have to do that," Why says, reaching for his own
wallet.

"No. I really do. For starters."

Why backs down and lets me pay for the drinks. We grab a
table and wait for them together. I break the silence first.

"Why, I'm so majorly sorry."

"I know."

"And Cooper told me he explained, but I wanted a chance to
tell you—"

"Yeah, he showed me what happened. And you know, part of
me gets it. I see it. I read through some of those comments, and
I just—I understand. But at the same time . . ." He pauses. I can
tell he's turning the words over in his head, not wanting to say the
wrong thing.

"Just say it. I deserve it."

"How could you think I would be like that? Like one of them. Why would you assume I would treat you that way?"

"When I came into Atomix that day, I didn't expect I would make friends with anyone. The idea of meeting someone cool there, after dealing with Brody, never even crossed my mind. And then we met, and you were funny and dorky and you reminded me of my friends back in Portland."

"Okay, so then why couldn't you have—"

"Because I thought you would hate me! Not because I'm a girl, but because I lied. I just wanted to keep being your friend as long as I could."

"You're pretty weird. You know that, right?" He laughs.

"Yes. I'm weird and dramatic, and I make messes out of mole-hills or whatever."

"Senior year is gonna be pretty interesting with you around— I'll say that much."

"Yeah?"

"Maybe you can help me figure out a way to ask this guy out to fall formal. I think he has a flair for dramatics too."

"Are you kidding? Of course! Anything you want, seriously."

"Because I've thought a lot about all of it. All of this. And I guess I realized . . . you're not the right guy for me." We laugh and pick up our drinks. "You gonna come to Atomix later?"

"Maybe."

"You should."

. . .

I take our chais and the cloak to Kozy Corner. The bell jingles, but there's no one at the register. I leave Lincoln's cup on the counter and wander through the aisles until I see Dotty, trying to fetch some yarn off a shelf just out of her reach.

"Let me help you!"

"Ah, Cameron's here to save the day. I'm almost done with my afghan," she says. I reach up on my toes and grab the skein she's after.

"Is Lincoln here?"

"You keep missing each other! He's off doing who knows what today." I wonder if she can hear the bobbin in my chest stop spinning. I missed my chance. This feels final. We're just going to keep missing each other.

"Can you give him this for me?" I hand her the cloak that we worked together to finish.

"You should be the one—"

"Please, Dots?"

"If you insist."

I tell her that I do and thank her again for all her help the other day. I want to stay and chat, but it doesn't feel right. Instead, I walk over the DeFazio Bridge and do laps of Alton Baker Park until it's time to meet up with Cooper.

. . .

"Hello?" The door is open, but the store is empty. Someone moved Dr. Strange so that he's watching over the cash register. I feel a bit of déjà vu, walking the aisles, looking for Brody or Why. But they're obviously not here.

I flip through comics; I sort through some dice. It's nearing closing time. Should I lock up and leave? Where does Brody keep the keys? Something crashes in the storeroom. I hear voices. I know Brody keeps a MagLite behind the counter. Lincoln used it once in our game. I keep it tight in my fist as I sneak up on the door.

The voices have stopped.

"Hello?" I whisper, hoping that I was just imagining things. I open the door a crack and peek inside.

There's Jade, in full elven garb, arms wrapped tightly around Wizzy. I've never seen an elf and a wizard make out before, but when one of them is your brother, you can't help but cover your eyes. They don't even notice that I'm here. I clear my throat, but Cooper just pulls Why closer. I have to break them up when he goes to grab Why's butt. It's too much.

"Excuse me!"

"Consider the favor returned, Clover." Wyatt laughs, red-faced.

"What are you guys wearing? When did you get these?" I can't believe the costumes fit each of them perfectly; even the little hat I made for Wizzy sits flawlessly on Why's head.

"I literally got them out of the literal garbage this morning. Here, put yours on." Cooper smiles while Why sneaks his hand back into Cooper's rear pocket. Both of them flush with excitement.

"Now hurry up before—"

"I told you it wouldn't fit!" Brody crashes out of the bathroom decked out in Tiffani's long blue gown. Underneath he is wearing a #PINZHASAPOSSE shirt. "I can't get the zipper up!"

"Oh. My. God." The three of us say in unison.

"You made it too small, dude." Brody keeps trying to reach the zipper. "I look like a fool. I wanted to look hot!"

"It doesn't look all that bad, actually." I try to comfort him. "If you only look at it from the front."

"Yeah? Come on, I need a wig," he announces, and goes to find one in the shop.

"Should I?" I hold up Clover's costume.

"Obvs." Cooper chuckles. "Hurry up!" He pulls Why along out of the storeroom.

I change out of my green dress and into Clover's clothes, careful to keep them from grazing the floor. The pockets are still stuffed with plastic baubles and treasures. It's soft and comfortable, a ton of cozy layers. I'm missing my crown of clover, but the costume holds up well without it. I feel so lucky I bet I could roll twenties all night long.

"Well, if it isn't Miss Clover. Hello." Lincoln smiles. His cloak is draped over his shoulders and down to the floor.

"Hi. I see you got my delivery."

"Now, where did we leave off?"

"I was apologizing."

"No, you rolled a twenty on a perception check."

"No, you, Lincoln. I was telling you how sorry I was for lying, and messing up the whole group."

"Cameron, I overreacted. You know, as a DM I think I can control everyone, and sometimes I take it too far. I should have understood what you were going through. I said I would fight the trolls, and I bailed. I'm sorry, not you. So, as I was saying . . .

"You were following the glowing staves of some evil drow elves. Trying to find the crown of Valzyr."

"Oh, right." I can't believe he jumps back into the game so quickly. I try to get into the right headspace. It's difficult.

"Every time the drow advance on you, walk near you, swing their staves in your direction, the crystals light up."

"My direction?"

"Yours."

"But there was nothing in the floor under me!"

"Nope. Wait . . ." Lincoln takes a step back and looks me over. "You're missing something."

"I am?"

"Yes."

I pat down my pockets; I open up my purple cape and check my vest. Lincoln laughs and pulls my wreath, my crown, out from under his cloak. "This."

"N-no," I stammer in disbelief.

"Yes."

"The whole time?!"

"The whole damn time." Lincoln places the crown on my head and bows ever so slightly. The bobbin in my chest kick-starts and spins into overdrive.

"Lincoln. Does this mean we can . . ."

"The crown of Valzyr gives you some bonus modifiers should you find yourself in a position to need them. For instance, let's say you got caught up in a big misunderstanding. One where you made quite a few people upset. The crown adds plus eighteen to your charisma. So, if you're wearing it while you try to, let's say, win back the hearts of a merry band of misfits . . ."

"What about just one heart? What if I wanted to convince a certain Dungeon Master to be my boyfriend?"

"The only way you could fail is if you rolled a one. So, what would you like to do?" He takes a silver d20 out of his pocket and holds it in his palm. I can't get over how he looks in the cloak.

Royal, the king of stories. His hair pulled back off his face, he breathes in the way only Lincoln can breathe. Like a hum, like music. I scoop it up, letting my hand linger on his. Our smiles identical, our hearts pounding.

"Roll it."

acknowledgments

You sit in a dimly lit room. Scratching away, scribbling words on a piece of parchment. But everything you write seems forced and cliché. Frustrated, you crumple the paper and throw it onto the ever-growing heap at your feet. You lay out a fresh sheet and try to start again. The blank page taunts you: *Really? Another book? Who thought that was a good idea?* You pick up your quill, ready to fight back, one word at a time. It's a challenge. You fight until you're exhausted, until you're in tears, until you realize you can't do it alone.

Thank goodness you have a merry band of adventurers to help you on your journey.

Brent Taylor, you fell in love with *Chaotic Good* before I wrote the first word. This book would not exist without your insight and constant encouragement. Thank you for literally everything, Snap.

Thanks to my die-hard Dazzler fan and editor, Stephen Brown. I can't think of a better editor for this uber-geekfest of a book.

Marisa DiNovis for all of your hard work and ceaseless enthusiasm. I'm thrilled we ended up working together, and I can't wait to see what the future holds.

Ray Shappell and Regina Flath designed my perfect cover. You managed to squeeze in more geeky references than I thought possible. And thanks to Kyle Hilton, who captured Cameron's likeness flawlessly.

Thanks to Uwe Stender and everyone at Triada US for your support and passion.

To Kaitlyn Patterson for falling in love with Lincoln before anyone else. Thank you for your notes, optimism, and all the DMs.

Blair Thornburgh, how did I ever manage to survive in the publishing industry without you? Thank you for the unending pep talks. Summer Heacock, you are a fierce warrior and you inspire me to be one every day.

To everyone who has my back in fighting off the orcs of my own making—Amy Spalding, Phil Stamper, Jen Gaska, Sarah Gailey, Nita Tindall, Laura Silverman, Jeremy West, Tiffany Jackson, Fredrick Arnold III, Lygia Day Peñaflor, and Sean Klein, who just happens to show up with a smile at all my major life events.

Brendan Simpson, you were my first, and best-ever, Dungeon Master. Thanks for not only making me feel welcome, but making me feel integral. I was so lucky to be adopted into your little family of misfits and rogues.

Thanks to Jon Anzalone for the decades of dorkiness and friendship.

To Joe and Jake Giani, thank you for always letting me play video games with you growing up. Joe, I think Link is still stuck in that water temple from *Ocarina*. Jake, I'm so glad that you turned into a comic-book-loving super-geek. Getting to live next door to my cousins was the best thing ever.

To my mother, who didn't judge her dice-rolling daughter. Thank you for teaching me to march to the beat of my own drum. And to Aunt Linny, who gives incredible advice and throws even more incredible parties.

Arielle. My sister. Your zeal for life and adventure is an inspiration. I'm so proud of you.

Brie. My rattlesnake twin. Thank you for believing in me and my work so emphatically. I can't wait to read every book you ever write. I'm so glad we're on this journey together.

Cara. My papergirl. The Taako to my Lup. This book would not be what it is without you. Thank you for being down for literally whatever new nerd hotness crosses our path. Just know, no matter what you do next, you're going to be amazing.

I don't know where I would be without you, Roger. You're the method to my messiness. Thank you for your patience and your love. When I met you, I rolled a 20.

Six stencils in and it's gone. Okay, the tag vanished by Stencil Number Two, but I have a point to prove. I'm not covering up your scribbled slur with just anything. I'm *making art* here. I'm creating. I'm on fire.

I've never thrown up such an intense piece—I was worried I wouldn't be able to pull it off in time. My arm flies across the wall, pink paint striping across the last stencil. It looks like it's going to work out. I chuckle to myself. This is what it's all been for, the hours of paint-pen practice, filling up every inch of every sketchbook with tags and words and pictures. All my hard work has paid off, and it's all up here on the wall.

I know I shouldn't be tagging the school. *I know that.* But I wasn't the first, and that mess had to go. Jordyn told the principal that someone tagged the gym, she had to. The vandal singled her out, and word gets around real quick at Kingston School for the Deaf. But three weeks went by, and "Jordyns a SLUT" was still there on the back of the gym for all to see. And good ole Principal Howard hadn't done a damn thing.

No one gets to call my best friend a slut, especially not up on a wall, not on my turf. She asked for help, and I took matters into my own paint-stained hands. I designed a killer piece, cut out the stencils, shook up the cans, and got to work.

I'm getting away with it. I'm about to get up. On my way

to becoming an all-city queen of street art. I rip down the last stencil, take a step back, and admire my work. It's killer. You're welcome, Universe. I check over both of my shoulders again, eyes on constant watch. I can't rely on my ears, so my eyes work overtime. It's nice and dark. I pretend I'm nothing but a shadow.

I'm so proud I just can't help myself and I text Jordyn a picture of the new mural on my way back home.

(λ_λ)

"**Y**ou don't have any proof!" I snap at our principal.

"Don't lie to me, Julia. You'll only make it worse." His hands are big, with stubby fingers. He might be hearing, but he signs perfectly. He has to, or he never would have gotten the job.

"I'm not lying! You can't say it was me." I know there are no cameras on that side of Kingston. I know there won't be any footage to review.

"I have all the proof I need. Look at your hands!"

I'm so stupid. I was being lazy. I'm going to need to buy gloves. Lots and lots of gloves.

"This was from art class." I sign as fast as I can before dropping my hands out of view and into my lap.

"I'm going to give you one more chance to tell the truth, Miss Prasad." Mr. Howard seems more agitated than angry. He keeps sighing, looking at me with droopy, tired eyes.

"I don't know what to tell you. Sorry." *Let me go already, you've got nothing.* He stares at me, waiting for a better answer. I'm not giving it to him. I'm not confessing to anything, as much as I want to take credit for it. He hangs his head and pinches the bridge of his nose.

"Well, what can you tell me about this?"

My heart shakes up in my chest like a paint can as he produces a cell phone from his desk drawer, the case dotted with red cherries. It's Jordyn's. He slides it across the desk like some detective on *Law & Order*.

I don't want to look. I don't need to. I know what's about to happen. And I know without looking that Jordyn, my best friend in the universe, sold me out. *How could she?*

"The paint on your hands, the picture on her phone. You can't tell me you didn't do it."

"Fine. But I was covering up—"

"That's not your job."

"Well, whose job is it? Because that nasty graffiti was up there forever."

"Not *your* job. We had someone scheduled to take care of it."

"But mine is art!"

"That's not art, it's vandalism. I'm worried about you; you're not exactly showing any remorse here," he lectures. My face flushes hot with rage. He's not worried about me, he's relieved he has someone to pin it on. I wonder if the slut-shaming toy-tagger got the fifth degree, too. I doubt it.

"I don't understand what the big deal is! I didn't hurt anyone. I didn't destroy anything. I've tagged the girls' room dozens of times. No one cared then—"

"You *what*?!" His face is turning as red as mine.

"So now, when I try to make something worthwhile, *art* even, you're up in arms, calling me a vandal?" Just tell me how much detention I have so we can all move on with our lives, and I can X-Acto–cut Jordyn out of mine. I wonder how long she had to sit here before stabbing me in the back. She's spineless, so she's always asked me to break the rules for her. Which I've done plenty of times, because I thought we were a team. I bet all Mr. Howard had to do was ask, and she rolled right over like a David Hockney dachshund. The light by Mr. Howard's door flashes, indicating first period is about to begin. All my anger fizzles away and I just feel weak, depleted at the thought of Jordyn heading off to her first class, no worries, all smiles, while I get interrogated.

Mr. Howard stands up and walks to his office door without saying a word. He opens it and my stomach flips; all my bravado turns bashful as he ushers my mothers into the room. It's one thing to piss off the principal. I can barely look at my parents as he tells them I'm expelled.

It's silent.

Who am I kidding? It's always silent, but this—I can *feel* it. Like for the first time, I know what the word really means. It pounds in my head. Silence is the loudest sound. Ma doesn't scowl in the rearview. Mee doesn't sign a word.

I messed up. It was beautiful. Not a masterpiece but, I don't know, close? Didn't matter, got caught. Shouldn't have done it on school property and definitely shouldn't have texted anyone evidence; those were toy mistakes and I knew better. I stood up for Jordyn, tried to save her dignity. She cried and cried the day we discovered it. And when it looked like the school wasn't going to help her, I did. I helped her, and she ratted me out—I just don't understand. I get expelled and Jordyn gets what? Nothing.

The expulsion was an overreaction, if you ask me. But that was the "final straw" and "the school won't be responsible" for whatever "mayhem" (really?) I cause next. My first real piece and I'm expelled. And now I need a new tag. Go ahead, call me a vandal, say I'm some sort of delinquent, it isn't going to insult me. It's not going to stop me. Please. *This is what I live for.*

Silence. I stare at the backs of my parents' heads, waiting for one of them to start in on me. Waiting for Mee's pointer finger to fly to her chin with that grimace she saves for special occasions.

Disappointed.

It never comes, so I kick off my shoes and rush upstairs as soon as we're home. If they're not talking yet, I'm not going to be the first. I crash-land onto my bed face-first and grip the quilt in clenched fists. I pound the mattress. *What's! Wrong! With! Her?!* Who would do something like that? She was the only real friend I had, the only one who knew me and my whole paint-splattered story. It eats at me, worming its way through my stomach and up to my brain. Neither organ can make any sense of it.

My phone vibrates in my pocket, and I'm hoping Jordyn has a damn good explanation for what she did to me. Because only one person I know would be texting me right now.

JORDYN: Srry :(

JULIA: щ(°Д°щ)
That's it?

JORDYN: They were gonna call the cops. On meeee!

JULIA: ¬_¬

JULIA: No. They weren't.

JORDYN: Mayb.

JULIA: They kicked *me* out!

JORDYN: I didnt think they would really do it.

JULIA: WHY

JORDYN: Idk. I mean u did break the law and stuff.

JULIA: Standing up for you!

JORDYN: U didn't have to. I didnt ask u.

JULIA: Are you kidding me?!?!

JORDYN: It's not like u care abt getting in trouble.

JORDYN: I did u a favor. Ur gonna be famous now.

JORDYN: Don't be so mad.

I stuff my phone under my pillow. I don't care what else she has to say. Nothing can make up for what's already been done. Nothing.

(⌐ ° ロ°)⌐

love gray days. Every tree, building, telephone pole highlighted against the gesso-colored sky. This past week has
been especially overcast and it's a relief. I thought getting
registered at a new school would take at least a month,
that I would get to stay out of the educational system for
a while. But with both of my moms at the helm, it only
took four days. Now, three weeks in at Finley, the spotlight
hasn't grown any dimmer. I welcome the clouds. Bring on
the fog.

It's getting to be that time of year when it's still dark
in the morning and the roads are empty. The drive to Finley is one of the few things I don't hate about the transfer.
You would think the forty minutes it takes to commute from
Queens Village would suck, but I love driving. Gives me time
to think. I drive through the 'burbs of Greenlawn with the
tree-lined sidewalks and traffic lights reflecting in the wet
road. The leaves aren't turning yet, but they're about to. I
spot a red leaf here and there, pilot lights to the season. Just
me and my car, Lee.

Good ole Lee. I bought her off of Craigslist this summer
for twelve hundred bucks, a 1994 Oldsmobile. She's older
than I am, but she's got some moves left. When I got her,
she was this horrible maroon color. Now she's perfect:
black and white, with flecks of color here and there.

Krasner meets Basquiat. That's Lee. She's the only real friend I have left, the only one who's never let me down.

I fish through my bag on the passenger seat, getting my morning ritual started en route. Pull out a can of Red Bull, hold it between my thighs (I'm an expert at driving one-handed), and crack it open. I hate coffee. It's either bitter or sour or chalky, not to mention the bad breath. Red Bull isn't the most delicious morning elixir, but a girl's gotta get a jolt from something.

Pulling into the parking lot of my new hellscape, I look for a spot up front in case I need to make a quick getaway. I haven't actually tried escaping from school yet, but you never know. Doesn't matter that the overly accommodating administrators reserved a spot for me next to the front doors. I refuse to park there. I can walk. Don't baby me.

I don't get the best spot this morning, but it's not a gym day, so I probably won't feel the need to flee. I reach to put Lee into Park when—*SLAM!*—she lurches forward and my seat belt digs into my chest. I swivel around in my seat and look out the rear window.

Kyle Fucking Stokers.

He tried to park in my spot, not noticing that my car was already there. What a tool. He's one of those people who's unaware of anyone or anything else in his vicinity. Bow down to him, the only person on earth who truly matters. So of course this whole ordeal is about to be blamed on me. Doesn't matter that I was already parked, minding my own business. I exist, therefore I am at fault.

I get out, not bothering to put on my shoes. My socks are getting damp as I walk around on the wet pavement. Lee's bumper is okay, no real harm done. Tough bird. Some of my paint job has come away, but the maroon showing through isn't a tragedy. I'm the only person who would even notice. Before I can get a closer look, there's hands on my shoulders and Kyle spins me around to face him. He's yelling.

"What———-———-parking here?!"

There's always a moment when one of these kids asks me a question and I have to figure out if speaking is worth the risk.

I cross my arms.

"You——-aint—my bum—r!" he rages. It's not easy to lip-read when people are yelling at you. Despite what the distorted-face yeller might actually think.

I stare back at Kyle. He probably spent more time on his dusty blond hair this morning than I ever spend on mine. He has great eyebrows, but that's beside the point.

"Well?" He gestures to his car again and again, trying to drive his point home.

Walking over to his slick silver car, I spit on my sleeve. *I* should be yelling at *him*. I should scream and say, "You ran into ME, dipshit!" Honestly? He's not worth it. I buff off the paint and gesture at the spot. *All better.* I raise my eyebrows and smile. He doesn't catch the sarcasm.

"Bitches shouldn't drive," he says slowly, deliberately. I catch every word. He turns and walks toward the school. I imagine throwing my keys at him, chasing him down, kicking his shins until he's on the ground. I slam my fists into his chest over and over and—

There's a tap on my shoulder and I snap to. Kyle disappears into school through the double doors.

"Julia! Where are your shoes?" Casey signs. She's looking at me like I'm crazy, not a hair out of place in her perfectly cut chin-length bob. Her eyes behind her black-framed glasses are magnified to a ridiculous size, like something out of a Margaret Keane painting. I point over to Lee.

"One minute," I reply. "See you in history." I shoo her away from me, because the last thing I need is Casey thinking she can solve all my problems *outside* of class, too.

I get back in the car and peel off my socks. Great. Now I'm going to end up with blisters. Mee bought me new Doc Martens before the transfer. She winked when she gave them to me—a signal she reserves for when something is to be kept just between us. Ma would kill her if she knew Mee was buying me gifts now. Rightfully so; I know I don't deserve them. But they make me smile. They're yellow, my favorite color. Problem is, they're impossible to break in and twice as impossible to drive in, so I drive in my socks and put the boots on before school. I squeeze my size 10 feet in and lace them up loosely.

I reach into the backseat to grab my hoodie, but the one I

pull out isn't mine. It's Jordyn's, all purple and pilly. It even smells like her. How long has it been in here? Sand spills out of the folds, and I remember that day on Coney Island when we shared a spicy mango on a stick. Like we always did. Like we never will again. Not any time soon. I shove it under the passenger seat. I can't stand to look at it right now.

I need my own hoodie, my trusty black-faded-gray-with-age armor. The sleeves and hem flecked with rainbows of spray paint. This is what I wear when I go out and tag stuff. I yank the zipper up to my chin, and I'm protected. The hood falls over my two loose black buns, down over my ears. I take my bag, open my second Red Bull, and drink it, heading toward the big blue building.

At first I thought transferring to Finley wouldn't be a big deal. School is school; I hated it at Kingston, I'd hate it at Finley. I mean, Jordyn is always going out with hearies and they seem fine, but it's not like I'm looking to make friends. I don't have time for that shit anymore. Not after Jordyn showed me what she's really made of. No one here would even notice me, right?

Casey took care of that right quick. Having an interpreter in every class is like having a giant neon sign hanging around your neck, blinking: *Freak Freak Freak*. I've been here three weeks and people are still confused about how it all works. It's not hard: teacher talks, interpreter signs, I understand. They act like Casey's conjuring black magic, waving her arms around, when really she's only blathering on about tariffs or decimal places.

I toss the empty Red Bull into the recycling bin and head for my locker. Mine is stuck in the freshman hall, even though I'm a junior, because it's one of the few left over from the start